## ALSO BY
# CHRISTIAN McKAY HEIDICKER

*Cure for the Common Universe*
*Attack of the 50 Foot Wallflower*
*Scary Stories for Young Foxes*
*Thieves of Weirdwood* (with William Shivering)
*Ghosts of Weirdwood* (with William Shivering)

CHRISTIAN McKAY HEIDICKER
ILLUSTRATIONS BY JUNYI WU

# SCARY STORIES for YOUNG FOXES

# The CITY

HENRY HOLT AND COMPANY × NEW YORK

## FOR C. CHAMBERS,
## WHO FOUND ME IN THE WOOD
## AND LED ME DEEPER

Henry Holt and Company, *Publishers since 1866*
Henry Holt® is a registered trademark of Macmillan Publishing Group, LLC
120 Broadway, New York, NY 10271 • mackids.com

Our books may be purchased in bulk for promotional, educational, or
business use. Please contact your local bookseller or the Macmillan Corporate
and Premium Sales Department at (800) 221-7945 ext. 5442 or by
email at MacmillanSpecialMarkets@macmillan.com.

Library of Congress Cataloging-in-Publication Data
Names: Heidicker, Christian McKay, author. | Wu, Junyi (Graphic designer), illustrator.
Title: Scary stories for young foxes : the City / Christian McKay Heidicker;
illustrations by Junyi Wu.
Description: First edition. | New York : Henry Holt and Company, 2021. | Audience:
Ages 9-12. | Audience: Grades 4-6. | Summary: Cozy and her littermates are driven from
their suburban den because something is killing the foxes in their area, and so they travel
to a strange new world, the City, to confront a new set of dangers, where they meet
O-370, an injured fox who has escaped from a fur farm and who gives them a new
mission—return to the farm, defeat the humans, and free the caged foxes.
Identifiers: LCCN 2021008642 | ISBN 9781250181442 (hardcover)
Subjects: LCSH: Foxes—Juvenile fiction. | Fox farming—Juvenile fiction. | Brothers and
sisters—Juvenile fiction. | Survival—Juvenile fiction. | CYAC: Foxes—Fiction. | Fox
farming—Fiction. | Brothers and sisters—Fiction. | Survival—Fiction.
Classification: LCC PZ7.1.H444 Se 2021 | DDC [Fic] —dc23
LC record available at https://lccn.loc.gov/2021008642

First edition, 2021
Book design by Liz Dresner / Series design by Carol Ly
Printed in the United States of America by LSC Communications, Harrisonburg, Virginia

1   3   5   7   9   10   8   6   4   2

# CONTENTS

# SCARY STORIES
## for YOUNG FOXES

# The CITY

**W**INTER HAD ARRIVED in the Antler Wood.

Clouds spilled across the sky, darkening as they came. Their faces were a drizzled gray that shifted with the wind. They sneered and mourned, cackled and wept, as they bled the warmth from the air and withered the last of the green things. The clouds stretched their mouths, miles wide, and emptied their frozen throats.

They buried the world in white.

Rabbits huddled in their warrens. Squirrels squeezed into their trunks. Deer sought pockets beneath the pines, lest the storm spot them with its shifting faces and end them with its claws of ice. The wood grew so deathly quiet no creature dared disturb it.

No creature save the foxes, that was.

Three kits romped through the first heavy snowfall of the season, discovering it with their whiskers and paws. They bounded up plumes of frost and tackled one another in gratifying crunches, disrupting as much of the pristine landscape as foxingly possible.

"I can make a blizzard!" the alpha said. She clamped onto a branch and brought an avalanche down onto her siblings' ears.

"I can make a snow lizard!" the beta said, belly-flopping in the white, legs splayed, leaving an impression behind.

The runt watched his sisters command winter with their very muzzles, and he stuck his face into the snow without any plan for what would happen next. The snow ran right up his nostrils, and he sneezed an icy spray.

"Nope!" the runt cried, trying to squint the flakes from his face. "I hate it! Let's go back to the den. Let's go back to the den forever."

The alpha panted clouds into the crisp air. "Mom said we can't set paw in the den without a fresh catch each."

"She also said she'd pluck a whisker for every snowflake we drag inside," the beta said, then gnawed a white clump from her tail.

The runt pawed at his numb muzzle, making sure it was still there.

The alpha tried not to laugh. "Move around," she instructed. "It'll thaw your hunting instinct."

The runt attempted a hop across a fresh stretch of snow and then vanished, his berry-brown fur enveloped in white. The alpha felt a squeeze in her chest. Because she was the biggest, she was responsible for her siblings when their mom wasn't there. Her whiskers worried over their every movement.

The runt's ears popped out of the snow, and the alpha's tail relaxed.

He paddled his paws as if he were drowning, trying to reach solid crust. "I can't do it! I can't even *walk*!"

"Guess you gotta starve then!" the beta said, romping deeper into the trees. "Ha *ha*!"

The runt gave up trying to escape the drifts and rested his muzzle on his paws, his shiny eyes reflecting the winter wood.

"Don't worry," the alpha said. She grabbed him by the scruff and helped him to a bare patch of earth beneath a branch. "If you don't catch anything today, I'll help you take our sister down, and we'll eat her."

The runt's whiskers curled into a wicked grin, then fell slack. "Wait—but not really, though, right?"

The alpha rolled her eyes.

"Come on!" the beta called. "Time to hunt, runt!"

The runt bounded after her. "Mom told you to stop calling me that! Why can't I just be *Omega*? Or how about what if you call me *the Fang*?"

The alpha let them go. She tested the snow with her paws until she found a section that held her weight, then delicately padded across it. It was nice having a little distance from her siblings. The runt and the beta were about as stealthy as forest fires. This hunt would most likely end with the alpha catching three critters and giving one to each of them so their mom would let them back inside.

The alpha tuned her ears downward. She swiveled them left, then right, searching for the tickle of rodent activity beneath the shifting ice. But she didn't hear a skitter. Not a squeak. The buried earth was frozen to stillness.

Ears still perked, the alpha noticed the prey wasn't the only thing that had gone quiet. Her siblings hadn't made a sound in minutes. Not a whimper. Not a yelp.

"Beta?" she called. "Omega?"

The snow-laden branches caught her voice and froze it.

She sniffed out her siblings' groove of doubled paw tracks and bounded along them. The snow grew deep, and deeper still, rising past her ears. Soon she had to leap just to see a single flash of the forest before falling back to white.

Her siblings were nowhere to be seen. Their scent was lost on the frosted air.

She went faster.

A few leaps later, the alpha smelled blood. Fresh blood. It colored the wind, salty and warm. Her nose twitched while her belly pinched in fear.

Was that a *fox*'s blood she smelled?

The alpha bounded ahead, refusing to let the snow get the best of her paws. The stench thickened, leading her to the green-needle scent of a pine tree. Its branches were weighted by piles of white, trapping the shadows within.

She took a breath. Then another. And then she nuzzled through the snowy needles, sticking her muzzle into the darkness . . . where she spotted two bushy tails. The runt and the beta. Their blood still in them.

"You are *so dead*," she said, slipping beneath the branches. The bed of brown needles was soft and prickly against her paws. "When I tell Mom you ran away, she's gonna nip your ears to stubs."

Neither responded. They stared at something half obscured by the trunk. The alpha saw the thing's fur and lunged forward, placing herself between it and her siblings. Her lips curled around her fangs while her hackles grew sharp.

A fox lay on his side. Blood foamed in the corners of his lips and crusted in the fur of his belly. He had a small cut at the base of his ear.

The alpha's hackles softened when she saw that the fox's chest was as still as the needles beneath him.

"What do you think got him?" the beta whispered.

"What do you mean 'got him'?" the runt asked. "Things don't *get* foxes. *We* get things."

The alpha sniffed toward the fox's wounds and smelled something like rotten eggs.

"Should we bury him?" the beta asked.

"Ooh!" the runt said. "Or what if we drag him back to the den? I call this as my catch!"

"*No,*" the alpha said. "He might have curses."

Now that she knew the fox wasn't a threat, she wondered what had killed him. Their mom would want to know. The alpha swelled her chest, trying to become bigger than her fear, and she took a step.

"*What are you doing?*" the beta hissed.

"I want to see what happened to him," she whispered, creeping closer.

"What if whatever killed him is hiding behind that trunk?" the beta asked.

"What if whatever killed him is burrowing around in his dead body, waiting to jump out and burrow into *you*?" the runt said in a single breath.

The alpha gritted her teeth. As always, her siblings were not helping.

She proceeded slowly and reached the fox. But she couldn't find his wound. She lowered her muzzle to nudge him over and—

"*Kkuuuhhhhh!*"

The fox gasped to life.

The beta yelped while the runt whimpered, and they both dove through the branches. The alpha backed away, muzzle lowered, lips snarling, hackles rising to deflect the Stranger's fangs.

The Stranger's eyes were wide with fear. "Who's there?" he said, his voice gummy with blood.

The alpha kept her distance. He was bigger than she was. She wasn't sure she could fend him off, even with his injuries.

"*Please,*" the Stranger said, his voice ragged. "I won't . . . hurt you. I need . . . your help."

The alpha bent her legs, ready to dive through the

branches, grab the runt, nudge the beta, and not stop running till they reached the den.

But then the runt popped his head through the needles. "Whaddaya need help with?"

"*Phht!*" the alpha huffed, silencing him.

"See?" the beta whispered to the runt from behind the branches. "Stuff like this is why you're not gonna survive till *spring*."

The runt scowled.

"We can't help you," the alpha growled at the Stranger. "You need to leave this place."

"Please," the Stranger said. "I must . . . tell you . . . what happened. If you don't listen . . ."

His voice trailed off in a gurgle, leaving the alpha to try and finish the thought.

Quiet fell beneath the pine. Four foxes breathed. The alpha gazed beyond the Stranger, through the pine tree's parting branches, along the smear of red, which trailed across the winter wood.

The beta stuck her head through the needles. "No hurt in listening, right? There are two of us and only one of him."

"*Three* of us!" the runt said.

"And he's hurt," the beta said.

The alpha looked at her siblings, heads poking through the needles, noses wet and shiny. She sniffed toward the Stranger's bloody path, as blinding red as the snow was white. She wished her mom were here.

"Go home, Omega," she said.

"No way!" the runt said. "*You* go home! Except, wait. Actually, don't. Stay here with me."

"You heard her," the beta said. "Go be with Mom. We'll come back soon."

"Fine. I'll go home." The runt flopped onto his side. "If you *drag* me."

The alpha considered doing just that, but the thought made her teeth hurt.

"We can listen for a while," she said. "But if I say run, you *run*."

The siblings slipped through the branches and shook the snow from their fur. The alpha sat before the bloodied Stranger, pointing her nose so her siblings sat a tail behind her.

"What did this to you?" the alpha asked the Stranger.

The Stranger licked red from his lips. "I cannot . . . start . . . at the end." His rattling breath refused to catch.

The runt kneaded the needles with his paws, seeming to have second thoughts about staying. "Is this a, um, scary story?"

"Yes . . . ," the Stranger said. "But there are no wild beasts . . . No starvation. No . . . frozen tails. Nothing found in a forest." Wincing, he raised his head to look at them. "This is not a story about survival."

The fox siblings glanced at one another. What other kinds of stories were there?

"It begins," the Stranger said, "on a farm . . ."

"I love farms!" the runt said. "Farms have chickens. I like chickens. I like to shake them till they die."

The Stranger closed his eyes. "It wasn't that kind of farm."

# THE WHITE
# BARN

# ONE

"**WHAT'LL IT BE** tonight? The Snow Ghost? Mr. Scratch?"

"*Golgathursh*."

"Ugh. You guys choose Golgathursh every night."

"Golgathursh! Golgathursh!"

"Fine. Golgathursh it is."

The Farm was shrouded in darkening blue save two sources of light. The farmhouse flickered with candle flame, small and inviting against the window lace. Across the yard, the wire dens buzzed with sharp red lines, making the fur of the foxes within glow like flames.

"Ready?" B-838 whispered from her wire den.

She was a beta breeder, pregnant with the next generation of Farm foxes, though her belly wasn't showing yet.

"*Ready*," O-370 said. He was an omega kit. His den was beside B-838's.

"You have to tell it *right* this time," R-211 said. The runt's den was behind O-370's, on the row closest to the wood that bordered the Farm. "Uly never bit the Golgathursh on

**13**

its thousand *butts*. Golgathurshes don't even *have* a thousand butts!"

B-838 raised an eyebrow. "Where do you think the food from its thousand mouths goes?"

O-370 snorted. He had never seen anything with a thousand mouths before. Let alone a thousand butts. But that didn't stop him from gazing through the mesh of his wire den, deep into the trees, where he imagined an impossible creature with enough mouths to fill the shadowed spaces.

"You have to make it *scary*," R-211 said. "Like this."

He clacked his teeth in a dozen directions, trying to imitate the many mouths of the story's swamp monster. But instead, he looked like he was trying and failing to catch a fly.

O-370 laughed. "Don't hurt yourself, Two Eleven."

R-211 leapt and pressed his paws against the wire mesh between their dens. "You're lucky I'm not over there, or else I'd Golgathursh your *face*!"

"I'll Uly your thousand butts!" O-370 said, throwing his paws against his own side.

The two battled through the twisted wire holes, fangs clacking, trying to use the flimsy wall to bounce the other onto his back. Like most fights, this one ended in a draw, and the kits fell into their dens, howling in feigned injury.

"My face!" O-370 cried.

"My *butts*!" R-211 whined.

They fell into hysterics.

R-211 was O-370's cousin, but he was also his best friend. The fact that their dens were right next to each other had decided that more than anything. But O-370 was convinced he had been placed next to the coolest, funniest fox on the Farm. They gobbled up the stories about Uly and Mia more ferociously than the feed they ate twice a day. And when the other foxes fell asleep, the two tried to re-create the adventures as best they could in their wire dens, which were two tails wide and two tails deep.

"A-*hem*." B-838 cleared her throat.

R-211 lay down, bundling his legs beneath him, but O-370 remained standing. He liked to be up on his paws during the exciting parts.

As the trees creaked and swayed, B-838 narrowed her eyes. "The swamp opened its dripping maw, and it *devoured* Uly and Mia whole."

"Heh heh heh," R-211 said evilly.

O-370 blurred his vision with his eyelashes and imagined the trees drooping with gray and pools of black water oozing up through the leaf bed.

"In the tangled branches high above," B-838 continued, "ghost-white birds spotted the kits and clacked their bills toward the sky."

Through O-370's lashes, the moonlight on the bare branches seemed to grow feathers.

B-838's voice became a snarl. "And in the bottomless depths of the slimy lake, something began to *bubble*."

O-370's legs felt as tense as a grasshopper's. He ached to break through the mesh and hunt the scaly Golgathursh, escape the howling Snow Ghost, or battle the bloody fangs of Mr. Scratch. He wanted to sniff out the yellow stench—a curse that turned foxes into mindless cannibals—and he wanted to guide the helpless kits of the world back to the safety of the Farm.

"Quit messing up the story!" R-211 snarled, making O-370 realize he'd stopped listening. "The raccoon never told Uly he had *beautiful fur*, and she never asked him to move into her swamp nest."

B-838 lifted her muzzle disdainfully. "Did so. That raccoon wanted to cover Uly's blackberry spots with slimy swamp kisses."

"Ugh!" R-211 rolled his eyes so hard he almost fell over.

"You insult our ancestors," a deep voice growled.

B-838 flinched while O-370's ears perked.

It was A-947, two dens down—a hazy silhouette through mesh walls. The alpha was three winters older than the kits. His fur was as bright as acorns, his ears were tipped as black as night, and the end of his tail was as white as the moon. The red of the heaters burned bright in his eyes.

"The Golgathursh would have crunched up that raccoon like a baby *mouse*," A-947 said, lips peeled over his fangs. "It would have turned its jaws on Mia and Uly and ended their lives in a flash of *fur* and *blood*. Uly was lucky to exit that swamp missing only a paw."

O-370 grinned at R-211, who grinned right back. *This* was more like it.

"If you knew what life was really like out there, Three Seventy," A-947 growled, "your tail would not be wagging."

O-370 jerked to attention and sat on his wagging tail.

The alpha fox stared between the trees into the gaping darkness. "Your ears would freeze, your paws would bleed, your tail would snap in two. A hunger would tear open inside you, so deep your ribs would *crackle* when you breathed."

"*Yeeshk,*" B-838 said.

A-947 fixed his red gaze on O-370. "Every creature in the wood would come sniffing after *you.* Every badger. Every owl. Every coral snake. All waiting for you to drop your guard for a single moment, before they dragged you into the darkness, opened your belly, and feasted on your insides. *RRAAAA!*"

The alpha lunged forward, jostling the mesh and making all three foxes—even B-838—jump.

"Ha ha ha!" A-947 gave a deep laugh, and O-370 snorted in relief. "*That's* how you scare the wild out of them, Eight Thirty-Eight," A-947 said. "That way they'll be grateful to enter the White Barn when their time comes."

O-370 gazed through the mesh toward the Barn, which stood on the edge of the lawn opposite the farmhouse. Its paint was as bright as September clouds. Its shingles beamed golden, even at night. Once the snows fell and the foxes' coats thickened red, the Farmer would take the runts and omegas into the Barn to join their ancestors. There, R-211 and O-370 would feast on peaches and centipedes and be forever warmed by the fur of their mothers and fathers, their grandparents and great-grandparents.

Some of the alphas and betas would remain in the wire dens to tell Mia's and Uly's stories to the kits who came fresh from the whelping pens.

"We do not tell these tales just to chill you," A-947 said. "We tell them so you'll know what life was like before the Farm. So you'll realize how lucky you are to be here."

O-370 shifted his focus from the forest to the wire mesh

that protected him from the cruel things that lived there. He felt the heaters toasting his ears against the chill of autumn's dying days. He tried to summon gratitude for the Farm and its many comforts. But gratitude wouldn't come.

The alpha fox gazed across the Farm with pride. "Mia's and Uly's sacrifices brought us here. A place even more precious than the Eavey Wood." He nodded to the farmhouse. "Humans like the Farmer and Miss Potter provide warmth and a roof over our ears and plenty of food to eat. For that, we owe them our tameness."

Of all Mia's and Uly's stories, O-370 liked the Beatrix Potter one the least. The kindly woman had taken Mia in from the dark of the wild into the light of her cabin, where she fed and cared for the young fox kit before sending her back on her adventure.

It was *boring*.

In his most secret moments, O-370 worried that the White Barn would be boring too. That it was the end of all adventures.

"I know you still have some wildness in your whiskers," A-947 told O-370. "But don't worry. We'll get it out. By telling the stories the way they *really* happened. Blood and guts and severed paws and all."

O-370's mouth ticked into an almost smile, and A-947 released him from his red-tinted gaze. "They're all yours, Eight Thirty-Eight." The alpha settled in his den.

"Okay, *fine*," B-838 whispered. "The raccoon never professed her undying love for Uly. But if Uly had looked deep into her eyes, he could have seen a hint of longing, as if only he could fill the bottomless swamp of her soul."

"Wake me up when this is over," R-211 grumbled.

O-370 gave one last sniff toward the trees, hoping for a whiff of yellow or lilac, of snowy fur or swamp breath. But adventure always seemed just out of sniffing rage.

*KLANG KLANG KLANG KLANG*

"Finally!" R-211 said, leaping to his paws.

The sound of the scoop against the feed bucket brought the Farm foxes fussing and whimpering to the fronts of their wire dens. O-370's mouth began to water as his ear began to itch. And all thoughts of the White Barn faded among the hungry yips of anticipation that echoed across the Farm.

# TWO

"**F**EEDING TIME!"

Fern, the Farmer's daughter, walked along the wire dens with her bucket, tossing wet scoopfuls of red through the mesh while the foxes nipped up the bloody bits—a gill here, a chicken foot there, and something that might have been an eyeball.

The Farmer watched from the farmhouse door—a shadow against the rectangle of light.

"Check the mesh!" he called to his daughter.

Fern hooked her fingers through the wire holes and gave it a jangle before continuing down the dens.

O-370 whimpered and pawstepped as Fern and her clinking bucket grew near. She gave double rations to B-838 and her unborn pups, then finally reached the end of the dens. The scoop flashed, and feed rained down around O-370 and his cousin.

R-211 fell to feasting, but O-370 pressed his ear against the mesh.

"Hiya, baby boy!" Fern said.

She reached around the wooden structure that held up the dens and hung her bucket from a nail that jutted from the side. She reached up and slid her fingers through the mesh to scratch around O-370's ear tag.

A grumble escaped O-370's throat while his eyes fluttered in relief. Fern's fingernails were long and smelled faintly of chicken grease. He was tempted to lick them clean, but the itch on his ear was more urgent than the pit in his stomach. He pressed his head into her fingers.

*"Aww,"* she said. "You're extra snuggly tonight, aren't ya?"

The area around O-370's tag had itched since he could remember. His first memory was a puncture—sharp and white—that had wrenched open his eyes. While his ear throbbed and bled, he had blinked at the bright-blue sky, waking to the pain and the beauty of the world.

The itch wasn't quite extinguished when Fern stopped scratching. O-370's hind paw started to thump, and he dug around the base of his ear, trying to finish the job. But his clumsy claws couldn't get around his tag like Fern's fingernails could.

*"Dad?"* Fern shouted toward the house. "Can we keep this one?"

O-370's ears perked. Would he go to live in the farmhouse instead of the Barn? Fern was nice. Her voice was as pretty as the autumn wind, and she always smelled of lemon soap. Being her pet would come second only to going on an adventure.

The Farmer shook his shadowed head. "You know the answer to that."

*"Please?"* Fern cried. "I'll really train this one! I'll teach him not to pee on the carpet!"

The Farmer stroked his chin. "Correct me if I'm wrong, but you still haven't sewn up my pair of thermals the last one destroyed."

Fern wrinkled her nose and gave O-370's ear one last pinch. "I would've named you Peaceblossom."

R-211 snickered, and O-370 flashed his fangs at him. O-370 would put up with a name like Peaceblossom for a lifetime of ear scratches.

"Forget something?" the Farmer called, holding up a shovel.

Fern's shoulders drooped. "Do I *have* to?"

The Farmer pointed the shovel's handle toward the three tails of space between the ground and the wire dens, held up by wooden posts. "You know if we leave the waste too long, the smell damages their fur."

It was true. The stinky brown piles beneath the wire floor made O-370's eyes water and his fur feel slimy. The Farmer and his daughter were always doing everything they could to take care of the foxes—shoveling their waste or testing the mesh to make sure nothing could break into their dens. O-370 wished he felt more grateful.

He turned to eat the morsels scattered along the floor. *"Hey!"*

While he was getting his ear scratched, R-211 had slid his long tongue through the mesh and stolen some of O-370's food.

R-211 licked his chops. "It's fair game if you're flirting, *Peaceblossom*."

"I'll show you peace!" O-370 snarled, and met his cousin at the mesh between them.

The fight was just getting good when B-838 hissed, "Boys! *Hush!*"

"What?" R-211 said, blinking up. "What is it?"

O-370 followed B-838's gaze to the Farmer, who had stepped off the porch and removed his cap to stare at the sky.

*"Come on,"* the Farmer mumbled toward the clouds. "Give me *something.*" He sighed and set his cap back on his head. "You may be saved from poop scooping after all, Fern. Time to harvest."

*"Really?"* Fern said, clasping her hands together.

"We can't keep waiting for that snowstorm," the Farmer said, scaling the porch and collecting two sets of gloves from inside the door. "The bank will pull this property right out from under us."

O-370 stared at the Barn, glowing softly in the evening light. Was it cold in there? Was that why foxes went inside only at the height of winter, when their coats were at their thickest? He had no idea. Fern and the Farmer said a lot of things that didn't make sense. Anytime O-370 had asked the older foxes what the humans meant, they told him that everything would become clear once they reached the Barn.

"We'll do the older alphas first," the Farmer said, bringing a pair of gloves to Fern. "Their coats should be thick enough, and that'll keep the lights on. Once it snows, we'll hit the runts and omegas. Breeders'll go once they've had their pups." He clapped his hands sharply and then spun his finger in the air. "Let's wrangle 'em up."

Fern squealed and slipped on her gloves.

O-370's heart squeezed. This was it. The twilight of his kithood. If the alphas were already going into the Barn, it wouldn't be long before he and R-211 followed. And they hadn't had the merest nibble of adventure.

"Well, my dear foxes," A-947 said, sitting tall as Fern and the Farmer came across the yard. "It looks like this is it."

"Aww," R-211 said. "But I like how you tell the stories best."

B-838 huffed. "Thanks a *lot*."

Fern reached A-947's cage and gazed wide-eyed at the large fox. "Will he bite?"

"Nah," the Farmer said. "Your granddaddy taught me to only ever breed the calm ones. That wrings the wild out of them bit by bit with each generation. That's why their eyes are wide and their ears flop like that. Teeth are pretty dull too. Just make sure those gloves are snug and keep his muzzle away from your face."

Fern nodded and then struggled to slide the key in the lock with her gloved hands.

A-947's chest swelled with pride. "Tell the stories as they were meant to be told," he said to B-838. "Keep the darkness in the forest, where it belongs. Keep the fear alive in young fox hearts so they remain grateful for the Farm. So no fox kit will ever experience what Mia and Uly went through ever again."

B-838 nodded solemnly. "I will."

"And you kits," A-947 said to R-211 and O-370. He winked. "Watch your tails."

The lock popped open, and Fern timidly reached a gloved hand into the alpha fox's den.

"There, there," she cooed. "I'm not gonna hurt ya."

Without so much as a snarl, A-947 let her take him by the scruff and carry him across the lawn.

"I won't change the stories too much," B-838 howled after him. "Except maybe have Mr. Scratch run off with Miss Vix in the end!"

A-947 didn't look back. He went toward the Barn with quiet dignity.

*"That was a joke!"* B-838 yipped.

O-370 watched as the Farmer opened the Barn door, just wide enough to fit through, and switched on the lights, which flickered before flooding the darkness with white.

"Wait here, Fern," the Farmer said, and stepped inside.

O-370 and R-211 pressed their noses to the mesh, trying to sneak a glimpse through the Barn's cracked-open door. But all O-370 could see was light. There had to be hundreds of foxes in there by now. *Thousands* maybe.

*How do they all fit in there?* O-370 had asked his mom when he was still in the whelping pens.

*The Barn extends through the wood for miles,* his mother had whispered. *It just goes and goes. Far enough to hold every fox you've ever met as well as every fox you haven't. My parents and their parents . . . all the way back to Mia and Uly.*

O-370 knew his mom must be right because he'd never

seen any foxes come out of the Barn. Only wooden boxes, carried by the Farmer to his truck bed. The boxes were too flat for a fox to fit inside. Still, O-370 tried to imagine all those foxes living in one space and found the idea wouldn't fit inside his head.

The Farmer stepped out of the Barn and reached for A-947.

Fern pulled the alpha back. "I want to help with all of it!"

The Farmer shook his head and smiled. "Gotta wait till your teens."

Fern made big eyes at her father and whimpered like a hungry baby kit.

The Farmer laughed and ruffled his daughter's hair. "I suppose anyone who's willing to shovel manure deserves to do the fun part too."

*The fun part?* O-370 thought. Was it fun in the Barn?

Fern stepped through the open door, and A-947 vanished in the white. The Farmer returned to the wire dens and carried the rest of the older alpha males, one by one, to the Barn.

Once the last of the alphas was inside, the Farmer pulled the Barn door shut behind him, sending a waft of air to the wire dens. It smelled of damp pine and mold. Of sweet dusty fur and . . . another scent. Something O-370 couldn't quite place. Something tingly.

From their dens, he and R-211 watched wide-eyed for the phenomenon they had only heard about. Everything grew still. Leaves jittered in the wood. A-947's open wire door creaked back and forth.

The electric heaters dimmed . . . the foxes' fur rose with static, and . . .

## *ZZT!*

The cracks between the Barn's slats flashed a Blue so bright it left ghostly stripes in O-370's vision.

"Whoa," R-211 whispered.

O-370 tried to blink away the stripes. The light was even brighter and more beautiful than he'd imagined. Painful almost. His mom had told him that the Blue flash came from the static shocks that leapt between foxes' fur when they were finally reunited in the Barn and allowed to greet one another muzzle to muzzle, with no wire in between. O-370 imagined A-947 nuzzling his mother and father, his sisters and brothers—maybe even Mia and Uly—at last.

"I can't wait till I'm in there," B-838 said. She curled her tail around her belly, keeping her unborn kits protected from the cold.

"Same!" R-211 said. "I'm gonna eat peaches and centi-pedes till they dribble out my ears."

"Yeah," O-370 said without much heart. "Same."

No Golgathurshes lurked in the White Barn. No Snow Ghost. No Mr. Scratch.

Only peace. And foxes.

No adventure whatsoever.

# THREE

**T**HE STARS CAME out, the heaters dimmed, and the Black Hours began. The wind spoke, dark and hollow, swaying the trees around the dens and clacking their bare branches. It blew in from all sides—through the floor and the walls—flapping the plastic covers and rattling the mesh, as if trying to find a way inside.

The Farm foxes had bundled themselves up for the night, burying their muzzles in the curl of their tails. Every fox was fast asleep—bellies expanding, nostrils whistling, eyelashes fluttering with dreams . . .

Except the two kits at the end, of course.

"And then that part where Uly tackles his dad like '*Rrraawww!*'" O-370 whispered as he made a mighty hop in his wire den.

"*Shh-hh-hh!*" R-211 said, trying not to giggle. He checked to make sure B-838 was still asleep. "Or how about that part where Mia bit onto that badger's tail like, '*Nuh-uh! You're not gonna hurt my friend.*'"

"That'd be me," O-370 said. "I'd totally save your life."

"No way. I'd save *yours*."

"*Psh.* My life won't *need* saving."

The cousins whispered adventures through the mesh, using their noses to point out monster shapes in the restless wood. O-370 tried to imagine Mia and Uly in the moonbright spaces, fighting back the monsters for all foxkind. But the trees wouldn't cooperate that night. The leaves remained leaves. The shadows only shadows.

"What's the first thing you'd do?" O-370 said, staring into the wilderness. "If you could go out there?"

"I'd try *all* the foods," R-211 said. "Everything Mia and Uly ate. Grasshoppers, squirrel hearts, even that weird lizard with gills. How about you?"

"Honestly?" O-370 said. "I just want to sniff a butt that isn't yours for once."

Laughter nearly burst from their muzzles, and they had to bite their tongues to hold it in. Now that she was pregnant, B-838 was snappish about her sleep. But the vixen's belly rose and fell, smooth and slow, faintly illuminated by the starlight.

### Creeeaaak

A sound startled the kits' ears.

"What was that?" R-211 asked, wide-eyed.

O-370 gulped and shook his head. He stared into the wood and waited for something to happen. For a tree to collapse on their dens and break them free. For a Golgathursh to show itself. For the adventure to begin.

### Creeeaaak

O-370's ears folded in disappointment. It was just the Barn door.

The Farmer stepped into the night, followed by Fern, whose pale face shone through the darkness.

"You all right?" the Farmer asked.

Fern gave one quick nod.

The Farmer grimaced. "You know they don't feel any pain, right?"

O-370's ear twitched. That's what the Farm foxes always said. The White Barn was the end of all pain.

Fern frowned at her father, her eyes shiny, her lips trembling. "I thought we just gave them haircuts . . ."

The Farmer sighed. "I knew I should have waited till you were older." He squeezed her shoulder. "This is what we do, Ferny. We got bills to pay."

Fern gazed back at the White Barn. "But they never get to run around again. Or smell the trees. Or . . ."

It was just as O-370 had feared. The Barn was the end of all adventures.

"That's true," the Farmer said. "They don't." He knelt down so he was eye to eye with his daughter. "But you saw how happy they were. Comfortable place to sleep. Meals twice a day. Honestly, I wish someone would give *me* that life."

Fern frowned at the grass.

The Farmer removed his gloves. "I was going to surprise you, but . . . You know how I could never afford to give you your own? Well, you're getting one this year. The person who does the work reaps the benefits."

Fern's scowl eased a little. She considered her father, then looked to the wire dens. O-370 caught her eye for just a moment, but she winced and looked away.

"Could I . . . wear it to school?" she asked.

The Farmer laughed. "You're testing me."

He stood and threw his arm around her shoulders, and she leaned into him as they crossed the yard to the farm-house and closed the door behind them.

O-370 quirked his head. "What do you think the Farmer meant when he said Fern was getting one of her own? And what did she mean 'wear it'?"

"Hmm?" R-211 said. He'd been nibbling an itch between his toes and hadn't been paying attention. "Oh. Maybe he's going to let her keep A-947 as a pet. You're probably too ugly for her."

O-370 didn't feel like play-fighting right then. He flopped onto his side . . . and he saw something new. The feed bucket still hung from the nail that jutted out of the wooden beam between his and his cousin's dens. Fern had forgotten it.

O-370 stuck his paw through one of the mesh's holes and batted at the bucket, making its wire handle swing back and forth. Soon, the snow would fall, and O-370 and R-211 would go into the Barn. And the only adventures they would ever experience were the ones they imagined from the safety of their wire dens.

He pawed the bucket again, angrily this time, making it swing farther. The handle slid along the nail, caught on its flat head, and yanked it a hair's breadth out of the wood.

O-370's head tilted. The month before, he had watched the Farmer hammer nails into the structure, making it less wobbly. O-370's eyes traced from the nail up the beam it held in place. The beam propped up the tin roof and stretched taut the wire mesh that separated him and his cousin.

O-370 swiped the bucket again, and the nail squeaked out another whisker.

"Uh," R-211 said. "Wwwhat are you doing?"

*What would happen?* O-370 wondered as he swatted the bucket again. *What would happen if this nail came all the way out?* And again. *Would the mesh open?* Two bats in quick succession. *Could he and his cousin slip out of their dens for just a little while?* Three more. *Just long enough for one quick adventure.* He was getting a rhythm now. *Before they went into the White Barn and put away their wildness forever . . .*

"*Three Seventy!*" R-211 whisper-hissed. "Did you hear what I asked?"

"We're"—O-370 said, giving the bucket another swing—"gonna"—swing—"have"—swing, swing—"an *adventure*."

"We're *what*?" R-211 said, watching the nail eke farther and farther out of the wood.

O-370 ignored him. He swatted harder, jerking the nail so far out that it started to bend under the bucket's weight.

*RRRKT*

The beam groaned. The wire mesh grew slack.

"Um, Three Seventy?" R-211 said, panicking.

O-370 swatted the bucket again.

*RRNT!*

"Three Seventy!"

And again.

*Crkkkkkkk!*

The beam started to lean outward. The ceiling started to droop.

*Tok!*

The nail popped out.

*Kkt!*

The wood split.

***FOOM!***

And the world collapsed.

# FOUR

**O**-370 COULDN'T MOVE. Something cold and heavy lay on top of him, pressing him into the wire floor. He opened his eyes and found that the bright-red zigzags were inches from his nose. The heaters sizzled like a dying insect, reflecting against the wavy tin ceiling that was crushing him.

He understood. His den had collapsed. He was trapped.

*"Three Seventy?"* a panicked voice said. *"Two Eleven?* Are you okay? *Answer me!"*

It was B-838. She sounded far away.

Straining, O-370 turned his neck under the weight of the roof.

*"Please!"* B-838 said in a rising panic. "One of you *say* something!"

O-370 opened his muzzle to respond, but the roof lay heavy on his chest. He wriggled forward until he saw a bend in the tin showing bare branches against the starry sky. Using his hind paws, he pushed himself toward it and slipped into the open. He sucked in breaths and panted with relief, grateful to be free of the crushing space.

"You *butthead*," B-838 snarled through her mesh. Her den had not collapsed. "That roof better have cut off your tongue, otherwise I'm gonna kill you for not answering me." Her expression softened. "Are you okay?"

O-370 awkwardly got to his paws and stepped on top of his roof. A dull pain bloomed in his hip. "I think so," he said, wiggling his joints. "My hip hurts."

"Good," B-838 said.

He glanced up, and his mouth snapped shut. For the first time in his moons, O-370 saw the Farm without the mesh. The twisted metal circles had broken up the world into small, understandable bits. He tried to take it all in at once—the lawn, the trees, the sky, the farmhouse. Everything was so . . . *there*.

It made him dizzy. But it was a soaring kind of dizziness.

This was a story.

"Two Eleven!" he said, spinning around, giddy with excitement.

His breath stopped when he saw that his cousin's den had also collapsed—now nothing more than a pile of tin and mesh.

There was a lump under the tin roof. The lump wasn't moving.

"*Two Eleven?*" O-370 said with a tremor.

The lump did not respond.

O-370 bounded around the edge of the collapsed roof, careful not to put weight on his cousin. He stepped onto the wooden frame beneath, snagged the tin corner with his fangs, and pulled as hard as he could. It wasn't easy, but O-370 gave it everything he had, shifting the roof a couple of inches.

R-211 lay on his back, eyes wide and frozen.

O-370's ears went cold. "Oh no," he said. "No, no, no."

R-211 blinked. "That was squipping *crazy!*"

*"Language!"* B-838 said.

The fear in O-370's belly melted. And then it boiled. "Why didn't you *say* something?"

R-211 pushed up to his paws. "You deserved that for breaking our dens!"

O-370 leapt forward, expecting a mesh wall to stop him, and was surprised when his paws struck R-211 full in the face. He was even more surprised when his cousin's fangs sank into his ear. He chomped R-211's scruff in retribution, and then felt every nip, every scratch, even the rumble of his cousin's snarl against his skin as they rolled across the top of their roof.

It was painful. And it was wonderful.

*"Guys!"* B-838 said.

O-370 unclamped his jaws from R-211's throat, while his cousin released his ear. The two panted. O-370 realized that when he and his cousin made contact, no sparks had jumped between their fur. They'd always been told this was what happened when foxes met in the Barn, creating that bright flash of Blue. The fact that it hadn't happened gave O-370 a squeamish feeling, but he wasn't sure why.

"What are you gonna do now, *geniuses*?" B-838 said. "You don't have anywhere to sleep."

The kits gazed around. The four walls that had once kept them safe were crushed beneath their paws. The sky hung cold and black above, the warm glow of the heaters replaced with icy stars. The wind swept their fur. The branches reached toward them. Invisible eyes watched from between the trunks.

O-370 shivered. He couldn't tell whether it was out of excitement or fear.

He sniffed toward the farmhouse, whose candles had been extinguished for the night. The collapsing roof hadn't woken the Farmer. O-370 and his cousin were out of their dens. And they weren't going back in anytime soon.

*"Rrrrn!"*

He heard a straining behind him and turned to find R-211, nuzzling under the bent roof.

O-370 quirked his head. "What are you doing?"

"Are you kitting?" R-211 said, using his head to try to get the roof to stand up straight again. "A monster could leap out of the trees any second! Help me!"

O-370 watched the forest. He waited for a badger to materialize in the shards of moonlight, for Miss Vix to step rickety from behind a bush, for Mr. Scratch to strike from the shadows with his bloody teeth.

Nothing happened.

O-370 stepped on the roof, weighing down his cousin's efforts. "Look *around*, Two Eleven! We're free until the Farmer sees what happened! We can do anything we want! Go jump on the truck! Get Grizzler to chase us! We can even go into the forest and hunt some lizards! We'll get real good at it and slowly work our way up to fighting the Golgathursh!"

R-211 let the roof slip off his muzzle. He glanced, worry-eyed, into the trees.

"This is what we've always *wanted*!" O-370 said. "The foxes of the Farm will be talking about the Great Den Collapse for *moons* to come. Long after we go into the White Barn. It isn't as exciting as the old stories, but it's something!"

His cousin frowned down at the roof. "What about our ancestors? What if they smell the wild in us and won't let us in the White Barn?"

"Think about it," O-370 said. "They let Mia and Uly in there. And they were the wildest of all!"

R-211 bit his tongue in thought.

B-838 sighed. "Now that Nine Forty-Seven's gone, I guess I'm responsible for you fuzz balls. And I have to say, Three Seventy, that this is the worst idea I've ever heard. I'd rather not watch you die, thanks."

O-370's excitement almost fizzled . . . until he realized B-838 was still locked up and couldn't stop him if she tried.

He gave his cousin a hopeful look. "Whaddaya think? Adventure?"

R-211 lowered his muzzle. "I . . . I *want* to. Except . . ." His right forepaw twitched up and dangled. "My paw. It got a splinter. When the roof fell."

"Lemme see," O-370 said. "Maybe I can pull it out."

"I don't think you can," R-211 said, turning away from him. "It's stuck deep."

O-370 noticed that his cousin's ears were folded, his eyes were watering, and even though the air was chilled and the heaters lay broken beneath them, he was panting . . . O-370 had always thought his cousin was braver than he was. But R-211 was *scared*.

O-370 couldn't imagine going on an adventure alone. Mia and Uly survived the stories only because they were together. Each had talents the other did not. Whenever the cousins imagined their own adventures, O-370 was the planner while R-211 was the *teeth*. But right then, R-211 didn't look like he could harm an earthworm.

O-370 stared into the forest. It looked darker, more tangled than before. The world was terrifyingly open. But it was open.

"I'm going," O-370 said.

R-211's ears perked. "Really?"

O-370 peered over the edge of the collapsed roof. It was a dizzying three-tail drop to the vast lawn. Within the confines of his den, he'd barely hopped two paws into the air.

He licked his lips and reminded himself that an opportunity like this came along once in a lifetime. Less than that.

"What if Grizzler catches you?" B-838 asked.

O-370 scanned the Farm, searching for the spot where the old hound had plonked his bones for the night. But Grizzler was nowhere in sight. Not that it much mattered. The hound may have been eight times O-370's size, but he was bulky and cross-eyed, and he moved at a waddle.

"The scariest thing about Grizzler," O-370 said, "is getting hit by spit when he barks."

R-211 didn't laugh. "What if Mr. Scratch is out there, waiting for you to jump down so it's easier to snap your neck?"

O-370 tried to keep his hackles from bristling. "If you see him, howl and warn me."

Before his fear could get the best of him, he positioned his paws at the sharp edge of the roof and wiggled his hips.

"Don't you dare, Three Seventy!" B-838 snarled.

He stared at the grass below. This was it. The start of his one great adventure.

"Three Seventy?" R-211 said.

O-370 looked over his shoulder.

"What if something happens to you?" his cousin asked.

"Yeah, but . . . ," O-370 said. "What if nothing ever happens to me?"

R-211's ears flattened.

O-370 jumped.

# FIVE

**T**HE GROUND RUSHED up and smacked O-370's paws, driving his knees into his stomach. His muzzle struck the grass, and his teeth clacked together so hard they felt as if they might shatter. For a horrifying moment, his breath wouldn't catch, and he thought he'd broken himself forever.

His lungs finally hooked and gasped in air. O-370 staggered to his paws and gave his head a shake, trying to lose the floaty spots in his vision. He searched the lawn, legs tense, waiting for Mr. Scratch to strike from the bushes or a Golgathursh to come flopping, slithering, chomping toward him.

But if any deadly creatures lurked in the wood, they remained hidden.

O-370 tested the grass against his paws. It tickled. He romped a few tails down the line of wire dens, then turned and romped back.

"This is fun!" he called up to his cousin.

B-838 peered down at him through her mesh. "How are you gonna get back up here, smart guy?"

"Oh, um . . ." O-370 eyed the three vertical tails between him and his collapsed den. "I'll figure that out when I get back."

"*If* you get back."

She vanished into the comforting red glow of her den, and O-370 was suddenly alone. R-211 was too much of a scaredy-paws to even peek over the edge. O-370 would show him. He'd go collect a hundred Golgathursh scales and drop them triumphant before his cousin.

O-370 faced the forest, trying to feel brave. The night was just as windy and haunted as it had been moments before. But now that O-370 was outside his den, every gust felt colder, the waving branches sharper, every forest click a threat.

He suddenly didn't feel bold enough to stick so much as a whisker into the wood. Not without R-211 there to keep an eye on his tail. O-370 glanced around the Farm, searching for other adventures. He huffed when he saw the White Barn. He certainly wasn't about to visit the place where all adventures ended.

That left the farmhouse.

O-370 smiled. He had it: the perfect adventure. He would go to the feed barrel and bring back a muzzleful of food, which he would devour in front of his cousin. R-211 would regret pretending to have a splinter.

O-370 trotted along the row of raised wire dens.

"*Tsk, tsk, tsk,*" a voice said above.

"Would you look at the wild in this one?" said another.

"Whatever happens to him will be *well* deserved."

It was three beta breeders, their silhouettes blazing against the faint glow of the heaters.

"You mustn't do this, little kit," one said.

"If the Farmer sees you, he might never take you to the Barn."

"Don't ignore us," snarled another.

O-370 avoided their eyes. If they wanted to live their whole lives without so much as a lick of adventure, then that was up to them.

He was going to have a story.


O-370 arrowed across the tickling grasses, keeping his nose aimed at the feed barrel. His paws felt stumbly on the unpredictable lumps of the lawn. His joints ached, and the cold dew numbed his pads. But he kept moving, wanting to reach the cover of the farmhouse as quickly as possible. Being out in the open made his senses twitchy. His heart jerked when the wind ruffled the grasses. Shadows grew claws in his periphery.

He was twenty tails from the feed barrel when a rumbling stopped him in his tracks. His head turned slowly. His forepaw lifted. There, between the house and the shack, was the Farmer's truck. For a moment, O-370 thought the Farmer had left the engine running. But then he noticed the fuzzy form lying beneath the truck's shadow. Grizzler snored as loud as a motor, his vibrating lips spraying ropes of saliva. The hound's meaty breath thickened the air.

O-370 waited to see whether his presence would wake Grizzler. Foxes were meant to be faster than dogs, and Grizzler was a lump of a hound, but O-370 had never walked so far in his life—halfway across a yard. His joints hurt too much to run, and his lungs felt ready to heave out of his throat.

Grizzler continued to snore, but O-370's ears buzzed with doubt. He looked around for less dangerous adventures and spotted something strange sticking up from behind the farmhouse.

It was a giant ear.

He headed away from Grizzler and the feed bucket, padding around the farmhouse to the driveway. Up in the sky hung a picture of a giant winking fox face. It smiled happily, like a human would, its tongue lolling over its chin. There were letters beneath, like the ones on O-370's ear tag, but he couldn't understand them.

At the end of the driveway, beneath the winking fox face, something else caught his eye. His heart began to pound before he understood what he was seeing. Out here, on the other side of the farmhouse, he could see the White Barn from a different angle. His eyes traced the building's side, expecting its slats to continue through the trees as far as he could see. But the Barn ended a few dozen tails from its front door, its side no longer than its front was wide.

As O-370 stared at the Barn, so much smaller than he'd imagined, questions burned to life in his mind. How could all the ancestors fit in there? What had Fern really meant when she said the foxes couldn't run around anymore? And why had no sparks leapt between his and R-211's fur when they finally had a chance to play-fight?

O-370 padded toward the Barn to investigate. Despite his itch to have an adventure, he had to admit that he was excited at the prospect of seeing his mom again. He hadn't seen her since the whelping pens.

With each step, the road seemed to stretch longer and longer while the White Barn grew larger and larger, until it nearly filled the sky. What had felt like a quaint building nestled among the trees was now a towering structure, with old bones that creaked in the wind. The Barn looked different up close. Its white slats were peeling gray, and the gaps between let the darkness seep out.

He reached the edge of the lawn and stepped onto the dry strip of earth beneath the Barn's eaves. He sniffed for A-947's scent, but all he smelled was mud and paint dust and just a hint of smoke.

O-370 hoped R-211 was watching as he moseyed up to the giant double doors. He tried pushing one open as the Farmer had, but it wouldn't budge. Instead, O-370 stuck his head through the narrow space beneath the doors.

It was dark inside the Barn. A dusty-brown dark. The air smelled stale—dirt and mold. And there was that electric scent, tingling underneath. The slats squeezed the wind to a high-pitched whine.

O-370 quickly pulled his head out and swiveled his ears around the lawn. Grizzler still snored beneath the truck. The leaves rustled lightly as the smiling fox sign creaked. The farmhouse was quiet. O-370 gazed toward the dens and saw R-211—a fuzzy speck in the distance.

"*Hmph,*" O-370 said, hoping his cousin could hear him.

He stuck his head back under the Barn doors and then wriggled and strained to squish the rest of his body through. He was in the dusty darkness now. Moonlight crept beneath the doors like fog.

The air was colder in here. The smells were all trapped together. Somewhere beneath the wood and mold and tingle, he could smell fur, but he couldn't see any foxes. The space stretched, dark and empty. The moonlight only reached so far.

"Hello?" O-370 whispered into the darkness.

His ears strained in the silence.

"Nine Forty-Seven?"

*whoooooooooooo*

The wind answered, whistling through the slats. O-370's aches turned to trembles. There were no foxes here. He wondered whether he had ruined something by sneaking into this place. By leaving his den. By tackling his cousin. He suddenly regretted ever swiping at that bucket.

The longer O-370 stared, the clearer the Barn became. Shapes pushed out of the darkness, like bones floating up through water. A sliver of moonlight shone on a bucket spilling over with black, the Farmer's gloves draped over its handle. There was something inside the bucket. A wet gleam that smelled of salt.

In the opposite corner was a large metal box. O-370 quirked his head at the rods and dials and spindly wires. The box hummed and smelled warm. There were slices in its sides, like fish gills. Worms of electricity coiled through its heart. They were Blue. They tingled his nostrils and made his heart knock against his rib cage.

*whoooooooooooo*

The wind whistled through the Barn's uneven slats, making shapes sway in the darkness above. O-370 looked up. Something was hanging from the rafters. *Many* somethings.

He squinted, trying to unblur the swaying shapes. They were a reddish orange. As thin and fuzzy as blankets. One was a sort of *acorn* red, with black triangles at its top. And hanging from the bottom was something long and bushy, with a tip as white as the moon . . .

O-370 took a step back. They were foxes. Hanging from the rafters. But there was nothing inside them. No eyes. No bones. No tongues to cry for help.

The sight stole the breath from O-370's lungs, but the wind screamed for him.

# SIX

"**B**ACK SO SOON**? Heh heh heh."

"You see Mr. Scratch, little kit?"

"Nah. He saw old Grizzler. Just look at the whites of his eyes."

"Get in your den, little one! Before the Farmer sees you."

O-370 ignored the breeders as he stumbled back to his collapsed den. He reached it and gazed up, and his heart sank into his paws. It was too high to jump.

R-211 poked his muzzle over the edge. "You're back."

"In one piece, no less," B-838 said through her mesh. "Did you see our ancestors? Did they banish you from the Barn forever?"

O-370's words dried up. His jaw shook.

"Did you try the peaches and centipedes?" R-211 asked, with wonder in his eyes. "How's Nine Forty-Seven?"

*A-947's not in his body anymore,* O-370 thought, and his skin rippled down his spine.

He looked toward the White Barn, which glowed like an eyeless skull in the moonlight.

"Three Seventy," B-838 said.

His eyes shifted back to the wire dens. And he realized that wasn't what they were. They were *cages*. The mesh wasn't meant to protect the foxes. It was there to stop them from escaping. The tags didn't show their names but the order in which the foxes would be taken into the Barn so the Farmer could . . .

"Hey," B-838 said. "Are you too good to talk to us now that you've been inside the Barn?"

O-370 blinked up at her and his cousin, and for a horrifying flash, he saw what they would look like without their skins—meat and teeth and lidless eyes. Just like the thing glistening in the bucket.

"They . . . ," he managed. "They threw the rest away."

"Who threw what away?" B-838 asked. "Did someone throw your brain away? You're not making sense."

O-370's muzzle was too numb to answer. He wanted this story to be over.

"Why's your lip bleeding?" R-211 asked.

Before O-370 had left the Barn, he had sniffed at the metal box, at the Blue that jittered in its heart.

Maybe it was the tingly scent or the way his whiskers stood on end. Maybe it was the Blue flash that came after the alphas had entered the Barn. Whatever it was, O-370 knew now that it was the machine that had stolen A-947's life. Just as it had done to hundreds of foxes before. Thousands.

*The Skinner,* he had thought.

O-370 had wanted to destroy that machine. But when

he lashed at its metal sides, the sharp edge had sliced open his lip.

"We have to get out of here," O-370 whispered.

"Out of where?" B-838 said.

"Out of these cages," O-370 snapped at her. "Away from the Farm!"

"Cages?" B-838 asked.

R-211 tilted his head.

"We . . ." O-370 tried to find the words. They didn't come. He stared deep into his cousin's eyes. "You have to trust me, Two Eleven. We have to go. *Now.*"

"I . . . I can't leave," R-211 said, taking the weight off his front paw. "My splinter."

"And I'd love to join you," B-838 said, bowing her back to stretch her legs, "but my den's still standing, so I have to stay here and get fed twice a day until I go to the White Barn and eat peaches and centipedes with all of our friends and family forever. Shucks."

O-370 realized that the foxes had unwittingly played along with the Farmer's plan. Believing that the humans were good and the Farm was paradise, they'd told the young ones stories, trying to scare the wild out of their whiskers so they wouldn't put up a fight when the Farmer took them.

B-838 adjusted her paws around her belly, and O-370's heart clenched. Soon, she would go to the whelping pens, where she would give birth before being taken to the Barn. Her kits would live in the cages until their fur was thick enough, and then the runts and omegas would be taken away while the alphas and betas would become breeders and story-tellers, and the cycle would repeat for moons and moons.

O-370 leapt up and threw his paws against the wooden support, hoping to tip it over and bring all the cages down with it. It didn't budge.

"Help me, Two Eleven!" he called up to his cousin, hitting the support again. "Start chewing through Eight Thirty-Eight's mesh! We have to get everyone out of here!"

R-211 only watched, head tilted, as O-370 sank his teeth into the wooden post, trying to tear it away splinter by splinter.

"We'll have none of your wildness, kit," a breeder called from a few cages down.

"You'll jump back up to your den if you know what's good for you," said another.

"Please, little kit! Do it now!"

O-370 continued to gnaw on the post.

"Three Seventy, *stop*!" B-838 said from above. "Tell us what's happening."

The wood wouldn't give, and O-370's teeth felt as if they were going to pop out of his gums.

He sat back hard and started to whimper. He had to convince the foxes they were in danger. He had to tell them the truth.

"The humans . . . ," he said, breathless. "They-they-they—" He tightened his muzzle and forced his lips to form the words. "They're going to take our skins. That's why we're here. On the Farm. The Farmer took Nine Forty-Seven's. Pulled it right off his bones. I saw it hanging in the Barn."

B-838 snorted. R-211 listened, brow furrowed.

"Hey!" one of the breeder foxes said. "We weren't kitting."

"Get back in your den before you get us all in trouble."

O-370 ignored them. "There was no feast or ancestors or anything like that," he whispered. "Just a big metal box with wires and tubes. And the skins. And . . ."

He swallowed. He couldn't tell them about the bucket.

B-838 laughed outright this time. "Skins aren't like human clothes. They don't just *come off.*" She bit her haunch and tugged, demonstrating. "See? Still on."

*"I'm squipping serious!"* O-370 barked at her.

B-838 clicked her tongue. "You're lucky Nine Forty-Seven isn't around to hear you talk like that."

A-947 would never hear again, O-370 realized. His ears were with his skin.

"But . . . ," R-211 said. "Humans are good. Beatrix Potter gave Mia shelter."

O-370 winced. For the first time he wondered whether that story was more horrifying than the Farm foxes realized.

"Get back in your den, kit!" one of the breeders yelled. "Now!"

"Climb that drooping mesh!"

"Whatever it takes. Just get back up there!"

O-370 looked to his cousin. "Do you believe me, Two Eleven?"

R-211 gazed deep into his eyes, as if trying to see what O-370 had seen.

"Now, little kit!"

"Before the Farmer wakes!"

The breeders continued to bark threats and warnings while O-370 gave his cousin an imploring look. He was determined to convince him. Even if it took all night.

*CLICK!*

The fur on R-211's face lit up, and O-370's head swiveled around.

The porch light had turned on.

"Farmer's up," B-838 said casually. "Breeders must have woken him."

O-370 gazed in horror as the farmhouse door started to open.

# SEVEN

**O-370 SLIPPED BEHIND** the wooden post as the Farmer's shadow stretched across the grass. The sight once put a wag in O-370's tail. But now the Farmer looked like a dead thing. A skeleton smiling in the darkness.

O-370 looked straight up and found his cousin peering down.

*"Jump,"* O-370 whispered. "If your paw hurts, walk on three. I'll help you."

R-211 swallowed. "I don't wanna play this game anymore."

"It's not a game!" O-370 said.

Back on the porch, the Farmer had laced up his boots and was setting off across the yard.

O-370 stared into the black spaces between the trees and hesitated. He looked up at his den. His cage. It would be so much easier to just stay on the Farm. To get fed twice a day and play with his cousin. To believe what he'd always believed.

*"Please*, Two Eleven," O-370 said. "Come with me."

R-211 stared at his paws. "Three Seventy . . . stories are just for listening."

O-370's ears wilted.

The Farmer reached the cages.

O-370 fixed his eyes on the forest, gave one last whimper, and then bounded out from behind the post. He was almost to the trees when he heard a deep huffing and the rattle of a chain dragging across the yard.

"Grizzler, *no*!" Fern shouted from the porch.

The hound was on O-370 in seconds, catching his head in his massive jaws. Gray teeth crushed O-370's throat while a massive tongue flopped sticky against his nose. Grizzler shook his giant muzzle, and O-370's body whipped back and forth, his head straining like it might pop free from his neck.

In the distance came a sharp whistle. *"Drop it!"*

The Farmer spoke, and the hound obeyed. The jaws released O-370's throat, and he fell to the grass, cold air rushing into his lungs. Grizzler stuck his nose into O-370's chest and snarled deep. Saliva dripped from the dog's black lips onto O-370's belly.

*"YAOWR!"*

The Farmer's boot struck Grizzler's chest, and the hound yelped and retreated.

"Stupid mutt!" the Farmer yelled. "That kit's worth a month's wages! I swear, if you harmed that hide, I'll have yours to replace it!" He pointed at O-370. "Fern, grab that kit!"

O-370 lay in shock as Fern knelt beside him. "You poor

thing." She took his ear between her long fingernails and rolled it in a soothing circular motion.

O-370's eyes fluttered shut. He was tempted to let her pick him up, cradle his paws as she placed him back in his den, where B-838 would clean his wounds through the mesh.

But then he remembered the question Fern had asked the Farmer: *Can I wear it to school?* And he realized she'd been talking about a fox's skin.

"There, there," Fern said. "I've got you."

The moment her hands scooped under his forelegs, O-370 snapped at her fingers, clamping his muzzle shut a whisker before his fangs met her skin.

*"Oh!"* Fern cried, flinching back and dropping him.

The moment O-370 hit the ground, he scrambled toward the trees.

"Fern, grab my gun!"

"No, Daddy! You can't shoot him!"

O-370 did not stop running when he reached the forest's shadows. He ran and ran until his lungs burned, his paws bled, and the world doubled in his eyes. When he couldn't take another step, he sank onto a pile of spotted leaves. Panting, he gazed back through the tree trunks. The Farmer scowled into the wood, searching for signs of his runaway kit.

"He's just a baby," Fern said, hugging herself. "He'll die out there."

"Yeah," the Farmer said. "There goes fifty bucks."

He looked toward R-211, who dutifully sat on his collapsed cage, looking small and helpless. "Looks like we've got one obedient kit, at least." The Farmer approached

R-211, took him by the scruff, and held him in place. "Fern, go cook up some chicken."

Fern frowned into the forest a moment longer. Then she headed back toward the farmhouse.

O-370 whimpered. His cousin loved the old stories as much as he did. Together, they'd imagined great adventures unfolding right outside their dens—their *cages*. But at the first sign of danger, R-211 had frozen up.

The wind ruffled O-370's fur and reminded him where he was. Out in the cold, dark wood. The trees creaked and moaned. Somewhere, a squirrel screamed in the talons of an owl.

When Mia and Uly had first entered the wilderness, they'd had their mothers' lessons to guide them. But O-370's mom had never taught him anything beyond the lies of what happened in the White Barn. She had never imagined he'd need more than that.

O-370 stared deeper into the wood. He still had Mia's and Uly's stories. And knew that if he stayed where he was, something would find him. An owl. A coral snake. A Snow Ghost. He had to move. He had to find food and shelter. He had to survive.

O-370 took his first step toward the unknown.

**A** **BREATH OF SNOW** whirled beneath the pine tree. The alpha used it as an excuse to shiver.

Her siblings sat stock-still behind her, as if worried the story itself could sniff them. The Stranger's head lay heavy on the brown needles. He winced in pain as he waited for his breath to return.

"Wh-what was hanging in the rafters?" the runt asked, his voice as small as a mouse squeak.

The beta scoffed. "Weren't you listening? It was the older foxes' sk—"

*"Don't,"* the alpha snapped at her. "Just . . . don't."

The runt whimpered in frustration, forever feeling left out because of his size.

"What kind of a name is O-Three Seventy anyway?" the beta asked.

The Stranger struggled to answer. "The kind . . . a human . . . would give a fox."

The alpha studied the Stranger's wounds, which seemed to have stopped bleeding. If the beginning of this story was about a skin-stealing farmer, how much worse was it going to get?

"Go home," the alpha told the runt. "Mom's probably worried."

"But-but she *loves* it when we're gone!" the runt said. "She says so all the time! Besides, Three Seventy's safe now, right?"

The Stranger took a moment to breathe. "The

Farm foxes might have been wrong about the Barn . . . But that doesn't mean they were wrong about the outside world."

"Oh," the runt said, ears folding.

"What was in the forest?" the beta asked.

"Nothing," the Stranger answered. "It ended as quickly as it began . . . at a field of chopped-down trees."

*The land beyond the tree stumps,* the alpha thought. She'd seen them, stretching toward the horizon like broken teeth. Their mom had made her and her siblings swear by their belly fur that they would never set so much as a paw there.

"This," the Stranger said, "is where we leave O-Three Seventy."

*"What?"* the runt said. "That can't be the end of the story!"

"It isn't," the Stranger said weakly. "Just the start of a new one." He coughed and winced. "Beyond the stumps was a land buried in concrete. Where foxes' dens have been dug up and human dens built on top of them. And any wild green that could hide a fox's fur has been uprooted and cut down."

The Stranger drew a stuttering breath, and the alpha gazed into the wood, trying to imagine a land where trees didn't exist.

"Foxes have found ways to survive in this place," the Stranger said. "Some even do well there. If you stay sharp and mind your tail, it's a sort of paradise, where no coyotes or badgers dare go. Where food can be sniffed every dozen tails." He found the fox kits with his clouded eyes. "And where some monsters are as invisible as the wind."

# A HOWL ON HAWTHORNE STREET

# ONE

TWILIGHT SWEPT OVER Hawthorne Street and drained the color from the sky. As the neighborhood fell to silvers and grays, the humans shut themselves inside. They locked their doors and drew their curtains, rattled their garages closed—as if protecting themselves from the night.

Once the antennas electrified the air . . .

Once the windows danced with staticky light and hummed with muffled applause . . .

Four shadows crept out of the graveyard—one large, three small.

They darted down the street, weaving through fences, slinking along leaf-gooey gutters, and arcing around cones of streetlight. The way was written in their whiskers and paws—every crack and broken post, every rut and patch of grass as familiar as the fur on the tops of their muzzles.

"What wickedness awaits in the gray of dusk?" Sterling, one of the boy kits, said.

*"Sterling,"* Dusty snapped, quieting him.

The vixen stopped every twenty tails to look, sniff, listen. Yard, hedge, garbage can.

*Look, sniff, listen.*

Porch, car, lawn mower.

*Look, sniff, listen.*

Sterling continued at a whisper. "Driven from the country by coyotes and wolves, kept from the City by the cruelty of humans, our heroes find themselves in an *in-between place*. A place between city and forest. Between shadow and streetlamp. Between bright of day and dark of—"

*"Sterling,"* Dusty hissed. "I'm serious."

The vixen paused and raised a forepaw, so the kits did too.

*Look, sniff, listen.*

To Cozy, the young vixen, the night smelled and sounded like any other—the rust-water scent of sprinklers, the drip of leaves, the tar cooling in the road. It didn't look the same, though. A white van was parked in the street, its metal belly ticking as it cooled. But Dusty didn't pay it any mind, so Cozy tried not to worry about it.

The foxes continued through the night, and Sterling's whisper shrank to a breath. "Hawthorne Street might *seem* like any other neighborhood. But who knows what evil lurks in its nooks and crannies?"

Julep, the other boy kit, snorted. *"Crannies."*

Dusty raised a lip, and Julep's muzzle snapped shut so fast that it made a sound.

"If our intrepid foxes aren't careful," Sterling said, narrow eyes glancing around the night. "If they don't sense every sight, every sound, every *scent*, they could stumble into a place I like to call—"

Dusty whirled with a snarl, freezing Sterling in his tracks. "If you get us caught tonight, so help me, I will throw you to the humans so the rest of us can escape." Her single fang flashed sharp. *"Got it?"*

Sterling dipped his head, and Dusty padded on.

The moment her tail was turned, he mouthed, *"The Crepuscular Zone."*

They reached the house with the black-and-white pinwheel, which spiraled hypnotically on the lawn. Dusty slipped beneath the side fence, hips collapsing like a folded leaf. The boys followed, wriggling and scraping under the splintered wood. Cozy took her time, careful not to get her tail fur caught on the nail again.

The foxes crept down the pitch-black crack between house and fence and entered the wild shadows of the Trash Yard. Most humans threw their old things away, but the Toothless Lady kept it all: towers of tires, nests of spokes, a mannequin and a broken window, a refrigerator, a stopped clock, even a sculpture of a human eye—all surrounded by stacks of magazines, grown fat with months of rain.

Cozy's tail relaxed; her ears softened. The Trash Yard was a rare comfort on Hawthorne Street, with its treats and many hiding places. Still, she stepped lightly, scanning the lawn for shards or loose staples, ready to bite like ants.

As Julep sniffed the yard's more interesting treasures, Dusty checked the house's back porch. A ghost of the Toothless Lady's perfume hung in the air, like wilting flowers. Her rocking chair swayed in a light wind. The old woman was in for the night. But she hadn't forgotten them. The cat food tin was open and waiting.

"*Phht*," Dusty said, and Sterling shot toward the wobbly steps, his silvery fur streaking through the night. Julep, who'd been distracted, sprinted after him, blurring his bluish splotches. Sterling was a whisker from the porch when Julep snagged him by the tail and yanked him back down.

"*Yipe!*"

Julep climbed over Sterling's back but stumbled before he reached the top. Sterling leapt to the side, pouncing on the loose step and making its other end bow up, cracking Julep under the jaw and flipping him backward down the stairs.

Sterling made it to the tin and panted in victory.

At the bottom of the steps, Julep scowled. "You almost made me bite my tongue off!"

"Good!" Sterling said. "With speed like that you'll never make it to the food in time to use it!"

Julep shook the pain from his muzzle and laughed despite himself. "I know where you *sleep*."

This was why Cozy always waited before climbing the stairs.

"It's *empty*!" Sterling said.

He nudged the tin off the porch, making it clink hollow down the steps and roll to a stop before Dusty.

The vixen narrowed her eyes toward the street. "Someone's been here."

Sterling and Julep looked at each other wide-eyed. Cozy's hackles prickled. She didn't feel so hungry anymore.

"The neighborhood foxes know this yard is ours," Dusty said. "We've marked it."

"I'll mark it again just to be sure," Sterling said. He peed on a tire.

"Does this mean no cat food tonight?" Julep asked sadly.

Dusty batted the can away. "Good riddance. It's wet garbage meat anyway."

Julep's ears wilted. "Take that back."

Dusty led the kits through the narrow crack to the front lawn. "You know the drill. The three G's."

"Gardens, garages, garbage cans," Sterling and Julep recited.

But the garages were all sealed up that night. Every trash can clamped shut with elastic cords. Even the garden fences had been mended, sharp wires placed along their tops, their boards extended into the earth.

"We'll have to cross the street," Dusty said, her voice tight.

Cozy caught the boys smiling at each other. The other side of the street was another fox's territory.

The foxes crossed beneath the dying twilight and snuck up to the house with the creaky weather vane.

Dusty paused in front of the fence. "Sterling?"

Sterling nodded and then dug into the grass as if his life depended on it. Once he'd made a hole deep enough, they all slipped through.

### BAOWRAOWRAOWRAOWR!!!

The next fence over bent and shook as the old dog attacked the wood, trying to snag the foxes through the slats. Dusty teased the hound with her tail while the kits bounded up a mulch pile, crossed another fence's wobbly top, and dropped down two yards over.

They waited in the shadows while Dusty padded along the wobbly fence, snarling death at the snapping hound, before bounding down beside them into the Chicken Yard.

The chickens sensed the foxes coming, and their coop filled with panicky warbles that made Cozy a little drooly.

"Cozy?" Dusty said.

Cozy closed her eyes and sniffed, sensing for wafts of human sweat and dander that slipped through the cracks of houses. *Snff snff.* This house's doors and windows were locked tight. *Snff.* She couldn't find the faintest hint of sweat. These humans had been gone awhile.

"Clear," Cozy said.

Sterling and Julep raced up the ramp of the coop. Sterling chewed on the twisted wire while Dusty sniffed the border for a way in.

She made a full rotation, then slipped her paws into the wire holes and scaled the mesh toward the tin roof. But she couldn't get over the lip. She dropped to the lawn and huffed in disappointment.

"You're lucky, ladies," Julep told the chickens, who stared at him, throats bobbing like frightened hearts.

"Whoa," Sterling said. "What's *that*?"

Beside the coop was a small box made of wires. It was just big enough for a fox to fit inside, and it smelled delicious.

Sterling bounded off the ramp, romping toward the box's entrance, but Dusty caught him by the scruff and dragged him back.

The metal box shone dully in the remaining twilight. Inside was a dish overflowing with kibble. The foxes had seen many traps since they'd come to Hawthorne Street. Dusty always said that humans blamed foxes for everything. Broken fences. Cat feces. Disease. If a house burned down, she said, humans would say the foxes' tails were made of flames.

"Julep?" Dusty said.

Julep sniffed at the kibble in the trap. "It's clean," he said, a little glassy-eyed. He always got that way when smelling for poison.

Dusty circled the box, studying its slanted wire entrance and the spring contraption within.

"Trap 'Em 2000," she said, reading the label on the back. "Clever."

She slid under the trap's opening. The door tried to snap shut behind her, but she blocked it with her fluffy tail. She snagged the dish with her front teeth, coiled her body, and wriggled back through the narrow space held open by her tail.

*Klak!* The trap snapped shut with a rattle.

Dusty scattered the kibble across the lawn, and the kits fell to crunching, Julep with more ferocity than the others. The kibble was soggy from the lawn sprinklers, but it filled Cozy's belly well enough.

"Doncha want some, Dusty?" Julep asked between crunches.

Dusty sneered at the kibble, then gazed into the night. "What I wouldn't give for a rabbit right now."

Cozy swallowed her last bite and licked her beard clean. There was one crumb left on top of her snout, just out of reach. She looked to Sterling and Julep for help, but they were busy cleaning each other's muzzles and playing Catch Your Tongue.

Cozy tilted her nose toward Dusty. "Mom?"

*Snrrrrr.*

The moment Cozy heard the snarl, she winced and dropped to her side.

*"What did I tell you?"* Dusty snapped. Her fang was a hair away from Cozy's ear.

Cozy's voice came in a hoarse whisper. "It was an accident." She showed the vixen her belly.

Dusty breathed heavy a moment, then huffed—*phht*—making Cozy flinch.

The vixen headed back toward the street, and Cozy rolled upright, fighting tears. It was easy to forget sometimes that Dusty didn't do mom stuff. Easy to forget Cozy's real mom was gone.

Two tongues were suddenly licking Cozy's muzzle from either side.

"We gotcha, Coze!" Julep said.

"We'll make ya as clean as a dog whistle!" Sterling said.

Cozy pulled away. Her heart hurt too much for a cleaning just then.

Twilight faded on the horizon, and night fell in earnest. The stars leeched the last of the grays away, and the windows' dancing lights clicked off. As the neighborhood dissolved to darkness, the foxes headed back toward the graveyard, trying to stay ahead of the Black Hours.

# TWO

**A** **SHADOW WAS WAITING** on the edge of the graveyard.

Cozy ducked behind Dusty's tail and peeked through her tall legs. It was a fox. They had seen him. He and his vixen lived beneath the garden shed at the end of Hawthorne Street. He was large, with fur as orange as autumn leaves. The Chicken Yard was his territory.

The adults considered each other in the starlight. Their lips were uncurled, their hackles smoothed, but Cozy could sense the tension in Dusty's limbs. Cozy tried to stand as brave as Sterling, but her legs felt like jelly.

"Something is killing foxes," the fox said. "I found a body near the reservoir last night. Fresh."

Cozy's heart gave a quake. And not only for the dead fox. On hot days, Dusty led the kits to the reservoir to cool their tongues. But Cozy always kept her distance. She could hear voices in the bubbles—drowning ones. She could see little muzzles under the water's surface, ready to leap out and drag her under if she got too close.

"Her scent was clear of poison," the fox continued. "Her tail untread by tires. Her fur dry and unscratched. I would have spent more time examining her, but I sensed a presence." The fox narrowed his eyes at Dusty. "I have reason to believe it was another fox."

Dusty gazed back toward the wild shadows of the Trash Yard. "Something stole our food tonight."

"I kept to my territory," the fox said. "Did you keep to yours?"

Sterling stepped forward with a snarl, but Dusty knocked him back. Cozy's breath came uneasy. Dusty could outrun the garden shed fox, but if the kits tried to escape, he would snatch them up like helpless prey and snap their necks with a single squeeze.

"There's another thing," the fox said. "The vixen's body had a single puncture wound. In the chest."

Cozy stared up at Dusty, her one fang jutting from her muzzle. Had the vixen killed that vixen so Cozy and the boys would have more to eat?

The fox took a step forward.

*"Phht,"* Dusty huffed, so urgently that even Sterling scrambled beneath her belly.

"You have more to gain from another fox's death than anyone else on Hawthorne Street." The fox nodded toward the kits. "By taking in these orphans, you've given yourself more mouths to feed."

Dusty started to back away, making the kits shuffle beneath her.

"I'm not trying to start a fight," the fox said, taking another step. "Let me smell your breath." Another step. "If there's no trace of the vixen's blood, you and the kits are free to go."

"Turn around," Dusty snapped at him. "Go back the way you came."

The fox lowered his muzzle in a growl. "You're hiding something."

Dusty lunged, leaving the kits out in the open. The fox met her in the air, jaws wide, their teeth clashing in a sickening crunch. They snarled and thrashed, trying to catch each other's throats as Sterling growled as if he were also in the fight.

**SSSSSHHHHHOOOOOMMMMMmmmmm**

A sound cut the night in two, like lightning striking sideways. It ripped a hole through the air, leaving behind a silence so complete it hurt Cozy's ears. Dusty and the fox collapsed to the grass.

Heart pounding, Cozy strained her eyes, trying to see what had happened. One of the foxes untangled itself from the other. Dusty. She was safe.

But the garden shed fox lay on the grass, tongue dangling between his teeth, eyes open and fixed on her. He was dead. Cozy could smell his life leaking from the single puncture wound in his chest. And beneath it, something like rotten eggs.

Dusty hunched low, glancing in one direction, then another, searching for the source of the thunderous sound.

Cozy tuned her senses to the night. *Look, sniff, listen.* Nothing stirred. Nothing breathed. *Look, sniff, listen.* The scent of blood clogged the air. *Look, sniff—* Her eye caught something at the field's edge. The wind ruffled the grass in a crooked, slender shape. Like a tree with two legs. Like the night itself was walking. Cozy blinked, and the figure vanished. Somewhere in the sweeping wind, she smelled burning leaves.

*"Rao!"* Dusty shouted something, but Cozy couldn't hear over the ringing in her ears.

The vixen took off across the field, and Sterling and Julep followed, scrambling around the body and vanishing among the headstones. For a horrifying moment, Cozy found herself alone with the dead fox and his rotten-egg scent and his wide, empty eyes.

She ran.

# THREE

**O**N THE OTHER side of the Howling Hour, in a den tucked deep in the graveyard, the kits were still awake.

"You were *so* scared," Sterling told Julep. "I smelled your pee."

"It was a *tactic*," Julep said proudly. "No one wants to bite a pee-covered kit."

"Oh yeah?"

Sterling bit Julep's haunch, hard, and the two chomped at each other, fangs clacking.

Cozy turned her nose away. Whenever the boys fought like this, their scents always grew stronger. Julep smelled like the soap at the Ladies' House. And Sterling . . . well, Sterling just smelled like boy.

Cozy tried to get comfortable, crinkling her bed of red and yellow leaves. She couldn't sleep. The ruptured air still rang in her ears. Every time she closed her eyes, she saw the dead fox staring back at her.

The boys finished their fight.

"What do you think it was?" Sterling whispered.

"All I saw was nothing," Julep said.

"*Nothing* looks like nothing. Unless something looks like nothing because it's *invisible*."

Julep gasped. *"Flamouflage."*

"Huh?"

"Like when something looks like the place it lives in so you can't tell it's there."

"Oh," Sterling said. "Camouflage."

"Right. That's what I said."

Cozy didn't know much about camouflage. Only that some prey had it—like lizards and insects. But living around humans with their endless sources of discarded food, she'd never had to learn to spot a prey's leafy-brown skin or grass-green wings.

She turned her head and studied the boys—Sterling, with his silver-streaked fur, and Julep, with his blue splotches—faint in the moonlit den. The kits' light brown fur helped them blend into the den's soil. That way, if a hungry badger peeked inside, it would see huddled clumps of dirt and nothing more.

But what sort of creature camouflaged with the night? What walked on two paws and smelled like burning leaves?

*"Zags,"* Julep said. "Gotta be."

Cozy rolled her eyes. Zags, the boys believed, lived in the clouds. They swept in with the storms, flashing the sky in blinding white, threatening to hurl electric death at any fox that didn't find cover. But Cozy didn't believe in Zags. The world had enough scary things in it without inventing more.

"It can't be Zags," Sterling said. "There weren't any clouds out there."

"It's the only thing that could kill a fox that way," Julep said. "Zags can shoot a lightning straight through your brain."

Sterling bit his lip in thought. "What if it's a *ghost*?"

Cozy's ear twitched. She hoped the boys didn't notice.

Back in the Linen Closet, when she was still a baby, her mom had taught her and her brothers about ghosts. Ghosts were sounds and scents, she'd said. What was left over after an animal's body had rotted away, leaving only the warning behind. If you were brave enough to listen to their whispers, the ghosts would tell you how to avoid their horrible fates.

But the ghosts Cozy knew stank like pipes and bathtubs. If she had smelled anything like that in the field, she would have turned tail from Hawthorne Street and never looked back.

"Ghosts don't make exploding sounds!" Julep said. "They sound like this: '*Woooooo*, I've come to chew your soul.'"

"Well, Zags sound like this," Sterling said. "'*Dzzt dzzt* Julep is as tame as a neutered poodle *dzzt*.'"

Julep scowled. "What do you think, Coze? Who's right? It's me."

"Don't ask *her*," Sterling said. "A moth will probably flutter out of her mouth."

Cozy sighed. She didn't like to talk much. Ever since she'd left the Linen Closet, her voice had lived at the bottom of her throat. Besides, she was still trying to make sense of the night—the explosion, the shifting green, the burning leaves . . .

"What if it's a human?" Julep asked.

"Ha!" Sterling said. "Humans don't have a camouflage. They don't even have *fur*."

Julep rocked his head back and forth. "It could have been hiding in some sand maybe. Or mud."

"There's no sand or mud in the graveyard!" Sterling said. "Just grass. And what I mean is, humans don't *need* a camouflage."

"Explain," Julep said.

Sterling quickly checked on Dusty, near the den's entrance. The vixen's breath was slow and even.

Sterling's voice fell low. "Why would humans need a camouflage when they have the *shovel*?"

Julep's ears drooped. "Or poison."

*Or sacks,* Cozy thought.

Humans had made each kit an orphan in a different way. Sterling had lost his family when a massive machine with smoggy breath and rusted teeth had caved in their den, burying them alive. Only Sterling was able to dig his way out.

Julep's dad had been poisoned. He'd insisted on trying a can of tuna fish before his son, and he'd died with his muzzle frothing pink.

Cozy didn't like to think about her story.

"Camouflage would be wasted on a human," Sterling said. "They've got too many tricks."

Julep nodded sadly, and Cozy quickly blinked before the boys could see the tears shine.

She used to love stories like these. Harrowing tales about Mia and Uly that her mom had told her and her brothers back in the Linen Closet. But that was before the sack.

Now, whenever Julep and Sterling talked about their families, Cozy wanted to hook her paws over her ears to keep the dark words from scrabbling into her mind like spiders. She was always grateful when Dusty snapped at the boys for dwelling on their tragic pasts.

But in the small of the den, with the vixen fast asleep, it was impossible not to catch splinters and shards of these terrible stories. Impossible to forget her own.

"Whatever's out there," Sterling said, "we have to get it." He gazed toward the den's entrance, autumn leaves twirling past. "Before it gets us."

"How do we get something we can't even see?" Julep asked.

The kits fell to thinking. Sleep came before any answers.

# FOUR

"**P**HHT!" **DUSTY HUFFED**, startling the kits awake. The boys leapt to their paws and romped toward the den's entrance, where dawn blushed the grasses. Cozy lingered behind, her stomach too full of knots to feel hungry.

"Keep to my tail," Dusty told the kits, sharper than usual. "We don't know what's out there, and I can't scavenge for all of us."

Sterling nudged Julep's side.

"What?" Julep whispered.

"Tell her," Sterling hissed through his teeth. He tilted his head and raised his eyebrows. "About the *Zags*?"

Julep swallowed, then slunk toward the vixen. "Um, Dusty?" he said nervously. "We-we think we figured out what's killing foxes."

Dusty glared at him. Cozy bit her tongue.

"So, um," Julep said, "we think what's doing it is probably a Zag."

Sterling nudged him again.

"And also," Julep said, "it has a camouflage. If we just

attack all the bushes, then maybe we can catch the Zag in our teeth." He gulped. "Or something."

Dusty's expression didn't change a whisker.

Julep sucked in his cheeks. "But now that I think about it, it's probably not that."

Dusty trotted out of the den.

Sterling started to laugh. "What happened?"

"I panicked!" Julep said. "Why didn't you say anything?"

"Because you were the one with all the good ideas," Sterling said mockingly. *"Zags."* He snorted. "That was so tame."

"I'm not tame! *You're* tame!"

"Where's your collar, *Tamey*?"

"It's sitting in *your* kennel with *your* name on it because it's actually *yours*."

Cozy had to grit her teeth to keep from chomping their noses. Her mom had worn a collar.

The boys began to fight again until Dusty stuck her head back into the den. "Come unless you want to starve."

Julep stopped fighting, but Sterling got one last chomp in.

The foxes slipped out of the den into the morning shadows. Cozy tuned her senses to look, sniff, listen . . . but she couldn't trust her eyes anymore. Not when the night itself could walk and split the air in two.

As the first warm winds ruffled the air and melted the night away, the foxes made their way out of the graveyard, through the leaves, around the headstones and over the grassy humps. Squirrels sensed them coming and scrambled up the cottonwoods, unaware that their stringy little bodies were too much trouble when just ahead was an entire neighborhood filled with feasts waiting to be plundered.

From the high hill, Cozy could see the bulky silhouettes of the skyscrapers, looming dead and gray in the distance, sparkling with ominous constellations. The sight of the City always made her chest swirl with fear and comfort both. A panic to keep far away fighting against an ache to return.

When the foxes reached the graveyard's edge, Cozy blurred her eyes, not wanting to see the dead fox again. But the body was no longer in the field. Something had taken it.

Cozy was grateful the fox was gone. Grateful she didn't have to see the birds pecking out those eyes. But the grass was still flattened in the body's shape. Blood crusted on the green. And every time Cozy blinked, she could see the dead fox staring back at her. Reminding her that something was out there.

The foxes made their usual sweep, stopping every dozen tails to look, sniff, listen. The air was clear of burning leaves, and there wasn't much green for a camouflaged thing to hide in. But Cozy still eyed every brick, sniffed every trash can, listened to the humans muffled in their houses.

The foxes passed the pinwheel, motionless without a breeze, and slipped into the tangled comfort of the Trash Yard. The dead-flower scent filled the air that morning, untangling the knots in Cozy's stomach. The Toothless Lady was out on her back porch, rocking in her chair and clipping her newspapers.

Dusty nodded, and Sterling padded toward the porch,

Julep close behind. They kept their eyes fixed on the old woman, who quietly chewed her gums and snipped her scissors.

At the bottom of the steps lay the cat food tin, upside down.

Sterling pawed it over. "Empty again!"

"Who's stealing our cat food?" Julep snarled through his teeth.

"Too slow, little ones!" the Toothless Lady called, sending the boys scrambling to the lawn's edge. The old woman cackled and wagged her scissors at them. "I put it out, but you were too slow!" She set down her newspaper and shuffled back inside. "Too slow, too slow."

Cozy's belly squirked. An empty stomach made the shadows darker, the grass sharp.

"Jackpot!"

Sterling had found something—a mound of soil at the base of the broken window. Cozy sniffed—*snff snff*—a meaty scent buried beneath.

Sterling started to dig, so Dusty and the kits joined him. The soil came loose and easy. About a foot down, they uncovered a cat's corpse. Its white fur was stained with earth. Its paws were black, and it still had a collar on.

"Why would the Toothless Lady stick this in the ground?" Julep asked.

"Maybe she was saving it for later," Sterling said, nosing the dead cat over and discovering a writhing white pool. "Sprinkles!"

"Those are *maggots*," Julep said, muzzle wrinkled with disgust.

"Whatever," Sterling said, chomping up a mouthful of the wriggling larvae and squishing them between his teeth. "I like it when they *pop*."

The foxes began to eat.

*SSSSSHHHHHOOOOOMMMMMmmmmmm*

A sound hooked Cozy's ears, jerking her muzzle toward the fence. She wasn't sure whether she had heard something in the distance or her senses were playing tricks.

The boys continued to chew. Not even Dusty seemed to have heard.

Once the cat was stripped to its collar and bones, the foxes headed back toward their den.

They froze at the graveyard's edge. There, beside a crumbling headstone, lay the body of another fox, stinking of blood and old eggs. It was the vixen from the garden shed. A hole ran straight through her throat, waking an invisible pain in Cozy's own.

The boys gave each other dark looks while Cozy swiveled her muzzle, searching the morning for clues. But the graveyard looked, smelled, and sounded as it always had.

"Quick now," Dusty whispered.

The foxes hurried to their den as fast as their paws could carry them.

Cozy was grateful the dead vixen's eyes had been shut.

# FIVE

**A**T DUSK, THE foxes prowled from their den and through the graveyard's twilit mist.

Sterling kept low, eyes narrow, while Julep made random snaps at the air, hoping to catch a Zag. Every hair on Cozy's tail was alert. Her ears strained; her whiskers stood on end. She searched the haze of evening for a walking tree. She sniffed for burning leaves. She listened to the wind, waiting for it to split.

Her senses did not relax until they reached Hawthorne Street.

Dusty passed by the Toothless Lady's house and led the kits across the road. They slipped beneath the white van Cozy had seen the night before, then crept behind the weather-vane house. They made the wobbly journey across the fence, over the barking hound, and then dropped down into the Chicken Yard.

Now that the garden shed foxes were gone, someone had to eat those chickens.

The trap had been reset, the dish within refilled. Dusty padded past it. She hooked her claws in the coop's wire circles and scaled the mesh. Once she reached the top, she pressed her nose between the tin roof and the wire, pushing her shoulders into one while bending the other with her paws, stretching the space between them. She had learned something from the Trap 'Em 2000.

Dusty slipped inside the coop, as the feathered meals began to flap and scream. The kits ate as well as humans that night.

As the Black Hours rose, the foxes padded back toward the graveyard, bellies full, muzzles sticky with red.

"What's your favorite part of the chicken?" Julep asked.

"The screaming," Sterling answered.

"I'm a leg fox myself," Julep said.

### GRAO!

A voice stopped them in their tracks. Their muzzles swiveled toward a swell of brambles on the graveyard's western edge.

### GRAO!

The voice wailed from within, urgent and mournful. But what it was wailing Cozy couldn't tell. She widened her eyes, trying to catch a shape, any shape. The brambles trapped the night on its thorns, all shadows against the stars.

### GRAO!

She winced. There was something horrible about that voice. Something strangled and strange. It sounded like a fox, but its words didn't make any sense.

### GRAAOOO!

The voice was growing desperate. It wanted the foxes to come into the thicket.

"Cozy?" Dusty said.

Cozy sniffed for human sweat or burning leaves. But the wind swept toward the brambles.

"I-I can't tell," she whispered.

**GRAO!**

Dusty tilted her nose into the air. "Who are you?" she called.

**GRAO! GRAO! GRAO!**

The voice seemed excited that it had received a response. Julep's breath shuddered.

"Phht!" Dusty huffed at the kits, turning tail away from the voice.

**GRAO! GRAO! GRAO!**

Cozy and Julep trotted after Dusty, but Sterling didn't budge.

"She's in trouble," he said, staring toward the brambles.

"I dunno, Ster," Julep said. "That fox sounds weird. I don't think we should listen."

Cozy's heart thumped. What if Sterling was right? What if this fox had been captured by the walking night? What if they could still save it?

**GRAO!**

Sterling took off across the grass, sprinting toward the brambles.

"Sterling!" Dusty hissed after him.

"She might be buried somewhere!" Sterling called back. "We have to dig her out!"

Cozy's stomach turned icy with fear. Julep's paws kneaded the grass.

Dusty huffed. "If he wants to get himself killed, let him."

She turned to leave. Julep whimpered but followed.

Cozy's limbs felt too tense to move. Sterling was half-way to the brambles now. His silvery fur blending with the night. The strange voice had fallen silent.

"*Phht!*" Dusty huffed at Cozy.

Cozy winced but kept her eyes on Sterling. She frantically searched for walking trees, but all she saw was thorny blackness.

"*Now*, Cozy," Dusty said, "or I'll drag you by your scruff."

Sterling reached the brambles, and a shadow separated from itself. A tree bent away from the others. Cozy strained her eyes and spotted a glint of metallic black right before—

**SSSSSHHHHHOOOOOMMMMMmmmmm**

The night erupted, and Sterling fell, tumbling across the grass. Somewhere, a headstone shattered.

Cozy bounded forward to save her friend, but Dusty seized her scruff.

"No!" Cozy yelped. "Sterling!"

**SSSSSHHHHHOOOOOMMMMMmmmmm**

Something zipped past her ear, and warm liquid sprayed against the back of her head, slamming her eyes shut.

When she opened them again, she found she was being carried back to the graveyard, her scruff clamped tight in Dusty's jaws. Blood ran down the vixen's throat. Someone was howling over and over.

*Oh*, Cozy thought.

It was her.

# SIX

**B**ACK IN THE den, the kits lay in a close pile on their bed of leaves.

Cozy could feel Julep's paws pressed against her back, Sterling's tail folded over her own. She stared at Dusty, who was passed out cold by the entrance. The vixen's breath came rapid and shallow. The fresh slash across her cheek, opposite her single fang, gave her a half-twisted grin. Cozy's own cheek stung just looking at it.

After the air itself had torn open Dusty's face, she had still carried Cozy back to the den. The vixen had bitten Cozy's scruff so hard she'd squeezed the howls out of her. Dusty had saved her life. But she had also prevented Cozy from trying to save Sterling. Cozy wasn't sure she'd ever forgive her.

"We've gotta stop it," Sterling whispered behind her. "Otherwise, it'll keep attacking us until we're all as dead as canned meat." He had the sort of snarl in his voice that he used when talking about hunting for tractors and ripping their shovels to pieces. "It almost got Dusty!"

"I thought it got you when you rolled across the grass!" Julep said.

"That was a *stealth* roll," Sterling said. "Did you cry for me?"

"No!"

"No, huh? Let me lick your whiskers. Ope! Tastes salty to me!"

Julep lunged at Sterling, and Cozy kept her breath slow and even, feigning sleep as the boys finished their fight.

"We gotta hunt it," Sterling said. "Tonight."

"How can we hunt it when we don't even know what it is?" Julep asked.

"Well, what do we know about it?"

"We know it's a fox," Julep said. "We heard it talk."

Cozy winced. That hideous *Grao!* still echoed through her ears. The walking shadow was burned into her eyes. She had stopped trusting her ability to look. Now she couldn't trust her ability to listen, either.

"What if it's not a fox?" Sterling said. "What if something stole a fox's voice?"

"Things can't *steal* other things' voices!" Julep hissed.

"Magpies steal voices all the time!" Sterling said.

While the boys argued, Cozy ran through the clues again, trying to cobble them together into a single creature. She imagined a thing that blended with the night, bending and stretching its body to fit in a patch of crabgrass or behind a single branch. Its fur was made of moss. Its nose was metal, glinting black. Its tongue was nothing but smoke, and from its skull stared the dead eyes of the garden shed fox.

"So we agree," Sterling said. "We go to the Trash Yard and listen for something that definitely kind of sounds like a fox, even though it might not be."

"Wait," Julep said. "Why the Trash Yard?"

"You haven't figured it out?"

"Figured what out?"

"The cat food!"

Dusty stirred in her sleep, and the boys' muzzles clicked shut.

A moment later, Julep whispered, "What about the cat food?"

"It started disappearing the same time foxes started dying," Sterling said. "Tell me that's a coincidence!"

Cozy felt a flutter. This was the first thing Sterling had said that made sense. She imagined the moss-furred thing in the Toothless Lady's backyard, licking the tin with its tongue of smoke.

"The Toothless Lady puts out that cat food every dawn and dusk," Sterling whispered. "If we leave now, we'll get there before that fox killer can steal it."

Cozy quietly sniffed toward the den's entrance, where the Black Hours still reigned. Foxes were meant to keep to their dens when all was black as pitch. Especially kits.

"We'll hide in the Trash Yard and wait," Sterling continued. "As soon as the ghost, Zag, fox, whatever it is, shows up, *that's* when we'll pounce and rip the thing to smithereens. We'll save the neighborhood! And our cat food, of course."

"Totally," Julep said. He squirmed against Cozy's back. "It's just . . . if we go out there, that thing might explode our faces."

"Don't go tame on me now, Julep," Sterling said. "This isn't a dentime story."

Julep's hackles sharpened against Cozy's shoulders. "I'm *not* tame."

"Prove it."

Julep's hackles softened. "Maybe we should wake up Cozy and ask her."

Sterling scoffed. "She'll say *no*. She's tamer than you are."

Cozy rolled upright. Sterling snapped his muzzle shut while Julep flipped around and cowered.

Cozy stared at them. "Let's go kill this thing."

Sterling's eyebrows leapt while Julep's furrowed.

"Ha!" Sterling said. He batted Julep's cheek. "See? Even Cozy thinks you're tame."

Julep's muzzle rumpled in anger.

Sterling trotted toward the entrance. "Come on," he whispered. "Before Dusty wakes up."

Julep scowled at Cozy. "Don't know why we're listening to a vixen kit, anyway."

She ignored him and followed Sterling.

Cozy didn't like hearing about sad things. They brought too many memories bubbling up inside her. But if she was forced to hear them anyway, if she knew foxes were in trouble, she couldn't just hide in the den.

Besides, the boys' imaginations kept running away with them, making them snarl at clouds and chomp at empty air. Whatever was killing foxes might have tricked her eyes and ears with its shadow walk and fox's howl. But she could still trust her nose.

The three kits slipped out of the den and into the Black Hours.

It was a long, chilled walk across the graveyard. The fox kits crept tail to tail through the endless black. There were no howls in the night. No glinting metal or walking trees. But that only made Cozy more nervous.

Halfway across the field, she thought she caught a whiff of burning leaves, but she couldn't tell whether it was her nose or her fear speaking to her. Still, she romped ahead of Sterling, leading him and Julep away from the scent, toward the moon.

They made it to Hawthorne Street. No streetlights shone. No windows glowed. Moonlight stretched the chimney shadows long and crooked across the roofs.

The kits passed the still pinwheel and slipped beneath the fence, through the crack, and into the Trash Yard. Sterling nosed open the rusted refrigerator, and they all hopped inside, hiding their tails in the musty shadows and sticking their noses into the crisp air.

They watched the back porch. And they waited.

The moon grew dull. The air fell still. The crickets played a lulling song.

Julep sighed. "I never thought hunting fox killers would be so boring."

In response, Sterling stank up the refrigerator. "Is that more interesting?"

Cozy held her breath while the boys tried to contain their giggles.

Soon, the stars melted into the brightening sky and gave the roof a shape. The screen door creaked open, and the Toothless Lady tottered out, slippers shuffling against the porch, her dead-flower scent blooming through the yard. The foxes watched, whiskers sharp.

There was a crisp pop as the old woman squeezed a tool into the tin, followed by a metallic crunch as she wound the handle. Julep licked his lips. The Toothless Lady hadn't fully opened the tin when her eyes caught something across the yard at the base of the broken window. The tool and the tin fell from her hands, clattering against the porch.

"No!" the woman cried. She shuffled down the steps toward the bones of the cat the foxes had eaten the day before. "No, no, *no!*" She fell to her knees and picked up the collar, clasping it tight in her withered fingers. *"Bootsie!"* She blinked the wetness from her eyes, then searched the yard. Her mouth pulled into a frown. *"Vermin."* She spat the word.

With a grunt, the old woman stood and hobbled back into her house, cradling the collar to her chest. The screen slammed shut behind her.

"What's her deal?" Julep asked.

Sterling shrugged. "Probably upset she didn't get to eat Bootsie herself. Right, Coze? Cozy?"

Cozy's jaw fell open. Her breath stopped. The boys followed her gaze, and their eyes went wide.

The thing did not come from the sky. It did not come from the shadows or the rooftops. It came from beneath the porch. It wriggled out from a hole in the latticework, fuzzy and indistinct in the thin dawn light. The thing was fox-shaped, but also not. Its ears were floppy. Its tail curled.

Strangest of all, a piece of metal dangled from the base of its ear.

The sight of the creature sent Cozy's heart racing. She wasn't sure whether it was out of fear . . . or something else.

The kits watched in silence as the thing hopped awkwardly up the steps.

"Is that a . . . *fox*?" Sterling asked.

*"Foxoid Being,"* Julep whispered. "It's a Zag! I *told* you guys!"

The Foxoid Being reached the porch and searched the yard with its moony, wide eyes. The kits tucked their muzzles back into the refrigerator, then reextended them as the Being sniffed at the tin. It licked its lips, showing teeth so dull that they didn't look as if they could bite through a feather.

"That's not a Zag," Sterling whispered. "It's a dog. Look at its face!"

"Zags can *disguise* themselves," Julep said. "They don't just have a camouflage."

"It has jewelry. Like dogs do."

"Dogs wear *collars*," Julep said. "Not earrings." He nodded to the strange metal tag. "*That* is Zag technology. That's how it hurt Dusty. It shot a lightning out of that thing."

"You can't shoot a lightning out of earrings," Sterling said.

"You can if they're Zag earrings."

Throughout this argument, the Foxoid Being pawed at the half-sealed tin and flipped it with its nose, trying to get it open. Cozy sniffed, hoping to get a sense of what she was seeing. The creature was a little boy. He had the most beautiful fur she'd ever seen, shiny and smooth. Strangely, he smelled like *nothing*. This reminded her of something she'd heard before—in a story maybe—but she couldn't remember where.

Sterling narrowed his eyes. "If that metal thing can give it a camouflage, then why isn't it using it *right now?*"

"It's eating," Julep said, as if that explained it.

The Foxoid Being finally managed to peel open a section of the lid. He slipped his tongue inside, licking the jellylike fats from the top of the food and whimpering hungrily. Cozy's stomach gurgled in sympathy.

"Whatever it is," Sterling said, "it kills foxes."

"*Yeah*," Julep snarled.

Surprise caught Cozy by the throat. The boys didn't actually believe that this little creature had killed those foxes, did they? Nothing about the Foxoid Being was green or smoking or glinting. He was too small to *Grao!* across the fields. And she didn't believe that metal tag could do any of those things.

"We gotta get it," Sterling said. "*Now.* Before it slips back under the porch."

"Ready when you are," Julep said, waggling his hips.

"Wait—" Cozy began.

But the boys were already lunging out of the refrigerator. By the time Cozy stepped out, they were halfway across the yard. The Foxoid Being jerked his head up in alarm, then cowered at the sight of two foxes bolting toward him. He tumbled down the stairs, but before he could slip through the latticework, Sterling leapt and pinned his throat to the lawn while Julep pounced on his tail.

"Quick, Cozy!" Julep shouted, putting his weight on the

Being's thrashing hind legs. "Chew off its earring before it chucks lightning at our heads!"

Cozy froze between the refrigerator and the porch. The Foxoid Being looked so frightened. He yelped in pain as Sterling shook his scruff and Julep chomped his toes. They were going to rip the poor thing apart.

Cozy tried to find the words to stop them. "I-I . . ."

### *BANG! BANG! BANG! BANG! BANG!*

For one awful moment, Cozy believed that the Being's ear tag was firing lightning and that Julep and Sterling were about to fall down dead, holes burned straight through them.

But then the screen door slapped open and the Toothless Lady shuffled onto the porch, banging two pots together. "Get on! Scat!"

### *BANG! BANG! BANG!*

With Sterling and Julep startled, the Foxoid Being wrenched himself from their grip and scrambled through the narrow crack between house and fence. The boys chased him toward the street while Cozy ran to keep up, just managing to dodge one of the Toothless Lady's hurled pots.

# SEVEN

**WHATEVER THE FOXOID** Being was, he wasn't fast.

The boys chased him to the end of the sidewalk, where Sterling managed to tackle him onto the grass. Julep leapt and tumbled them both, and their bodies became a confused tangle of fur and gnashing teeth, yipes, snarls, and gasping.

Cozy watched helpless as the boys ripped at the poor thing's ears and paws. The smell of the Being's fear roiled her stomach.

*"Stop!"* she yowled.

The boys looked up, shocked to hear her cry so loudly. Cozy was pretty shocked herself. But her distraction gave the Being a chance to wriggle out from under the boys and slink away. His fur was disheveled, his shoulder bleeding.

"Come on, Julep!" Sterling said. "It's gonna get away!"

Before Julep could move, Cozy nodded toward the silver tag, dangling against the Being's cheek.

"Why isn't he shooting lightning right now?" she asked.

"Because." Sterling snarled toward the Foxoid Being. "It knows if it tries, we'll turn it into dog food."

Julep nodded. "The *gross* kind."

The Foxoid Being had flopped to his belly, exhausted. He kept his nose on the boys, in case they tried attacking again. Cozy looked into his strange wide eyes.

"Why don't we try talking to him?" she said.

"Because it can't speak fox, *duh*," Julep said.

"I can speak fox," the Being said in a trembling voice.

The boys' heads spun around.

Sterling swallowed his shock. "You can't fool us."

"Yeah," Julep said. "We know Zags steal voices."

"And dogs can say a few words," Sterling said. "Stupid ones."

"I'm not a dog," the Foxoid Being said. He lifted his muzzle, showing blood crusted around his throat. "A dog bit me."

Cozy's own throat started to sting in the same spot.

"I never said dogs don't fight," Sterling said. "They're not smart enough to work together."

The Foxoid Being swallowed.

Sterling stepped toward him. "You thought you could get away with killing every fox on Hawthorne Street. But you made a *big* mistake when you hurt Dusty."

"And when you ate our cat food," Julep said, closing in.

The Foxoid Being started to retreat, eyes jerking from Sterling to Julep. "I-I don't know who Dusty is. And I didn't know that food was yours. I was hungry."

Sterling stopped approaching. His grin grew sharp. "You were *hungry*, eh?"

The Foxoid Being shifted his paws and licked his whiskers.

"Why didn't ya say so?" Sterling said. "We'll feed you."

The Foxoid Being's floppy ears perked. "Really?"

"We have special food just for visitors," Sterling said. "Right, Julep?"

Julep caught Sterling's wicked expression. "Right."

Cozy started to worry.

Sterling trotted back down the sidewalk. "Come with us."

The Foxoid Being swayed, then crept after him, head lowered. Julep bowed his muzzle, allowing the Foxoid Being to pass, then followed behind. Cozy padded after them. It was only when Sterling crossed the street that she realized where they were going.

She ran to catch up with him. "He couldn't have killed those foxes, Sterling. *Look* at him."

Sterling stopped in the middle of the road and considered the Foxoid Being. Cozy could see in his eyes that he didn't believe it either. But he had an anger that would not be tamed. Sterling had needed to kill something that hurt foxes since the day his family had died.

"He still crossed into our territory and ate our food," Sterling said. "And now he has to pay."

Before Cozy could argue, the boys led the Foxoid Being behind the house, up the mulch, across the fence, and into the Chicken Yard. The house was still locked up tight. Every light was off. The humans were still away.

"Your food's in there," Sterling said, pointing his muzzle. "Eat up."

The Foxoid Being saw the trap, and his floppy ears flopped even lower. "That's a cage."

"Nah," Julep said, padding up behind him. "It's a food giver. Like the ones humans put up for birds. It just looks like that so animals that aren't foxes can't get inside."

"No need to lie to him now, Julep," Sterling said with a sneer. "We got him this far." He grinned at the Foxoid Being. "Yeah, it's a cage. And you're getting in it."

"But," the Foxoid Being said, "I just got out of a cage."

Sterling and Julep stood tall, blocking the way back to the street.

The Foxoid Being sighed pitifully and then nuzzled beneath the trap's slanted door. The door slapped shut behind him with a rattled *klang*.

"And that's how you catch a fox killer!" Sterling said.

Julep jumped onto his back and gnawed his ears with approval.

The Foxoid Being turned circles in the cage. The scent of fear was so sharp it stung Cozy's eyes.

*Hsssssss!*

A wet hiss scared Cozy off her paws, and she bounded onto the planters and back to the fence before the sprinkler water could touch her fur. The boys took their time, giggling and romping through the droplets.

Cozy watched the Foxoid Being desperately sniffing for an exit while the sprinklers drenched his fur. He howled in misery, sounding nothing like the voice in the fields. The boys laughed as they hopped up the planters and onto the fence.

Cozy whimpered. "He could freeze."

"It shoulda thought of that before it ate our food," Sterling said, and trotted along the top of the wobbly fence.

Cozy couldn't tear her eyes from the Being. Even if he survived the night, the humans would return eventually. And they would kill him.

A damp muzzle nudged her side. "It was either him or us, Coze," Julep said. He followed after Sterling.

Cozy watched the Being shiver. She couldn't get the trap open. And if she watched his fur drip any longer, her heart would break beyond repair. It reminded her of her brothers.

She turned away and followed the boys.

"Dusty! *Dusty!*" Julep called, romping triumphant into the den. "We did it!"

Dusty was only just waking as the sun crept bright and golden across her fur and bloody cheek.

"We found what was eating our food!" Sterling said, bounding in beside him.

"And we caught the killer!" Julep said.

They told her the story while Cozy sat in the den's entrance, biting her tongue, which was starting to feel raw.

When the story was finished, Dusty scowled, showing her single fang and stretching her wicked gash until the kits, even Cozy, started to cower.

"If you ever leave this den without my permission again," Dusty said, "I will not let you back inside."

She pointed her nose toward the bed of leaves in the

corner, and the kits understood. No scavenging for them that morning.

"You'd think she'd be grateful," Sterling whispered as he slumped against the soil.

Julep sighed and lay beside him. "Our reward will be the satisfaction of no more dead foxes. And also cat food."

Soon they were both asleep.

It was only now, in the quiet of the den, that Cozy remembered that whatever was killing foxes was still out there.

# EIGHT

**T**HAT NIGHT, THE boys bounded out of the den with a prancing confidence. Cozy kept to Dusty's tail. She watched the vixen's sniffing nose, her rotating ears, her forepaw lifting to investigate every rustle, every click. There were no fox barks. No burning leaves. The shadows held their shapes.

Cozy's heart began to beat steadily. What if the Foxoid Being *had* killed those foxes with his tag?

The moment they set paw on Hawthorne Street, the streetlamps flickered on. They took their practiced path through the neighborhood, darting in and out of yards, weaving through fences, and slinking down gutters.

They passed the pinwheel, which spiraled mesmerizingly, and entered the Toothless Lady's backyard, which bloomed with the comforting scent of wilting flowers. The shapes were all familiar—the eye sculpture and the broken clock, the newspapers and tires. Julep paused to scratch his side against the bicycle spokes.

"Cat food's back!" Sterling said.

He and Julep raced toward the porch, extra anxious after skipping morning rounds.

Something was wrong. A silence filled Cozy's ears. Her whiskers wouldn't stop twitching. The old woman sat hunched in her rocking chair, a gray silhouette, wet eyes gazing into the dusk of the yard. She was not snipping her scissors as usual. Her chair was still.

The moment the boys reached the base of the steps, Cozy smelled it. Beneath the perfume, so faint it was almost nonexistent, was a nauseous tinge of burning leaves. She widened her eyes and saw a gleam of black metal—a stick, as straight as a broom handle, leaning against the back door.

"*Wait*," she said, her voice barely a squeak.

Dusty heard and sniffed toward the porch.

The boys were already halfway up the steps. The old woman was standing from her rocking chair. She stood taller. She stood *thinner*. She peeled her hair off her head as her face contorted in a crinkled smile. The Toothless Lady had *teeth* now.

*No,* Cozy thought. *Not the Toothless Lady.*

"The Hidden Man," Dusty whispered. "Boys!"

Julep stopped and looked back, but Sterling continued to leap up the steps.

The Hidden Man had tricked their eyes. He had tricked their ears. And now . . .

Cozy watched in horror as the Hidden Man, cloaked in the scent of wilted flowers, grabbed the black stick and raised it. Sterling paused at the top of the steps and slowly looked up at the man, who grinned down over the stick. Sterling didn't run. Instead, he frantically scraped his claws against the porch. Like he was trying to dig. Trying to escape.

**TTTTTHHHHHEEEEEEOOOOOMMMMMMmmmmm**

The sound was deafening in the tiny yard. And Sterling was rolling limp down the steps. His body reached the grass, and he slumped to stillness, red on his chest.

*"Sterling!"* Julep cried, and bounded toward his friend.

The Hidden Man clicked the stick—*chk-chk!*—as Dusty lunged and clamped Julep's scruff, dragging him across the yard and through the crack as the stick traced their movements.

Cozy stood in shock, feeling an impossible pain in her chest where Sterling had been hit. It was only when the Hidden Man swept the stick across the yard, looking for more foxes, that she startled, realizing she was still alive.

She scampered behind the stack of tires before the stick could put a hole in her too. She held her breath and waited, trembling uncontrollably, until she heard the *thunk* of metal against the porch. Cozy peered from behind the tires and sniffed at Sterling's still form. She couldn't smell his breath.

On the porch, the Hidden Man slipped off the Toothless Lady's dress like a second skin, revealing clothing printed with sticks and leaves and releasing a waft of old smoke. Cozy couldn't look away. For all her looking and sniffing and listening, she hadn't been able to sense the danger before it was too late.

The screen creaked open, and the Toothless Lady, the real one, stepped out of the house, rubbing her arms and staring down at the hump of fur that had once been Sterling.

"It didn't feel any pain, did it?" she asked.

The Hidden Man laughed. "What do you think?" He nodded to Sterling. "Clever little buggers." He reached in his pocket and pulled out a cylindrical wooden object. "Usually, all it takes is a bit of this."

He put it to his lips and blew.

### *GRAO!*

The sound sent a shiver from Cozy's nose straight to her tail. Sterling was right. The Hidden Man had stolen a fox's voice.

"They even avoided my blind after they picked up my scent," the Hidden Man said. He held up a bottle of golden liquid and grinned. "Thanks for making me smell pretty."

The Toothless Lady snatched the bottle and held it to her chest. She frowned at Sterling's body. "Poor thing. I never would have called you if they hadn't eaten my Bootsie."

*"Poor thing?"* The Hidden Man stuck a white stick in his mouth, flicked a fire to life, and touched it to the stick. Orange glowed on his wrinkled eyes, and the air grew

choked with smoke. "You put out food every day, attracting these pests and creating a problem for your neighbors. Then, once the foxes eat your precious dead pet, you need *me* to come and clean up after ya." He puffed again and laughed. "'Poor thing.' You killed this kit yourself, lady."

The Toothless Lady coughed and waved a hand in front of her face. "I wish you wouldn't smoke on my porch."

The Hidden Man blew smoke at her. "Pay me."

The Toothless Lady stepped inside while the man grabbed a cardboard box from under the rocking chair. He descended the steps, snagged Sterling by the tail, and lifted him. The moment Sterling's body began to sway, Cozy looked away.

Somehow, her paws managed to slink back through the crack. She found Dusty and Julep at the end of the sidewalk. Julep stared at his paws, eyes leaking.

"*Phht*," Dusty said, padding down the street.

"We can't just leave him," Julep said quietly.

Cozy didn't want to tell him she'd seen the red spray. Almost like feathers. Or that Sterling's body had gone into a box.

Dusty turned back. "What do we say when we lose someone?"

Julep sniffed. "Fewer tails to watch over."

Dusty looked to Cozy.

"M-more food for us," Cozy said, stifling a whimper.

Dusty nodded. "Instinct prevails."

Cozy hated these words. And she hated Dusty for making her say them. She often imagined running away from the graveyard den and Dusty's heartless rules. But how could one small kit possibly survive in a world of humans?

"Where we're going," Dusty said, "we won't need a digger anyway."

She padded off, leaving Cozy and Julep to look at each other. What would life be like without Sterling? Quieter. Not as funny. Maybe not as mean either. But one thing was certain. If it had been Julep or Cozy with holes in them, Sterling would be sprinting back into that yard to try and save their lives. For better or worse.

*"Phht!"* Dusty huffed.

The kits followed.

At the end of Hawthorne Street, Dusty made a hard turn, away from the graveyard.

"Where are we going?" Julep said. He sounded afraid.

Dusty gazed back toward the gray roofs of the street. "While the Hidden Man prowls the neighborhood, we'll have no chance here. He'll hunt us down wherever we hide." She gazed toward the sharp silhouettes of the skyline, purple with twilight. "We'll have to return to the City."

A thrill ran through Cozy's heart. Horror and excitement both. *The City.* Where the humans swarmed, and hiding places were common but treacherous. Where trash cans overflowed with food, but many were laced with poison. Where a fox could find paradise as easily as death. Where Cozy had been born.

Based on Julep's expression, he saw only terror in the towering structures. Even Sterling, the bravest of the three kits, had been running from the City ever since it spread into the fields, unearthed him from his den, and buried his family alive.

The ghostly pain reared to life in Cozy's chest again. Her eyes began to burn. The City had finally caught up with Sterling.

"Maybe the old den is still there," Dusty said. She started toward the skyline.

"Wait!" Cozy said.

Dusty stared back at her, and Cozy's heart started to pound.

"There's a fox kit," Cozy said. "Back in the trap. He might still be there."

"That was a dog, Cozy," Julep said.

Cozy blinked at him. That wasn't what he'd said before.

"It spoke fox," she told Dusty. "We can still save him."

Dusty considered a moment. "A kit?"

Cozy swallowed. Despite Dusty's sharp ways, she had taken Cozy, Julep, and Sterling in, playing mom to three kits with nowhere else to go.

"Yes," Cozy said, hoping she was right. "A kit."

Dusty stared at her, and for one falling moment Cozy believed two fox kits would die that day.

"Show me," Dusty said.

# NINE

**T**HE FOXOID BEING was still in the trap. His fur
had dried, but the smell of his fear was sharper than
ever.

Dusty sniffed a circle around him. "Floppy ears. Dull
teeth. Wide, mopey eyes . . ."

The Foxoid Being growled at her unconvincingly.

"And timid," Dusty concluded. "It's a dog, Cozy."

"Toldja," Julep mumbled.

"It's none of our business what happens to it," Dusty
said, and looked toward the street. "Its owner must be
around here somewhere."

Cozy worried her paws against the lawn. "If it's a dog,
then why can it talk? Watch this. *Speak.*"

"Wh-what do I say?" the Foxoid Being said.

"See?" she said.

Dusty turned to the Foxoid Being. "Sit!"

The Being, startled, sat.

"Some mutts," Dusty said, "retain enough of their

wildness to communicate with us. But they're still trained to follow human commands."

Cozy whimpered. She couldn't stand the thought of leaving the Being in the trap, his spine hunched, his tail smashed up, his fur drenched by sprinklers, until the humans came for him.

"Maybe he can help us with something," she said. "Y'know, like I sense humans, and Julep sniffs for poison, and Sterling digs"—her throat tightened—"*dug* under fences."

Dusty sighed and scowled at the Foxoid Being. "What can you do? If anything."

"Um . . . ," the Foxoid Being said, and then gulped.

Julep scoffed. "Let's just leave him, Coze."

Dusty and Julep padded toward the fence.

Cozy took one last look at the Foxoid Being, shivering in the trap. "I'm sorry," she told him. "I tried."

She followed Dusty and Julep, tail tucked between her legs.

"I can break through mesh!" the Foxoid Being burst out.

Dusty and Julep turned around.

"I know a trick," the Foxoid Being said shyly.

"How?" Dusty asked.

The Being considered his paws a moment. "I'm not telling unless you help me out of here."

Julep rolled his eyes. Cozy gave Dusty a hopeful look.

Dusty considered for a second, then returned to the trap and wriggled her head beneath its slanted entrance. She released the spring with her teeth, and the Foxoid Being crawled out. Cozy's paws tingled with relief.

Dusty sniffed at the bit of metal dangling from the Foxoid Being's ear. "Your name's Oleo?"

"Huh?" he said.

"It's written on your tag," Dusty said. "O-L-E-O."

The Foxoid Being tried to read the tag on his own ear but succeeded only in going cross-eyed. "It says 'O-Three Seventy.' That's my name."

"That's not a *name*," Julep said.

"We'll call you Oleo," Dusty said. "It's easier."

"But that's not . . ." The Foxoid Being gave up with a huff. He squinted at Cozy's ears, as if expecting to see a tag hanging from them. "What are your names?"

"Don't worry about that," Dusty said. "You won't be with us long."

She led the kits out of the yard and back to the street. They resumed their journey toward the horizon.


The foxes left the suburbs and crossed what seemed an endless field of tree stumps.

Julep sniffed the last of his tears away. "And now we know what wickedness awaits in the gray of dusk," he said in his best Sterling impression.

"Not you now too," Dusty grumbled.

For the first time, Julep didn't listen. "Forced to leave the place they called home, the foxes and their new pet dog headed toward the pulsing heart of the unforgiving City. What choice did they have when trying to escape an evil that could disguise itself as grass or a fox or an old lady? An evil that defies sight, sound, and smell . . . The kind of evil that can only be found—"

*"Julep,"* Dusty snarled.

Julep's muzzle snapped shut. So Cozy finished for him, under her breath, as quiet as quiet.

"In the Crepuscular Zone."

"**T**HIS STORY IS *squipped*!" the beta said.

"Oooooooh," the runt said. "Mom's gonna chew your tongue out!"

*"Hush,"* the alpha said.

Outside the pine tree, the flurries were aswirl again. The alpha scanned the frozen wood, making sure every bush was a bush, every snowy branch a branch. She sniffed deep, but all she could scent was dead needles and icy air and the Stranger's blood.

She didn't think anything was hiding out there. But after that story, how could she be sure?

"Poor Sterling," the runt said.

"Yes," the Stranger wheezed. He closed his eyes, as if pained by his wounds . . . or a memory. "Poor Sterling."

"Did they ever see the Hidden Man again?" the beta asked.

The Stranger took a labored breath. "Not before he saw them first."

The alpha's stomach tightened. Her eyes made another sweep of the wood.

"Which of these foxes are you?" the beta asked. "Are you Oleo? 'Cause you don't look like a dog, I don't think."

The Stranger's eyes remained shut. He was either ignoring the question or trying to get on top of his pain. The alpha sniffed at the Stranger for clues to his identity, but she could only smell his wounds. She couldn't tell if his ears were pointed or floppy because of the way he lay.

"No way!" the runt said. "He's Julep." He pointed his nose at the Stranger's fur. "Look at his blue splotches."

"That's *blood*," the beta whispered. "I think. Besides, if he's Julep, how does he know about all the stuff that happened on the Farm?"

With each new guess, the siblings sniffed closer to the Stranger until they were within snapping range of his muzzle. The alpha caught them by their tails and pulled them back, one after the other, but with less urgency than before.

The Stranger's eyes leapt open as if he'd been drifting off. "The foxes left the long stretches of human dens, and they came to a new territory. A place where everything is connected—from the holes in the ground to the running water to the sidewalks shared by paw, foot, and claw alike. A place with a million lights and eyes. A place with poison to turn a fox's guts inside out, traps to snap off their paws, and great rumbling machines that could squish a fox as flat as the skins in the White Barn. A place with strange miracles that can bring a fox back from the edge of death . . ." The Stranger drew a ragged breath. "Or drag them howling over it."

# THE TOMB
# OF VETERI

# ONE

**THE OLD STORIES** had never sounded this uncomfortable.

O-370 tried to keep up with the three wild foxes as they crossed what looked like the end of the world. Mounds of soil loomed over vast pits that stank of chopped-up earthworms and gasoline. Soot-stained moths flapped drunkenly through the air. It was as if the land itself, even its insects, was slowly transforming from nature . . . into something else completely.

The wild foxes didn't seem fazed by the dead landscape or the vast distance they had traveled. Their movements were smooth and low as they slunk like water around the dirt piles and arrowed across narrow bridges of soil. They didn't even pant.

O-370 panted like a broken engine. He limped on splinter-filled paws. His hips and shoulders burned like bee stings, and his legs felt ready to snap. Every inch of him ached to be back in the comfort of his wire den, cradled by mesh and toasted by the glowing heaters while being lulled to sleep by the Farm foxes' breathing.

But he had asked for this adventure, and now he couldn't take it back.

"Oleo."

Every step O-370 took away from the wire dens put a little more strain on his heart. But he couldn't make his paws turn back. Grizzler and the Farmer were back there. The Skinner and its writhing Blue light.

"Oleo, I'm talking to you."

Whenever he'd listened to Mia's and Uly's stories, O-370 had imagined them happening in a space about the size of the Farm. But out here, the world kept going and *going*. Like the White Barn was supposed to.

*"Oleo!"*

O-370 jumped and nearly bit his panting tongue.

Julep, the boy kit, was staring back at him. He had blue splotches scattered through his fur, and he smelled like the purple flowers the Farmer brought Fern on her birthday. O-370 used to like that scent.

"Didn't you hear me say your name?" Julep said, still trotting.

O-370 bounded to catch up, feeling wobbly-pawed on the strip of earth. "I-I thought you were just making a weird sound."

He didn't understand a lot of the words the wild foxes used. Keeping up with their conversation felt like trying to catch a fly before it zipped past his muzzle.

"I *was* making a weird sound," Julep said. "Oleo's a weird

sound. Is that why you have that name tag? So you don't forget your own name?"

"My name is *O-Three Seventy*," O-370 said. He gave his head a turn, flopping his ears and making his tag briefly whip into sight. "This is my ID. It's so we know each other's names on the Farm, and . . ." *So the Farmer knows when we're old enough to be taken to the Barn.*

He didn't finish the thought. Even though his tag itched something fierce, it felt comforting against his cheek. It was his only remaining connection to the Farm. And the foxes caged there.

"You know," Julep said, "your owner probably misses you. Maybe you should go find him."

The young vixen, Cozy, frowned back at Julep. Her fur was a light, creamy orange, and her eyes were mismatched—one green, one gold. She smelled like the air after a rainstorm.

"I don't have an owner anymore," O-370 said. "I come from the Farm."

Julep laughed. "Foxes don't come from *farms*. Farms are where chickens and sheep happen. How'd you learn to speak fox anyway?"

O-370 tilted his head. "Because . . . I am one?"

"With floppy ears and dog jewelry?" Julep said. "Nah. You're a mutt, plain as whiskers."

The foxes reached a low mound, and Oleo struggled to follow them up and over it as the loose soil tried to swallow his paws. It was true these wild foxes looked different from the ones on the Farm. The red of their fur was duller. Their ears were stiff and pointy. Their narrow eyes were slivers of gold, and their fangs stood out as sharp as thorns.

But that didn't mean O-370 was like Grizzler . . . did it?

A growl built in his throat. "I'm not a squipping *mutt*."

Julep scoffed. "Where'd you get that word? Your *grandma*?"

O-370's ears folded.

"Tame," Julep said, and romped ahead.

O-370 limped behind, head low. Every fight with R-211 had always ended in laughter.

The foxes reached the end of the pits and passed strange machines that resembled the Farmer's truck, only bigger. Their metal was rusted at the edges, their wheels bundled together so they would have to crawl like caterpillars. Their fronts held massive toothy scoops.

Julep let out a heavy sigh. "He never even got to fight a tractor."

Cozy looked away from the machines and sniffed.

It was only then that O-370 realized a kit was missing.

"Hey, what happened to your friend?" he said, trying to catch up again. "The one who locked me in that cage?"

Julep and Cozy stared at the ground before them.

"Oh," O-370 said sadly. "I lost my cousin. Back on the Farm. His name was—"

There was a snarl, and before O-370 knew what was happening, Dusty, the vixen, had bounded from the front of the line and pressed her nose to his. Her lips curled, exposing one fang and stretching the gash on her cheek into a half-jagged scowl.

"We don't care where you're from," she said, quiet and dangerous, fixing him with her narrow golden eyes. "We don't care what happened in your past. We only care how you can help us *survive*."

O-370 tried to keep his eyebrows from trembling, wishing he had some mesh to protect him from the terrifying vixen.

"Foxes die," Dusty said. "The survivors learn, and we move on. We don't whine about it."

With that, she turned away, twirling her iron-orange tail.

"I can't believe we replaced Sterling with a mutt," Julep said.

He and Cozy ran to catch up with Dusty.

O-370 gulped. After Dusty had stopped him from saying his cousin's name, R-211 had become a lump in his throat. He tried swallowing it again and again as he padded after the foxes. At least it stopped the panting.

The end of the world finally ended at the base of a concrete slope. The wild foxes bounded up with ease, but O-370 was left scrabbling, his paws backsliding with every step.

Dusty and the kits reached the top of the slope, and the light on their fur changed.

Cozy nodded sideways. "Aren't we going to the old den?"

"Not until Oleo proves himself," Dusty said.

O-370 didn't know what that meant, but whatever waited at the top of the slope was bright enough to light the clouds. A massive sound trembled the air, so loud that

O-370 could feel it vibrating his whiskers. He finally got his slippery paws to reach the top, but what he saw nearly made him tumble back down.

His eyes were overwhelmed with blazing lights and towering shadows. He blinked, trying to untangle the sight. There were hundreds of structures. Some rose like sheer glass cliffs, while others bulged like diseased tree trunks. A constant noise howled from the center of it all, echoing down the streets and into the night beyond.

O-370 turned his muzzle toward the soothing darkness. He tried to squint away the spots left by the blinding lights, tried to twitch the deafening roar from his ears.

"You say you're not a dog?" Dusty asked him. "Prove it."

She, Cozy, and Julep padded toward the City. O-370 stared after them, heart thumping. His paws ached. His stomach was hollow. He needed sleep. He gazed back down the concrete slope, across the impossible miles toward the Farm. He couldn't turn tail and run. He needed the wild foxes to survive.

O-370 padded toward the City. It felt just like falling.

# TWO

**T**HE FOXES REACHED the first of the City's structures, squat and separated by wide spaces. They kept to the dark patches, slipping down sidewalks with the breeze and creeping down alleys, away from the rush of cars. Their fur flashed bright against gray brick before vanishing behind the next cardboard box, the next trash can.

O-370 tried to mimic the foxes' shadowed movements, but he felt as slow and obvious as an insect with a missing leg. The scratchy sidewalks rubbed his pads raw. The buildings breathed cold from their bricks, making him shiver the last of his warmth away. His eyes couldn't keep still in their sockets, trying to make sense of the crushed and broken objects littering the street or the bright and colorful new ones that shone through clean windows.

The stories had never mentioned anything like this. Where was the Eavey Wood? The Boulder Fields? Had they been torn down? Crushed? Scraped away and dug up like the chopped forest outside the City? He'd even take the Lilac Kingdom over this concrete nightmare.

*"Phht!"* Dusty huffed.

The wild foxes vanished among the debris moments before a human stepped onto the sidewalk. O-370 panicked, then quickly wriggled beneath a nearby newspaper, heart throbbing in his exposed tail. The human swayed past, smelling of smoke and rotting wood and mumbling to herself.

As her heels clicked by, O-370 dared a peek from beneath the tented newspaper. He instantly regretted it. The woman wore a dead fox around her shoulders. The vixen's head dangled, limp, off the woman's arm. Her eyes were squeezed tight, still flinching from whatever had killed her.

Had this skin come from the Farm? Did O-370 know her? Was she . . .

*"Phht!"*

As the woman's footsteps faded around the corner, the wild foxes rematerialized and continued down the sidewalk. O-370 followed, breath shuddering.

The buildings began to multiply, smashing together tighter and taller on either side of the street. The largest of them stretched up in titanic walls of metal and glass. The windows had silhouettes behind them now. Some of the silhouettes moved.

The foxes hugged tight to the buildings, heading toward a river of light that shimmered between the structures. This vein of the City was brighter than the rest. Liquid lights of white and gold pierced and slashed the night. The air swirled with sizzling meat and wafts of waste and the tang of sweat. Hordes of humans flowed down the sidewalks while an endless snarl of motorized beasts grumbled down the street.

O-370 could no longer hear his heaving breath over his pounding heart. He hadn't known there were this many humans in the world. He wondered whether they were all like the Farmer.

The foxes came to a wooden fence and wriggled through its splintered corner. O-370 couldn't follow quickly enough. The alleyway's bricks were dripping damp, reflecting a yellow light that shone through a greasy haze. At the end of the alley was a chain-link fence. Above it buzzed an odd coiling of wormlike lights, forming what looked like a giant winged lizard. Its body was serpentine, and two twirling whiskers grew from each side of its muzzle.

Steam billowed through the fence, carrying a scent both sour and sweet—sizzling fat and gooey dough. Just sniffing it made O-370's stomach feel a shriveled sort of empty. Back on the Farm, he would have already eaten twice today.

Cozy licked her lips. Julep drooled on the concrete.

Only Dusty seemed unaffected by the scent. "Julep?"

Julep stuck his nose through the chain link and sniffed toward the dumpster on the other side. "Clean as a stream," he said.

Dusty glared at O-370. "Go on then. Show us what you can do."

O-370 froze. Was she really expecting him to break through this fence?

Julep snorted. "How's Oleo gonna do anything without his owner here to command him?"

Cozy scowled at him, then gave O-370 an almost smile, igniting a bit of warmth in his chest. The first warmth he'd felt since the cage's heaters. He took a deep breath and trotted up to the fence. It resembled the wire mesh of his cage, only the diamond holes were much larger, the wire ten times as thick. No buckets hung from its screws.

O-370 started to panic. The only reason these foxes were keeping him around was because he had promised he could break through mesh. But he hadn't been counting on something like this.

He took the wire in his side teeth and bit down. A jolt shot through his gums. His jaw began to throb. If he bit any harder, his teeth would shatter.

O-370 released the wire and turned back to the foxes, ears folded. "I . . . can't do it."

Julep snorted. "Duh."

Cozy kneaded her paws, still looking hopeful.

Behind the fence, a door clattered open—*Aroo-roo-roo!*— and a tan ball of fluff came yapping out, startling O-370 off his paws. He scampered behind Dusty.

Julep laughed. "Don't worry, Oleo. That pug's probably your cousin."

O-370 peeked around Dusty's tail at the wall-eyed little dog who rattled the fence, snorting and huffing. O-370 felt embarrassed he'd been scared by something so goofy looking.

Dusty sighed. "Let's go check the dumpsters."

The foxes trotted back down the alley and wriggled through the wooden fence. O-370 followed, tail tucked between his legs. He tried slipping through the fence's broken corner, but his head struck something fuzzy—*"Oof!"*—and he sat down hard.

"Not you," Dusty said, blocking his way.

"Go find your owner," Julep said through the fence. "He'll probably give you a treat."

Cozy said nothing.

The foxes padded away, and O-370 poked his head through the fence, watching them fade to silhouettes in a plume of steam.

The City spun in his vision. Streets curved and split and came to dead ends. They rose toward glittering lights or descended into darkness. Dusty had made so many turns and shortcuts, he couldn't possibly find his way out. This City would chew him up and spit out his bones.

O-370 started to shake.

A honk swiveled his head toward the river of cars. Beyond the billowing wall of exhaust, in a building across the street, he smelled fat—simmering and golden brown.

"Wait!" he called toward the steam.

One of the silhouettes stopped.

O-370 pointed his nose toward the scent. "What's that smell?"

Cozy stepped out of the steam and sniffed toward the building. "That's steak."

Julep followed after. "The rarest scavenge in the City."

O-370 gazed into the howling road, trying to convince himself that it wasn't the scariest thing he'd ever seen.

He sat tall, fighting the shiver in his bones. "I'm gonna

cross," he said. "And I'll bring back a steak big enough for all of us."

Before his nerves could get the best of him, he headed toward the street.

Julep romped to catch up. "Oh, this is gonna be *good*."

# THREE

**THE STREET WAS** a blur—wailing streaks of rubber and metal with blinding slashes of white and red. A crumpled piece of paper tumbled off the curb, was whirled into the air by the rush of one car, and then crushed flat by the tires of another.

The fox kits crouched beneath a blue metal box near the sidewalk's curb. They tucked their tails close to keep from being spotted by the river of humans hustling behind them.

"Don't do it, Oleo," Cozy said, imploring him with her mismatched eyes. "If your tail doesn't get crushed by a tire, your head will."

"And that's if you're lucky," Julep said.

O-370 looked back to the alley where the vixen's silhouette watched, unmoving. "If you leave me here," he said, "I'll die anyway."

Julep scoffed. "He won't cross," he told Cozy. "His owner'll swat his nose for misbehaving."

O-370 ignored him. He fixed his eyes on the opposite curb, knees tensing with each passing car, ready to spring the moment there was an opening.

*whoosh . . . whoosh . . . whoosh whoosh . . . whoosh*
*whoosh whoosh . . . whoosh whoosh whoosh . . . whoosh*

But the moment one side of the street opened, a car roared down the other. O-370 felt disoriented. He couldn't focus. Smog hung thick, stinging his eyes and making his throat clench.

He remembered the old story where Uly leapt across a crack. Once Uly had made it to the other side, he'd realized that the crack wasn't so intimidating. Of course, the street was considerably wider than a crack. And it was filled with cars instead of snakes.

O-370 refocused his eyes, gazing beyond the cold rush of cars to the building with its sizzling steak scent.

*whoosh . . . whoosh whoosh . . . whoosh*

"It doesn't matter when you go," Julep said. "You'll get squished no matter—"

Just then, a gap opened on both sides of the road, and O-370 bolted off the curb.

"Whoa!" Julep yipped in surprise.

The cars were faster than O-370 had anticipated. The first screeched and swerved around him while the next howled overhead, its scalding underbelly scraping his ears. He scampered between the speeding tires of the next, then skidded to a stop as a silver hubcap buzzed the tip of his nose. He slunk ahead half a tail, then cowered when a truck nearly took his head off. The moment it passed, O-370 bounded ahead and then bounded right back, barely missing the car that came hurtling from his right.

Another zoomed past. And then another and another. More cars rushed behind him. He was trapped. A step forward would crush his muzzle, a step back would take his tail.

"I can't see him!" Cozy cried. *"Oleo?"*

O-370 could barely hear her. He was blinded by headlights, choked by exhaust, deafened by rattling engines. A bit of gravel whipped his snout, and the road grew even blurrier.

O-370 squeezed his eyes shut, waiting for the end to come. But then an image of his cousin smiled to life in his mind: R-211 gazed through wire mesh, ears perked, tail wagging, waiting to hear the story where O-370 bravely crossed a road.

*So then what happened?* R-211 asked.

O-370 opened his eyes, and the world seemed to slow. The cars gleamed like beetle shells. The headlights dragged. The tires showed every rotation. O-370 pranced forward, then to the side. He ducked, leapt, and cleared the first line of tires. His vision flooded with white, and he froze as headlights bore down on him.

### *EEEEOOOooowww*

Three tails before his muzzle, the car swerved, laying on its horn as it passed and ruffling his tail fur. O-370 made one last jump and scrambled up the opposite curb. He panted as the feeling crept back into his ears, then his muzzle and paws.

Across the street, Cozy yipped, dizzy with happiness. Julep's shock twisted into anger.

The door to the building opened with a burst of smoky, fat-laced air, and O-370 slipped beneath the shadow of a nearby bench. Now all he had to do was find a steak and make his way back across the street. The foxes would have no choice but to keep him.

"Julep, *no!*" Cozy shouted over the roaring engines.

O-370 looked up to see Julep leap into the road, his blue spotches flashing in the headlights. He hustled forward a tail and then scooted back, flinching at the rush of spinning tires.

O-370 didn't breathe. He didn't blink. His paws kneaded the sidewalk, mentally instructing Julep when to pause and when to run. Julep waited for a car to pass, trotted forward, cowered again, then sprinted the final stretch. He leapt onto the curb and slipped under the bench.

"That was *easy*," he said, panting. "I think I did that faster than you. A *lot* faster."

He grinned at Cozy on the opposite curb. Her ears remained folded.

Julep slunk out from under the bench, and O-370 followed, around the side of the building to an alley. Julep snagged a trash bag by its corner, bit through the plastic, and pulled out a piece of meat bigger than his head.

O-370 reached his muzzle into the bag and found a piece the size of his ear tag and mostly gristle.

He looked at Julep's steak, so big it dragged on the ground. "Can you carry that across?"

"*Psh,*" Julep said, mouth full. "I'd take a whole *cow* if they had one." He tripped over the steak, dragging it back out of the alley.

He and O-370 waited until the crowd of humans thinned on the sidewalk, then stepped back to the curb.

*whoosh . . . whoosh*

After only two cars passed, Julep bounded into the road, hauling his steak across the asphalt. O-370 waited for an opening and leapt.

He knew how the cars moved now. He knew where to duck and when to pause. The steak dissolved between his teeth in salts and fats, leaving a pattering trail of saliva behind. If he ever made it back to the Farm, he would have to tell R-211 that the foods of the world were even more delicious than the stories made them seem.

Ahead, Julep reached the road's center, between the rows of snarling cars. He paused to adjust the steak in his mouth, and O-370 quickened his pace, ears tingling with pride as he passed the wild kit. He dared Julep to call him a mutt after this.

O-370 hopped onto the opposite curb and found Cozy back in the alley. He plopped his bit of gristle in front of her.

"One *steak*," he said, panting heavily.

### THUNK

Cozy gasped, and O-370 turned to see Julep's body rolling between the speeding tires. O-370 held his breath, hoping this was a tactic he hadn't thought to try. But when Julep stopped rolling, his paws flopped still in the street.

O-370 went numb with shock. Cozy began to whine.

"Instinct prevails," Dusty said, stepping from the steam. "What do we say, Cozy?"

Cozy stared at the ground and clamped her muzzle shut.

O-370 watched the fuzzy shape in the road, desperate

for signs of movement. Julep's chest didn't rise. His whiskers didn't twitch. His fur wavered beneath the rush of cars. O-370 whimpered.

"Come, Cozy," Dusty said. "We'll get by without a poison sniffer."

Cozy looked at Julep one last time, then followed the vixen. O-370 watched them fade back into the steam. He felt the City close in around him. Was life outside the Farm always this cruel?

A screech flipped him around. A car had stopped in the road. Others honked while a woman got out and hustled toward Julep. She removed her jacket, scooped up his limp body, and carried him back to her car.

As the door swung shut, O-370 could have sworn he saw Julep's ear *twitch*.

"His ear!" O-370 yelped down the alley. "It moved!"

Cozy came scampering back and gazed into the road.

"It was a breeze," Dusty said from the steam. "Wind coming off the cars."

"But-but," O-370 said, "a human picked him up. If he's really dead, why not leave him?"

Dusty sneered. "Humans don't want corpses stinking up their streets."

The car pulled away, and O-370 worked his paws, trying to keep the hope in his heart from wilting.

When the car took a left turn, Cozy's mismatched eyes went wide.

"Veteri," she whispered.

"What's . . . Veteri?" O-370 asked.

"It's a tomb," Dusty said. "It's where the City's injured animals go to die."

Cozy gulped. "It's full of curses."

"Curses," Dusty said, "don't exist."

O-370 stared toward the corner where the car had turned. When Cozy had convinced Dusty to release him from the trap, she'd said each fox kit had a special skill that helped them all survive. And Dusty clearly didn't want O-370 around if he couldn't do anything for them.

Back on the Farm, he and R-211 had always told each other that if they ever went on an adventure, they would save every last fox, no matter what. O-370 couldn't break through fences, but maybe he could be the fox that rescued other foxes.

"I'm going after him," O-370 said.

Cozy's ears perked.

"No fur off our tails," Dusty said. "Cozy?"

O-370 didn't wait for them to leave him again. He slipped out of the alley and padded down the sidewalk, doing his best to keep to the shadows. He didn't know what horrors waited ahead. But neither had Mia and Uly.

When he reached the corner, a muzzle nudged his hip, scaring a yelp out of him.

"You forgot this," Cozy said, laying the gristly bit of steak before him. "You'll probably need it."

"Oh," O-370 said. "Thanks."

He gulped the steak down. It was cold and salty and did little to calm the storm in his stomach. As he chewed, he gazed down the sidewalk toward Dusty. He thought he saw a look of hurt on the vixen's face, but the moment she saw him looking, it turned into a sneer.

"Why are you trying to save a fox you barely know?" Cozy asked. "He called you a mutt."

O-370 stared into her mismatched eyes and found he couldn't tell her the truth. That he was only doing this so Dusty would keep him around. That the City would kill him if she didn't.

He shrugged. "What if Mia and Uly had given up on each other in the forest? Foxes are supposed to watch each other's tails."

Cozy considered him a moment, giving no clue she knew what he was talking about. She looked back to Dusty, then turned and padded past O-370 and around the corner.

O-370's paws hopped to catch up with her. "You're coming with me?"

"Someone has to show you how to get in," Cozy said. "Unless you suddenly remembered how to break through fences?"

O-370 licked his teeth, which still ached from gnawing the wires at the restaurant.

Cozy smirked. "Come on."

Cozy led O-370 to the City's outskirts. The streets plunged into a calming quiet. The stars grew sharp again. The foxes walked in the open now, crossing through empty lots, the concrete broken by scraggly weeds.

"Your mom's kinda mean, huh?" O-370 said.

"Dusty's not my mom," Cozy said.

"Oh. Where's your mom?"

"She . . . died."

His ears folded. "How?"

"Just"—she turned her eyes away from him—"in the normal way."

O-370 wondered whether he'd said something wrong. "My mom died too. I was just a baby when—"

"We're almost there," Cozy said. "We should be quiet."

"Oh, okay," O-370 said, again with a lump stuck in his throat. The bit of warmth he'd felt when Cozy had smiled at him fizzled out.

They continued through the dark, empty streets. The air grew dry, and the wind spun trash and dust into little twisters that stung O-370's eyes.

Cozy stopped and looked up. "This is it."

The sandstone building was a perfect cube. Its walls were covered with brightly colored symbols, dripping and strange. At the very top, near the roof, big red letters buzzed like the heaters back on the Farm. The first few, **V E T E R I**, glowed bright, but there were more after that had burned out.

"How do we get in?" O-370 asked.

Cozy closed her eyes, tilted her muzzle, and sniffed deep. "This way." She trotted around to a fenced yard, which smelled strongly of animal leavings. She padded up to the fence's door and gazed at a flat latch two tails above her ears. She jumped and hooked her paws around the latch, making the door pop open, before dropping back down.

O-370's eyebrows leapt. "Where'd you learn to do that?"

"Shh," she said.

The little yard lay in the shadow of the building, but O-370 could just make out the fuzzy outline of a whirring fan box beside a pale brown door. Cozy pointed her nose toward a black rectangle embedded in the door's bottom center, just tall enough for a fox's ears.

"Dog door," she whispered.

O-370 didn't know what that meant, but he trotted ahead, paws splashing in a surprise puddle, as dark as the ground around it. One of the pipes that led to the fan box had a tiny hole, which hissed water onto the ground.

He stared at the dog door, nothing more than a plastic flap, bulging slightly from the air within. He nosed open the flap, just a whisker, so he could see inside. It was dark in Veteri. Clammy cold. The walls breathed through their vents—*sssswsss ssswsss ssssss*—sending stale gusts down a long black hallway. A scent caked the walls, reeking of urine and sickness.

O-370 jerked his head back through the flap. Cozy hadn't budged from the fence. Her eyes were locked on the puddle he had splashed through.

"You coming?" he said.

She swallowed and looked away from the puddle. "Can't. Curses."

She sounded like R-211 had when he'd lied about his splinter.

"We can't just leave Julep in there," O-370 said.

"That's brave of you, Oleo," Cozy said. "Going in alone."

His ears wilted. That wasn't what he'd meant at all.

"Be careful," Cozy said.

He gulped. Was there any other way to be?

He closed his eyes, imagined R-211's smiling face, and he entered the tomb.

# FOUR

***C*LACK*!***

    O-370 jumped when the dog door fell shut behind him. The dark passage stretched ahead, barely lit by the bit of moonlight that eked through the translucent flap. The building whispered—*ssss sswss sssss*.

"Julep?" O-370 whispered.

Nothing answered.

He padded down the hall, whose floor was slippery with a thin layer of soapy water. The click of his nails echoed against the walls, making it sound as if invisible things walked behind him. Every few steps he checked over his shoulder to make sure the echoes hadn't solidified into real creatures. He tried to pad more softly.

His heart thumped against his chest, telling him to turn around, *leave*. His lungs drew shallow breaths so the stench of sick and urine couldn't creep inside him. His whiskers told him that something was watching him. But he didn't know where. There were no hiding places here. And he didn't think he could outrun anything down the long, slippery hallway.

He turned a corner and found a row of doors running along each wall, faintly illuminated by a green-lettered sign that hung high at the hall's end. He placed his nose to the crack under the first door and sniffed for Julep's flower scent. The air was dry and pungent. The next room was earthy and nauseating. Sounds came from the third—panicky whimpers and scuttles. There were critters in there. They could smell him.

The fourth door was slightly ajar. O-370 held his breath as he nuzzled it open. The first thing he saw was a neat row of glass bottles sitting high on a shelf. The bottles were filled with clear brown liquid in which floated the bodies of beetles and frogs, an eyeball, a coiled intestine, and other unnameable things.

A writhing shape drew O-370's eye to the room's corner. A fuzzy white body twisted and jerked, as if it were trying to tie itself in knots. O-370 took a step back, and the thing spotted him with its gooey pink eyes.

*Grnt! Clang!*

O-370 tried to run, but his paws slipped on the soapy floor. He landed with a thud and scrambled away, only looking back to see whether the thing was about to attack him. His breath settled when he recognized the familiar pattern of crosshatched wires. The thing couldn't get him. It was in a cage.

O-370 sniffed. *Rabbit.* But this didn't look like the kind of rabbit he knew. Its face was twisted. Its blood-pink eyes were gummy and narrowed, its lips peeled back around fiendish buckteeth. Its movements were jerky and unpredictable, and its little head kept seizing in painful-looking spasms.

Whenever O-370 had spotted rabbits through the wire mesh, they had always seemed like soft, panicky things, fleeing the Farm the moment they smelled the foxes.

But this rabbit wasn't afraid of him.

*"Grnt!" Clang! "Grnt!" Clang! Clang!* The gooey-eyed rabbit grunted and kicked at its cage with its forepaws—*"Grnt!" Clang! "Grnt!"*—as if trying to reach him.

Its scent was as twisted as its face. Its breath was hot and strange and smelled faintly like the soiled straw beneath the wire dens. Or mold maybe. Or . . . O-370 didn't know what. He couldn't quite get his nose around it. Was this what Cozy was talking about? Was this rabbit cursed?

Another white shape caught his eye, hanging above the cage. Another rabbit, dangling by its hind paws. This one was missing its head.

O-370 scrabbled backward out of the room and didn't stop until his tail struck the wall on the opposite side of the hallway.

"Julep?" he whispered with more urgency.

Silence.

The next two rooms were just as unsettling, but in different ways. One smelled so strongly of dog that he left it shut. Another was stacked with towels and cloths and smelled of fabric dust. It had a shelf lined with needles filled with brown liquid that smelled faintly like the rabbit. In the corner sat a pile of soiled rags, reeking like meat left too long on the Farmer's grill.

Julep wasn't in either room.

At the end of the hall, beneath the glowing green sign, was a dark staircase. It led underground. O-370 stared into the pit of the building, paws positioned on the top step, heart leaping in his throat.

He thought of Dusty's silhouette, and he descended.

The stairs creaked beneath his paws—*reent, rrnt, reent, rrnt*. He reached the bottom and crouched on icy tiles. The black of the basement was complete, but his whiskers could sense corridors, tight and narrow. The air was still down here. Stale. Difficult to breathe.

*Mrrraaaooooroooaaarr*

*Hss*

*Mrrrrrrrr*

The underground came alive with hisses and yowls, growing louder and louder until it filled O-370's ears, drowning out his own heartbeat and making his bladder release. There were things in the darkness, and they knew he was there. He was about to turn tail, run up the steps, down the hall, through the dog door, past Cozy, out of the City, and never look back . . .

But then more crosshatched wires gleamed into view. These creatures were also locked away. They covered the walls on both sides, dozens of them, high to the ceiling and low to the floor, each behind their own wire door. O-370 had never seen anything like them. They had short ears and even shorter muzzles and strange colors and patterns in their fur. One was wrapped in white, its breath raspy and slow. Another was slumped on its side, its patchy fur pressed through the wires. Another smelled of scabs.

Dozens of eyes shone down at him. They spoke with scratchy, garbled voices.

"Why, who is *this*?"

"Better yet, *what* is this?"

"It's a puzzle!"

The creatures' sharp pupils widened with interest.

"That's not a puzzle. It's a puppy. Look at its ears."

"Look at its *eyes*. It's a cat."

"That is a *wrap*. My owner wears one all around town."

O-370's skin crawled beneath the creatures' gazes. He had to remind himself that they couldn't do anything to him from those cages.

"How did it escape its kennel?"

*With a bucket,* O-370 thought. But he knew that wasn't what the creature meant.

"I-I-I'm not from here," he said. "I'm looking for my friend."

*Mrrraaaooooorrr*

*Mrrrrrrrr*

*Hss*

The creatures' faces wrinkled and purred. They seemed to be *laughing*.

"Did you hear that? It thinks we're *from* here."

"No one is *from* here."

"We're here because we misbehaved."

"Some of us scratched up the couch."

"Some of us had too many kittens."

"So they're removing our claws."

"Or other things."

O-370 flexed his toes to make sure his claws were still there.

He cleared his throat. "Anyway, my friend—"

"Her Hissness is different, of course," one of the creatures interrupted.

As one, they turned their noses toward the corner kennel, where a striped, orange creature lay, face hidden behind her tail.

"Poor thing."

"Best paws this side of the river."

"You should have seen her sitting on her fence, as pretty as a sphinx."

"We all hated her at first, of course."

"She has an *eye* that's misbehaving."

"Accident with the vacuum cleaner."

"Shame."

O-370 tried to blink the sudden ache from his own eyes, wondering how they could possibly *misbehave*.

"That's what the words on her kennel say," one of the creatures said.

"They say, 'Rotten eye.'"

"They say, 'Please pluck it out. We're humans, and we can't be bothered with it anymore.'"

"Her Hissness was so beautiful."

"Best paws this side of the river."

"Shame."

"She doesn't deserve this sort of treatment."

"She deserves freedom."

O-370 blinked at the orange creature, then started to back away. "Okay, well . . . good luck with everything."

"Back to the question," one of the caged creatures said, fixing her green eyes back on O-370. "If it isn't a puppy or a cat or a wrap, what is it?"

"Does it matter?" another said.

"It's small like a cat."

"*Mrraoo*. Its muzzle is short enough."

"And its fur *is* orange."

"It's *cat enough,* if you catch my meaning."

One of the creatures lifted a paw and gave it a flick, spattering O-370's muzzle with something wet. He sniffed. Blood. The creature had flicked its *blood* on him.

*Hss*

*Mrrrrrrrr*

*Mrrraaaoooorooooaaarr*

The creatures continued to hiss and yowl as O-370 hurried away. He came to another hallway that swallowed all light. The floor grew sticky, his pads peeling up with every step.

"Julep?" O-370 whispered.

Something answered. *"Mmm-hmm-hmm—hmm-hummm!"*

His ears perked.

*"Mmm-hmm-hmph!"*

Julep.

O-370 bounded ahead, and a metal door materialized out of the darkness. He leapt and hooked his paws around the handle the way Cozy had outside. The door swung open, and he nearly gagged. The scent of urine and fear was overwhelmed by the gummy tang of old blood. The inside of the doorframe was covered in scratches. Animals had tried to escape this little room.

Against the far wall was a table. On top of the table was a figure wrapped in white. Patches of bluish-orange fur stuck through the wrapping, as well as two sharp ears, sticky with blood.

"Julep!" O-370 cried, then leapt onto a trash can and onto the table.

*"Mrrph mrph mmph,"* Julep responded, his muzzle clamped shut.

O-370 set about chewing away the wrapping. Julep's head had been bound tight, as if the humans were trying to squeeze out whatever life was left in him. With one last nip, the wrapping fell away from Julep's muzzle.

*"Mother-ssuckling sson of a tail twitch, dog pee and appless!"*

*"Shh!"* O-370 hissed, glancing toward the hallway. Then he snorted with relief. "Well, there's the curses Cozy was talking about."

Julep woozily lifted his head and, with one eye closed, squinted at O-370. "Dad?"

O-370's whiskers twitched with embarrassment. "Um, no. It's me. Three Seventy."

Julep scrunched up his face. "Oleo? Ugh. That's the *worsst.*"

His head thunked back onto the table. He was talking funny. He jawed at his words, tongue loose, his voice as slow as tree sap.

"I'm here to save you," O-370 whispered.

*"Pffshh."* Julep sprayed spittle. "You fink I need a *mutt* to ssave *me*? I can ssave my*self*. I jesst don't feel like it right now."

O-370 gritted his teeth. "I'm not a mutt."

Julep snorted. "Aw, come on. I'm jesst winding your whisskerss. *Ob-vee-uss-lee.* Don't getcher leash in a tang, um, tang . . . um, yeah, tangle."

O-370 tried to relax his jaw.

Down the hall, the hissing creatures were whispering:

"He's in the Cutting Room."

"He's hurt."

"He's got blood on his muzzle."

"If you swap him, we'll give you our food."

O-370 sniffed at the blood crusting around Julep's ears. "Does your head hurt?"

"No!" Julep shouted. "I'M AS SSTRONG AS FIFTY MOONSS!"

*"Shh!"* O-370 said, eyes leaping to the doorway. "Can you stand?"

"Nope!" Julep said. He made a a pathetic roll onto his belly and then flopped back again. "Ssorry. Don't have legss anymore."

O-370 nudged Julep's foreleg. "Yes, you do. They're just wrapped up."

"Nope! They're gone. In the trash."

O-370 bit Julep's paw *hard*. Julep didn't flinch.

"What did the humans do to you?" O-370 asked.

A creak swung his head around. Had the door just opened wider? A scent drew his nose to the dark space behind it. Sitting in the shadow was a pile of soiled rags, reeking of charred meat.

O-370's fur prickled. Had those rags been there when he entered? Were they the same ones from upstairs?

"We have to get out of here, Julep."

Julep's half-lidded eyes leapt open. "Oh *yeah*. Fer *sure*. Lemme jesst . . ." They fluttered shut again.

O-370 seized hold of Julep's wrapping and yanked him off the table. Julep practically belly-flopped onto the ground, but he didn't seem to feel it.

"Can you stand?" O-370 asked.

"*Pffshh*. I can *run*!" Julep said, wavering onto his legs, as wobbly as earthworms. "Now that I got hit by a car, I abssorbed all of itss . . . itss, um, *fasst*." Wooziness overtook him again, and he collapsed.

Behind the door, something rustled. Out of the corner of his eye, O-370 could have sworn the pile of rags *moved*.

Jaw trembling, he grabbed hold of Julep's wrapping and rotated him so that his paws faced the doorway. He walked backward, tugging Julep in sharp jerks toward the door. As they passed the rags, O-370 tried to convince himself that those weren't wet eyes staring at him from between the folds.

Once O-370 had dragged Julep into the hall, he dared to look up. Black fingers reached out of the darkness of the room and creaked the door wider. The scent of charred flesh seeped through the air.

O-370 pulled faster.

Julep started to giggle. "Walkin' iss for *sssuckers*."

*"Shh!"* O-370 hissed through gauze-filled teeth.

"'Kay," Julep said. "But I'm jesst ssayin', thiss iss how I'm traveling from now on."

They passed the walls of creatures, who watched in silence. O-370 could hear their wet smiles.

The moment his tail hit the bottom stair, the pile of rags shambled into the hallway. It walked on two stumpy legs, dragging its knuckles and trailing ghostly strands behind it. It paused just outside the room and stood crooked, its breath ragged in the darkness.

"Blech," Julep said. "Who *peed*?"

Right next to his nose glimmered the yellow puddle O-370 had left when the creatures first hissed at him.

"Never mind that," O-370 said, breathless. "I can't drag you up the stairs. I need you to climb as *fast* as you can."

*"Psh,"* Julep said. "I eat stairss for *breakfasst*!"

He rested his muzzle on the first step and started to snore.

*"Julep!"* O-370 said.

Julep didn't stir.

O-370 peered behind him. The pile of rags stared from the end of the hall. His lungs began to panic. He needed Julep to move and he needed him to move *now*.

"Um, um, um . . . ," O-370 said. "I'll race you to the top!"

Julep woke with a snarl and started to scale the stairs like a boneless frog.

O-370 nudged Julep's tail along. "That's it . . . You've got this. Just a dozen more . . ."

Julep huffed and climbed. "'F coursse I got thiss. I'm fasster than *you*."

O-370 placed his paw on the first step. He peered over his shoulder to make sure the pile of rags hadn't moved— And his nose almost touched a face. O-370's muscles seized. His heart froze. The smell of charred meat enveloped him. The face was wrapped in bandages, parted in places to show wet black eyes and dull lower canines, which jutted from a massive underbite through blackened lips.

The face grinned.

O-370 couldn't even yelp before a hand, just like a human's, clasped his tail and jerked him off the steps. His jaw cracked the bottom edge before he was dragged down the hallway, past the caged creatures, and into darkness.

*Mrrraaaoooorooooaaarr*

*Hss*

*Mrrrrrrrr*

Halfway up the stairs, Julep looked back and, slurring, said, "Sssso long, Oleo."

# FIVE

**T**HE RAGGED THING dragged O-370 down the hall, its bare feet slapping the tile.

*slap-slap slap-slap*

O-370 dug in his claws, shrieking them against the floor. But it was no use. The Ragged was strong. It was half the size of a human, hunched, with stumpy legs and long arms. It was wrapped head to toe in white and swayed as it walked. Tufts of black hair poked through in mad patches, while dark liquid seeped through the crusted wrapping. The flesh beneath was pink and twisted.

The Ragged brought O-370 to a corner and released his tail. O-370 tried to spring away, but the Ragged caught him with one strong hand, pinning his neck to the floor. O-370 aimed his muzzle at the staircase to yelp for Julep, but the Ragged's other hand pinched his muzzle shut. It released his throat and picked up a roll of white material. Using its fangs, it yanked a strand from the roll and wrapped it around O-370's muzzle.

Wrap. The basement vanished. Wrap. The sounds grew muffled. Neck, chest, paws, tail. Wrap. Wrap. Wrap.

Soon, O-370 was bound so tight that he couldn't do anything but pant through his nostrils. His lungs heaved against the binding around his chest. The stench of burned flesh made it even harder to breathe.

He watched through a crack in the wrapping as the Ragged used its canines to bite the strand free from the roll. Huffing, it pressed its twisted face to O-370's. O-370 winced, unable to move as the Ragged extended a blackened fingernail toward his muzzle. He waited for the creature to scoop out his eye, his brain, *both*.

But the Ragged simply dug into O-370's nostril and ate what it found there.

O-370 felt another tug on his bound tail as he was dragged back down the hall. A wire door squeaked open. The Ragged gently removed the orange creature's frail form from the kennel and then tossed O-370 inside, slamming the door shut behind him.

As the Ragged toddled away, the kennel creatures hissed their appreciation.

"Her Hissness is safe!"

"Spared by the pharaoh!"

"All hail the pharaoh!"

O-370 couldn't move. He couldn't yelp. He could only whimper through his nose.

"Hush now," a creature said from a kennel above.

"There's nothing to be afraid of."

"It's a good thing you're doing."

"A heroic thing."

With his muzzle wrapped tight, O-370 couldn't ask what exactly he was doing. His eyes searched, frantic, through the crack in the wrapping, and he saw the label dangling from the kennel's wire door. An answer snapped in his mind like a bone.

*Rotten eye,* the creatures had said. *Pluck it out.*

O-370's muzzle was short, his body small enough to be mistaken for the creature that shared his orange fur. Every other distinguishing part, including his ear tag, was bundled tight. He started to wriggle. But the more he moved, the tighter his binds became.

There was a sound upstairs. A door opened. Keys jangled. The creatures fell still. Something had entered Veteri.

A shadow descended the stairway, broken against the steps. It reached the bottom and clicked a switch, and a nauseating light blared to life, casting a sickly pall over the creatures in their kennels.

The human was dressed head to foot in pale blue. It had two glass eyes—round like an owl's. Material covered its hair and mouth, and its scent was drowned in something so clean that it burned O-370's nose.

He continued to struggle against his binds as the human stepped from kennel to kennel, examining the labels with its eyes of glass. It crouched at O-370's kennel and lifted the label from the wire door.

The creatures watched, pupils wide, as the human looked from the label to O-370 and then back at the label. O-370 tried to control his shuddering breath. All he could do was lie there and hope the human realized the mistake. This was not his kennel. His eye was not misbehaving. He didn't belong here.

The wire door squeaked open, and fingers curled beneath O-370's forelegs, scooping him up.

The creatures purred as he was carried away.

"Farewell, little puppy."

"Little wrap."

"Little cat."

"Cat enough anyway."

# SIX

O-370 WRIGGLED AGAINST his binds as the human carried him to the room where he'd found Julep. It laid him on the cold metal table and then flicked on the light, so bright the cracks in the wrapping grew almost unbearable to look through.

The human became a blurred silhouette, its movements skeletal and strange. It plucked empty rubber hands from a box and pulled them over its own—*Snap! Snap!*

*Rubber Hands*, O-370 thought with a shiver.

Rubber Hands picked up a needle and filled it with clear liquid, flicking its side before spraying droplets from its tip. Then it grabbed another sharp object. This one had a tiny blade at the end.

O-370 strained against the wrapping, hoping to bite the human's fingers before it stole his life with the silver instruments. Before it chopped him up and placed his parts in the upstairs jars.

Rubber Hands picked up a wobbly yellow tube and tied it high around O-370's hind leg—so tight his paw went numb. A whimper escaped his bound muzzle as Rubber Hands parted the wrapping in the bend of his hind leg. His eyes watered over as the needle worked its way into his skin, cold and metallic.

*CLANG!*

Something crashed upstairs, and Rubber Hands's glass eyes whirled toward the hallway. Sounds thumped against the ceiling while rattles and grunts echoed down the staircase. The needle was plucked from O-370's leg, and Rubber Hands swept out of the room.

O-370 tried getting up, but he couldn't feel his hind leg. Had Rubber Hands cut it off? Was the human taking it to the jars?

No. Julep had thought his legs were missing too. The stuff Rubber Hands had given him only made it *feel* that way. Still, O-370's hind leg felt as useless as oatmeal. And he couldn't open his muzzle to chew off his binds.

Focusing hard, he told his hind paws to *push . . . PUSH.* And soon, he found himself sliding along the metal table, inching closer and closer toward the edge. His shoulder reached the corner, and he slid off, his bound body slapping the floor. It hurt, but the impact loosened the wrapping around his neck.

O-370 rocked himself up onto his belly and shook his head until the wrapping started to unwind from his muzzle. He stretched open his jaw, then yanked the binds from his forelegs and chest. But he couldn't unwind them past the rubber tube, which was tied tight, holding in place the binds on his hind legs and tail. The more he jerked at the tube, the tighter it squeezed. He needed to get out of there before Rubber Hands returned.

Using his forepaws, O-370 slowly dragged his bottom half toward the door. When he reached the hall, he fixed his eyes on the staircase as he pulled and wiggled toward it.

Upstairs, the human was shouting. "No, no, no! Where did it go?"

O-370 reached the kennels, and the air ignited with hisses.

"Get back in there!"

"You'll ruin everything!"

The creatures sounded like the Farm foxes, telling O-370 to return to his cage. He pawed faster toward the stairs, legs dragging.

*"Pharaoh!"*

"Pharaoh, come quick!"

"Escape!"

At the end of the hallway came a rasping breath.

*Slap-slap thunk-thunk slap-slap thunk-thunk!*

O-370 gazed back, eyes watering with terror. The Ragged was running toward him *on its fists.*

Working his forelegs as fast as he could, O-370 reached the stairs and was just able to haul his legs up the first two when the Ragged seized the binds trailing from his tail and yanked. O-370's chest *thunk*ed down the steps, teeth clacking. He wriggled and strained, trying to get his numb legs to shake the wrapping free, but the Ragged pulled him closer.

WHUMP—*grmph!*

O-370 heard a thud behind him. A smoky grunt. The tension on the wrapping fell slack. Without looking back, he scrambled frantic up the steps, slipping, whimpering, banging his knees against the corners.

It was only when he reached the top that he dared look back. The Ragged had fallen. There was a streak of liquid beneath it. O-370's pee puddle. The Ragged had slipped. And now it was was trying and failing to get to its feet, grunting and huffing in a bone-chilling scream.

**OOH-OOH-OOH-AH-AUGH-AUGH-AUGH-AUGH!**

Footsteps echoed down the upstairs hallway, and O-370 quickly shuffled his hind legs behind the stairway door as Rubber Hands rounded the corner and hustled down the steps.

O-370, too afraid to move, peered through the crack beneath the door and down the stairs. Rubber Hands crouched over the Ragged, seizing its wrapped wrists and wrestling its strong arms. Once the screaming settled, Rubber Hands's fingers moved through the air in strange shapes. The Ragged signed back with its twisted black hands.

Rubber Hands gently lifted the Ragged's arm and slowly uncoiled the wrapping in crusted rinds. O-370 considered running while the two were distracted, but the human was so gentle with the burned monster that he couldn't look away.

The wrapping removed, Rubber Hands drew an orange tube from its pocket and squirted sharp-smelling goo onto its palm. The Ragged breathed wretched and slow as Rubber Hands rubbed the twisted pink flesh of its exposed arm. O-370 could almost hear its dry skin drinking up the goo.

Rubber Hands spotted something in the corner and sighed. "What now?"

O-370's ears perked. Rubber Hands spoke with a woman's voice.

She stepped toward the wall of creatures, then came back into view holding a roll of bandages. She frowned down at the Ragged. "Have you been wrapping up my patients again?"

The Ragged closed its eyes and breathed.

Rubber Hands crouched and unwound the wrapping on its other arm. "I've told you—you're only allowed to wrap up the *dead* ones." She spoke slowly as her fingers moved through the air. "*I* wrap the live ones. Understand?"

The Ragged made a shape with its fingers, and Rubber Hands continued to goo its skin.

The tension melted from O-370's muscles. His fur lost its prickle. He realized that within Veteri's walls, Julep's wounds had been tended to, just as the Farmer tended to the nicks and scrapes that the Farm foxes suffered from broken cage wires.

Back on the Farm, O-370 had thought the Beatrix Potter story was boring. But now that he was in the City, he ached to believe there really were humans like Miss Potter—taking in foxes and caring for them before sending them back out into the cruel world.

He wondered whether Cozy and Dusty were right. Was Veteri where animals came to die? Or was it where animals were saved?

He quietly crept from behind the door and slid his hind legs down the hall. He reached the dog door and pushed through to the night's starry softness.

*"Oleo, look out!"* Cozy cried.

She was on top of the fan box, Julep lying beside her. The twisted rabbit, somehow freed from its cage, leapt at the box again and again, spitting and hacking, trying to nip Julep's paws.

*Clack!*

The dog door fell shut behind O-370, and the rabbit whirled its gummy pink eyes. It came bucking and choking toward him. O-370 tried to back away, but he tripped over his wrapping. The rabbit bounded forward, sinking its buckteeth into his haunch . . .

O-370 didn't feel anything. The rabbit's teeth had caught on the rubber tube, and it was shaking it ferociously. He kicked the rabbit in the face, and the tube split with a *snap*, uncoiling the last of O-370's wrapping and freeing his legs. The rabbit continued to ravage the tube as it hopped in abrupt zigzags around the yard and through the open fence.

O-370 watched it go in shock, as feeling tingled back into his hind leg.

*"That,"* Julep said, flopping off the fan box and splashing in the puddle, "wass the ugliesst baby I've ever sseen."

Cozy leapt over the puddle to dry ground. They all stared after the rabbit.

"How did that thing get out of its cage?" O-370 asked.

Cozy frowned at Julep.

"It wass sso *cute*!" Julep said with a smiling sort of snarl. "I wanted to *hunt* it."

The rabbit faded into the night, and O-370 wondered . . . Had they just released a curse?

Julep snorted. "Leave it to Oleo to be afraid of a *rabbit*. You shoulda sseen him in there, Coze. He got beat up by *laundry*. It wass the tamesst thing I've ever—"

He fell to his side and began to snore.

# SEVEN

**T**HE FOXES MADE a long, slow journey around the edge of the City. They crossed a trash-strewn field and padded through a short tunnel that passed beneath a road. They balanced along slippery steel beams crossed with splintered planks and came to a bridge streaked with pigeon droppings. The bridge arched over a muddy, leaf-strewn river that smelled of wild honeysuckle.

"Where are we going?" O-370 asked.

"We're already here," Cozy said.

They helped Julep down the embankment to the river-side. Lying beneath the shadow of the bridge was an upside-down truck. It was white and rusted, its four flat tires sticking harmlessly in the air. Its front was all smashed up, and its side was painted with blue symbols.

"What's that say?" O-370 asked as they padded through the bank's goopy mud.

"It's a milk truck," Cozy said. "The humans don't stop drinking it after they're grown. And they get it from bottles instead of nipples."

Julep snorted. "Humanss're *weird*."

"Watch your paws," Cozy said as she nuzzled open the truck's double back doors, which squealed in argument.

Julep limped inside, lay in the doorway, and immediately fell asleep. O-370 had to step over him to get in.

All was fuzzy shadows as O-370's eyes adjusted. The inner walls were a foggy silver. The floor—the truck's roof—was unevenly stacked with wooden crates. The air smelled like a baby kit's milk breath. Bottles were scattered everywhere, shattered and sealed.

"I thought you were dragging in garbage," Dusty said.

She stuck her nose out of a cave made of crates and stared at Julep, his wrappings leafy and soiled from the journey.

"Look, Dusty," Cozy said. "Julep's alive. Oleo saved him."

Dusty padded from her crate cave and sniffed at Julep's bloody wrapping. He didn't stir.

"He's hurt," she said without feeling. "He'll probably die soon."

Cozy whimpered.

*Is that true?* O-370 wondered. Had he done all that for nothing?

"Can Oleo stay?" Cozy asked.

Dusty stared at O-370. He couldn't look her in the eye, afraid she'd see that he had only saved Julep so that she would keep him safe.

"I guess I don't have a choice," Dusty said. "He knows where the Milk Truck is now."

She stepped through the back doors and slipped into the night.

Cozy helped Julep get to his paws and settle on some straw in the corner, as pungent as a forest floor. The moment his head touched the straw, he started to snore again.

O-370 gazed around the Milk Truck, looking for a place to sleep.

"Hey, Oleo?"

He turned back to Cozy. "Yeah?"

"Thanks."

He nodded, feeling just a flicker of the heater's warmth.

He sniffed out a crate and nuzzled it onto its side. He stepped in, turned three circles to make sure he wouldn't lie on a splinter, and then curled up behind his tail. Starlight streamed through the cracked-open doors and the crate's barred side. It wasn't the crosshatched comfort of his wire den, but it would do.

O-370 rested his muzzle on his paws, sighed deep, and waited for sleep to take him away from this place. The City grumbled in the distance. Its sounds still vibrated in his whiskers. Its smog still coated his fur.

Living in a story was more terrifying than he ever could have imagined. The cuts were sharper. The horrors smarter. Death was always a mistake away. Stories, O-370 realized, didn't happen because you wanted them to. In fact, they seemed to happen when you were least ready for them.

As his eyes fluttered shut, he imagined telling the tale of Veteri to R-211. An adventure so much bigger and more harrowing than any they'd heard before. He wondered how his cousin would react. He wondered what he would think of the name Oleo.

"Oleo," O-370 whispered to himself as he drifted off to sleep. "Oleo, Oleo, Oleo."

A rusted shriek stirred Oleo awake. Dusty was creeping back into the Milk Truck, a snow-white body in her jaws.

Oleo gazed wide-eyed through the slats of his crate. He recognized the creature's curled lips, its gummy pink eyes, its yellow buckteeth.

It was the rabbit from Veteri.

Oleo wanted to leap up, to tell Dusty about the stench and the snarling, to warn her that the rabbit might be cursed . . . But Dusty didn't believe in curses. And her single fang was already sinking into the rabbit's stomach, ripping up a strip of wet flesh, bloodying its white fur.

The rabbit looked twice as horrifying with its guts inside out, and Oleo got a good sniff of its oddly tinged insides, which stank of soiled straw. Stories couldn't describe smells. Not really. The understanding of them had to come from experience.

And this was one scent his nose still couldn't place . . .

**T**HE ALPHA KNEADED her paws against the dead pine needles, making sure she could still feel them. She noticed her siblings doing the same.

Outside, the blizzard had calmed. The fox kits could continue their hunt. But the prey would be buried under layers of white. Tracking would be easier once the sun thawed the wood a little.

Besides, the alpha's siblings were clearly dying to hear what happened next.

"So what is the Ragged?" the beta asked.

"Yeah!" the runt said. "Is it a human that got shriveled like an old berry?"

The Stranger didn't respond. He had closed his eyes again and seemed to be waiting for his breath to catch up.

"Oleo's safe now that he's got friends, right?" the runt said. "They'll team up and go back to the Farm and bite that Farmer until he's nothing but a skeleton!"

To demonstrate, the runt snapped up a fallen pine twig and shook it side to side. Just as quickly, he spat it out, whimpering at the needle jutting from his lip like a brown whisker.

"Ow ow ow *owrooooo!*"

"Hold still," the alpha said, pinning her brother's squirming body so she could delicately nip the needle from his lip.

"Some Farmer hunter *you* are," the beta said.

The runt grumped in her direction.

"Better pine needles than glass shards," the Stranger said.

The alpha's jaw tightened.

"The beasts of the City aren't like the ones in the forest," he continued. "They have glass eyes, and gears for teeth, and black blood, scalding hot . . ."

The alpha didn't believe a beast like that could possibly exist. But she still leaned in as the story began.

RA-DA
THUNK!
RA-DA
THUNK!

# ONE

**O**LEO JERKED AWAKE.

He blinked, waiting for his eyes to find their focus. He couldn't understand why the walls of his den were made of wood, why the sky beyond was *metal*.

*Snff snff*

The scent of sour milk brought the last few days rushing back. He was in the Milk Truck.

Oleo rolled onto his stomach and waited for his paws to wake. The truck had grown as cold as stones overnight. The crack of morning light coming through the back doors was thin and gray. Winter was descending. But it wasn't snowing yet.

Oleo breathed a little easier. The Farmer had said he wouldn't take the runts into the White Barn until winter began in earnest. R-211 was safe. For now.

"Is that more comfortable? I hope so." In the truck's opposite corner, Cozy was worrying over something. Julep. Wrapped in white.

Oleo padded up beside them. Julep was so weak he couldn't lift his head. His whimpers were small and distant, as if he were lost in the bottom of a deep hole. Whatever Rubber Hands had given him had worn off, and now his body seemed to finally realize he'd been hit by a car.

Cozy kept rearranging his head and paws, trying to ease his whimpers. "I've cleaned his wounds a dozen times," she said sadly. "I don't know what else to do for him."

Oleo sniffed. The blood seeping through Julep's wrapping smelled wrong. Thick. Sure, the kit had teased him, called him a mutt, but Oleo didn't want him to die.

"*Phht!*"

A huff turned Oleo's head toward the back doors. Dusty was a silhouette against the crack of morning light.

"Time to scavenge," she said, and vanished.

Oleo's belly squirmed with hunger. The bit of steak he'd eaten the night before was barely a scrap compared with what he ate back on the Farm. But after the horrors he'd seen in the City, he didn't want to leave the Milk Truck.

"You go ahead," Cozy told Oleo, not taking her eyes from Julep. "He might need his head adjusted. Or his itches nibbled."

Oleo gulped. He'd hoped Cozy would make up an excuse for him. "Guess I'm going alone then . . ."

When Cozy didn't respond, he stuck his head through the doors into the crisp morning. The sky was barely a shade above black. The honeysuckle drooped, heavy with frost.

Dusty was already a hundred tails down the riverbank, and he had to trot to catch up. The mud was cold and gloppy underpaw. Every step felt heavy. His legs shivered while his stomach whined. A frozen wind pinched his ears to numbness. Back on the Farm, R-211 and the other Farm foxes would be eating breakfast soon. He ached to be back there with them, toasty and safe beneath the steaming heaters.

Oleo finally caught up with Dusty's tail, and she glared back at him, her one fang gleaming.

"Where's Cozy?"

"She, um," he said between pants, "wanted to stay with Julep."

"Hmm," Dusty said, and padded faster.

Oleo let her get ahead of him. Her breath still stank of cursed rabbit meat.

A ways down the river, Dusty bounded up the bank, and Oleo did his best to follow.

They came to an open road, where a high whine drew his nose upward.

*eeeeeeeennnnnnnnnnnnnnnn*

Swoops of thick, humming cables stretched across the sky, between massive metal towers.

Oleo shrank from the sound. "Where are we going?"

"Dog food factory," Dusty said, nearly gagging on the words.

*"Dogs?"* Oleo tried to swallow. The bruises from Grizzler's fangs were still fresh on his throat.

"There are no dogs there," Dusty said, annoyed. "Just machines."

Oleo stopped walking. The pain in his throat was replaced with a prickling fear. The Skinner was a machine.

Dusty noticed he'd stopped following her and looked back. "Machines are dangerous, but they aren't made to kill foxes."

Oleo started to tremble. He knew one that killed foxes. Stole their skins right off their muscles. But Dusty had made it clear that she didn't want to hear about his past.

The vixen continued down the road. "There are three things a fox needs to know about machines."

Oleo gazed back the way they'd come. The Milk Truck was no longer in sight. He ran to catch up with Dusty.

"First," she said, "never bite one."

The scab on Oleo's lip tingled. He knew that much already.

"Their metal skin will break your teeth. And if you bite their black tails, their wire veins will shoot Blue through you. It will cook your flesh and melt it off your bones. I've seen it happen to a raccoon."

*eeeeeeeennnnnnnnnnnnnnnnn*

Oleo flinched at the drooping wires. Their eerie vibrations wormed into his ears and made hanging skins flash through his mind. These wires were crawling with Blue. And there were *dozens* of them.

"Second," Dusty said, "machines are obedient. They can't work when humans aren't around. That's why we're going to the factory before the first whistle." She nodded toward the City skyline, its streets quiet, its lights glittering faintly through the gray morning. "We'll need to be long gone before the sun clears the horizon."

"Wh-what's the third thing?" Oleo asked, not sure he wanted to know.

"Once we're inside the machine," Dusty said, "watch your tail. There are gears everywhere. Each with hundreds of teeth. If one catches you, it will coil you in and chew you to bloody bits. It will never let go, no matter how much you scream."

Oleo swallowed a whimper. He couldn't turn back now. The Milk Truck was too far. He followed Dusty on numb paws and wondered why a fox would ever go *inside* a machine.

# TWO

**T**HE **MORNING AIR** was fouled by smoke as the power lines led Dusty and Oleo to the heart of a metallic forest. Silver trunks stretched high above, roaring with limbs of flame that billowed leaves of steam. Their nauseous fumes wiggled the sky and made Oleo's lungs wheeze.

He kept close to the reassuring swish of Dusty's tail, but he still trembled uncontrollably as they padded past pools of oil and beds of shattered glass. After a long walk through falling ash, they arrived at a massive wooden building with peeling purple paint. The humming cables slanted from the sky into the building's corner. Oleo's whiskers could sense the Blue crawling through them, feeding whatever lived inside.

Dusty sniffed along the outer wall of the factory and then vanished down a window well. Oleo padded to the well's edge. The window was so filthy he could only make out blurred silhouettes on the other side. A stench cut through a crack in the glass—raw meat and old oil, dust and dry grain, the tang of urine. And beneath that, Blue, coiling through metal.

Dusty pressed her muzzle into the bottom of the window frame and nudged it open with a rusted crumble.

*"Wait,"* Oleo said, heart pounding. "Wh-what were the rules again?"

Dusty stared up at him. "You, of all creatures, shouldn't be afraid of machines."

Oleo swallowed. "What do you mean?"

"Humans made you too."

He felt his shoulders bunch.

"Why do you think you have that tag in your ear?" Dusty said. "You belong to them. You may look like a fox, but the humans changed you to fit their needs. Your teeth, your ears, even your instincts—they've all been dulled to serve humans."

Oleo flattened his floppy ears, trying to hide them. He remembered the Farmer telling Fern that they bred only the tamest alphas so the kits wouldn't bite. The Farm foxes had been fed and cared for, slowly tamed over years and years, generation after generation . . . just so the humans could wear their skins.

"Look on the bright side," Dusty said, not so brightly. "Dogs might be slow, stupid beasts, but at least the humans think they're cute."

The words made Oleo want to chew his tag off his ear. But he worried that if he did, he would start to forget the Farm. And R-211.

Dusty glanced up at the sky, which was slowly blushing pink. "Come. This place will be crawling with workers soon."

She nuzzled through the open window and vanished inside. Oleo tried to shake the electric hum from his whiskers, but it was no use. He took a breath, dropped down to the pebbles in the well, and squeezed through the window.

He landed with a dusty *PAF!*

He was on a high stand overlooking a cavernous space, much larger than the White Barn. Light strained through smeared skylights, casting a brown hue over the factory. A hulking shape sat at its center, but it was too dark to make out.

Ears pulsing, Oleo sniffed the ceiling for hanging skins. Then the corners for buckets dribbling black. He couldn't smell anything over the meat and oil, urine and Blue.

Oleo followed Dusty as she dropped down the levels of shelves. The moment their paws touched the concrete floor, the shadows shrieked to life. Beady eyes clustered along the factory's edges. Fuzzy bodies, hunched and gray.

Rats.

Dusty padded straight toward them, and the furry mass scrabbled away from the vixen like shadows from a flame. Oleo scampered to keep up with Dusty's tail as wet noses sniffed after him and hollow eyes stared unblinking. He spotted a small trap in the corner, its wire bar clamped down on a fuzzy corpse, an explosion of guts against the wall.

They approached the floor's center, and the hulking shape gained definition. Oleo's fur stood on end. The Machine filled the factory. Pipes protruded from its sides. Dozens of glass eyes stared blankly. A square maw hung open at the front in an eternal howl. The Machine seemed to be asleep, but Oleo could sense its Blue crackling within.

Dusty sniffed at a vat of ingredients near the Machine's side and huffed. "Horse fat."

She trotted toward the Machine's front and leapt up onto a long black strip that extended across rollers and into the open maw—the Machine's tongue.

"Well?" Dusty said.

"I—" Oleo's voice caught in his throat. "I can't go in there."

"Then you aren't eating. And neither is Julep."

Oleo's paws felt stuck to the concrete. His eyes blurred. His lungs couldn't draw a full breath.

He nodded to the Machine's long black tongue. "I can't jump up there," he lied. "It's too high."

Dusty sighed. "Dogs can't jump to save their lives." She squinted toward the skylight, which was growing pinker. "I'll snag any kibble that fell between the gears, and we'll each carry a mouthful back to the Milk Truck. Got it?"

Before Oleo could answer, *No, he didn't have it, not at all,* Dusty slipped into the open mouth, her tail dissolving in the greasy darkness. Oleo watched the Machine's glass eyes, waiting for them to blare to life, for its insides to sizzle Blue, for Dusty's skin to come shooting out the tail end.

As he trembled in the dank factory air, the fuzzy shadows gathered around him. Hollow eyes. Dripping noses. Twining naked tails. Oleo took a step back.

*KRNCH!*

He jumped. The sound had come from inside the Machine. His head filled with visions of gears catching Dusty's tail with their hundreds of teeth, rolling her in and grinding her to bloody bits.

"Dusty?" he whispered, keeping an eye on the encroaching rats. "You okay?"

From within the Machine came a gagging sound. "How do dogs eat this trash?"

*Kibble,* Oleo thought with relief. The crunch was nothing more than Dusty eating kibble in the Machine's hollow belly.

He continued to back away from the rats, hoping Dusty was almost finished.

"*Hck! Kaff!*" Inside the Machine came more gagging and then a distinctive wet splat. *Gsh!*

Oleo's ears perked. Had Dusty had just thrown up?

*THOCK!*

A sound punctured the warehouse, shifting the pressure, and sending the rats scattering.

"Welcome to the gold mine!" said a scratchy human voice.

The factory door had opened, and two men were walking in. Oleo froze. Dusty had said the workers wouldn't show until the sun cleared the horizon. What were they doing here?

One of the men punched a button by the door, and lights sputtered to life across the ceiling. Oleo slunk toward the shelves that led to the window, found himself out in the open, and quickly rounded to slip beneath the Machine's black tongue. The rats scrabbled to the corners and became shadows again.

"Your shift's over, you creepy buggers!" a man with a mustache called after them.

A man with a hat laughed.

As they approached the factory's center, Oleo pressed into the darkness beneath the tongue. He aimed his muzzle toward the Machine's oily underside. *"Dusty!"* he tried to say. But fear had him by the throat, and the word came out as air.

The mustachioed man carried a sack to the Machine's tail end and hung it from a pocket on a strange metal tree.

"The job pays garbage," he said. "So I skim a little kibble off the top and sell it to friends. They pay less. I make more. Win-win."

*"Dusty!"* Oleo tried again, hoping she could hear the sound of his breath. *"Get out of there!"*

"We got half an hour till the whistle blows," the mustachioed man said, heading toward a table covered in buttons. Copper hairs ran from its base into the Machine. "Watch. I'll fill that sack before the workers get here."

He slammed his fist on a big red button, and a deafening

buzz rattled every object in the factory and split Oleo's ears.

### RRRRNNNNTTTTT!

The Machine began to wake. Its rusted skin shivered as its glass eyes blazed to life. Its tongue began to roll as the metal parts within picked up a gnashing rhythm.

### RA-DA . . . THUNK RA-DA . . . THUNK
### RA-DA . . . THUNK

The Machine's maw howled, thickening the air with a hot, metallic wind. The rhythm rose to a roaring clatter.

### RA-DA THUNK RA-DA THUNK RA-DA THUNK

*"Yipe!"*

"You hear something?" the man with the hat asked.

"This machine's old," the mustachioed man said. "The owner don't take care of it."

Oleo cowered beneath the spinning tongue. Dusty had made that sound. The Machine had caught her in its gears, he was sure of it. He wanted to get out of there. Escape before the Machine licked him up and rolled him into its open throat.

"Now we enjoy the morning and let the machine do her thing," the mustachioed man said, leading the other toward the exit.

Without thinking, Oleo darted after the men, toward the light of the open door, where the breeze blew cool and the air was free of deafening rhythms. The rhythms that were currently *digesting* Dusty . . .

### RA-DA THUNK RA-DA THUNK RA-DA THUNK

Oleo's paws skidded to a stop halfway to the exit. He gazed back at the Machine's open maw, its whirling tongue, its flashing eyes. When he had left the Farm foxes behind, it was because he'd had no choice. They wouldn't listen to him.

Dusty thought he was made to serve humans? He'd show her.

Oleo ran back, leapt onto the spinning tongue, and was swept inside the Machine.

# THREE

*RA-DA THUNK RA-DA THUNK RA-DA THUNK*

**O**LEO **HURTLED DOWN** the metal throat, a confusion of wires and darkness. The rhythm was all-consuming now, vibrating his bones.

*RA-DA THUNK RA-DA THUNK RA-DA THUNK*

He flattened his ears and wrapped his tail and kept his eyes ahead. All around him, gears gnashed, squealed, and rattled. He passed a section splashed with Dusty's vomit.

*RA-DA THUNK RA-DA THUNK RA-DA THUNK*

As the black tongue rolled him deeper and deeper, the gray light of the Machine's mouth grew fainter until he could barely see two tails in front of him.

*SHHHHHHHHHHHH!*
*Pok! Pok! Pok! Pok! Pok! Pok!*

Oleo yelped when hard objects rained from above, pelting his ears. He squinted down at the tongue and saw they were dried corn kernels, as hard as hail.

### VRRRRRRRRRRRR!

Something sharp whirled in the darkness ahead. By the fading light, Oleo saw two metal bars covered in hundreds of tiny silver teeth. They rotated inward, slashing against each other, grinding the corn into a fine powder. The tongue swept him straight toward them.

Oleo turned and sprinted back toward the open mouth, but the tongue moved too quickly beneath his paws. There was nowhere to jump—walls surrounded him on all sides. The space between him and the spinning teeth closed, little by little, until—

*"Yipe!"*

The grinding mill ripped the fur from the tip of his tail. He tucked his tail between his legs and tried to run faster, but his knees burned, his lungs felt full of needles. He gazed back toward the slashing teeth, wondering if this was what had gotten Dusty . . . and he noticed that there was no blood. Only corn dust.

Dusty had made it past this part. But *how?*

Oleo sprinted in place, panting, limbs throbbing, frantically searching for an escape. The belt was slowly outrunning him, bringing his hind paws closer and closer to the grinding teeth.

### SHHHHHHHHHHH!
### Pok! Pok! Pok! Pok! Pok! Pok!

Another waterfall of corn poured from above, and Oleo saw the answer. With the last of his strength, he bounded ahead. As the metal flaps of the corn dispenser started to close, he leapt up the golden waterfall and hooked his fore-paws around one of the flap's edges.

Wincing at the rush of kernels against his face, he scrabbled to pull himself up into the golden pool, slipping his tail through the closing flaps before they came together with a *clang*. He wriggled up through the kernels and found himself in a vat of corn. He waded to the side and climbed onto the vat's rim, kernels spilling from his fur.

He was outside the Machine now. On top of it. The metal trembled beneath his paws. Dusty was nowhere in sight. Balancing along the vat's edge, Oleo padded to its opposite side. Below, the tongue whizzed on, now piled with a fine golden powder.

*That could've been me,* he thought.

*"Yaowr!"*

Deep in the guts of the Machine, Dusty cried out again.

"Coming, Dusty!" Oleo called over the rattling howl.

**RA-DA THUNK RA-DA THUNK RA-DA THUNK**

He breathed once, then again, then dropped back down to the conveyor belt in a plume of corn dust. The gears were dirtier here. The walls crusted.

***SSSSSSSSSSSSSSSSSSSS!***

The rolling tongue hurtled him toward a metal tube that hissed with sweltering steam. *The Machine's stomach.* Even from several tails away, the steam was hot enough to scald his nose. If he went in there, he'd be cooked.

A whisker before he was swept beneath the steam, Oleo wriggled his hips and leapt on top of the tube. The metal burned his paws as he scampered across, slipping and sliding until his pads felt ready to melt. He tumbled off the tube's opposite end, nose over tail, and—*PLOOF!*—landed on a hot bed of corn paste.

The tongue rattled now, breaking up the paste and carrying him toward a precipice where cooked corn spilled over the edge in a steaming golden waterfall. Something sliced sharply below.

**SHINK! SHINK! SHINK! SHINK!**

Before the tongue could hurl him over the precipice, Oleo rolled sideways to a narrow strip of metal between the whizzing tongue and a steep fall into darkness. He bundled his paws together, one in front of the other so they barely fit. Balancing carefully, he crept to the tongue's edge and peered over.

There was Dusty, jaws clenched around a chain, dangling over a pit of spinning blades.

**SHINK! SHINK! SHINK! SHINK!**

The blades chopped the waterfall of cooked corn paste, spitting hot debris up into Dusty's fur. Her eyes were squeezed shut. Her ear was bleeding, her tail looked *singed*. And she was slipping. The drop would take her straight to the choppers.

**SHINK! SHINK! SHINK! SHINK!**

Oleo reached out for her. He snapped his muzzle, trying to snag the chain and pull her to safety.

Dusty heard and opened her eyes. *"Puh deh teh!"* she screamed through her teeth.

*"What?"* Oleo said.

"Deh teh! Deh *teh*! *Puh eh!*"

Oleo could only shake his head. "I don't understand!"

Dusty breathed heavy through her nose. Her jaw trembled. Her single fang slipped lower on the chain.

**SHINK! SHINK! SHINK! SHINK!**

Using her eyes, she gestured to the side over and over again toward the Machine's back end.

"Pull the *tail*?" Oleo said.

*"Yesh!"*

"With my *mouth*?"

Dusty snarled at him.

"But you told me not to bite the Machine! It'll melt my skin!"

*"Don baht harg!"*

Oleo strained his ears, trying to understand her over the slicing knives. *"What did you say?"*

Dusty shut her eyes and clamped her muzzle tighter around the chain. She slipped lower.

"Okay, okay!" Oleo said. "Just . . . hold on!"

He spotted a flat metal surface opposite the pit of knives. He steadied his limbs and leapt, briefly feeling the warm wind of the slicing knives against his belly.

**SHINK! SHINK! SHINK! SHINK!**

His paws touched down to the metal surface and slipped on a layer of fat. Oleo cracked his head on the metal, then dropped, bouncing off the outer edge of the knife pit and falling back onto the rolling tongue.

Before he could get his paws under him, he was swept into another hissing tube. Sprayers gurgled and spat above, and Oleo winced, waiting to be cooked. But the sprayers only coated his fur in a warm layer of liquid fat.

He and the glistening kibble were swept out of the hissing tube and into a rotating drum that spun and howled with an icy wind. Oleo was tumbled and whipped by kibble before the drum rotated downward, dumping him and the food into a pocket of the strange metal tree.

He tried to leap up, but more kibble pelted his face from above as the kibble below swallowed up his paws, then his legs, then his body and tail.

"*Dust—*" he called out, and was consumed.

Oleo couldn't breathe. He couldn't move. Kibble crushed in around him like a rockslide. But then something gave out beneath his paws, and he was falling through open air again— right into the mustachioed man's sack.

Oleo struggled to pull himself up and out before flopping onto his side. He lay still, panting and waiting for the factory to stop spinning. He was back on the floor. He had made it through the guts of the Machine in one piece.

But his work wasn't done.

Oleo staggered to his paws and sniffed until he found a fat wire coiling out of the Machine's tail end and followed it to a plug in the wall. He understood now. The Blue shot through cables across the sky into the factory, where it fed the Machine's blazing eyes and whirring gears and slashing teeth. If he just pulled its tail from the wall, he could stop it from digesting Dusty. So as long as the Blue didn't melt his skin first . . .

Oleo opened his mouth around the Machine's thick tail. He could almost taste the Blue surging within, prickling his tongue and humming in his teeth. He closed his eyes and tried to bite down . . .

He couldn't do it. His jaw locked open. He furrowed his

brow and reminded himself that Dusty was in trouble. That she would *die* if he didn't unplug this tail. But his mouth refused to bite.

A skittering sound opened Oleo's eyes. The fuzzy shadows had gathered around him again. A rat stepped forward. And another. And another. Their naked tails writhed while their buckteeth worked as if they could already taste his flesh.

Oleo released the tail and leapt over the rats, which lunged and nipped at his chest. He ran toward the Machine, a wave of shrieking shadows surging after him. He bounded onto the metal tree, over the rotating drum, across the top of the fat sprayer, and back onto the spinning tongue. He sprinted against its movement toward the pit of knives.

### SHINK! SHINK! SHINK! SHINK!

The rats followed, surging over one another and up the Machine's seams, chomping at his tail. Oleo reached the tongue's edge and leapt. His teeth caught high on the chain, his haunch striking Dusty as a wave of rats poured over the edge into the pit of blades.

### SHNK!squee!SKSH!eek!SHLP!skreee! SHKWRT!eeee!SHLG!

The sound—a metallic chewing of meat and bone, high-pitched gurgles and grinding—was the worst he'd ever heard. The remaining rats heard their dying siblings and skittered back down the tongue toward the safety of the factory floor.

Beside Oleo's tail, Dusty's teeth slipped from the chain and dropped into the pit. He squeezed his eyes shut, expecting to hear that same wet crunching sound mixed with Dusty's screams.

But the blades had fallen silent.

And the Machine . . .

**_ra-DA . . . THunK rA . . . DA thrnk ra—_**
**_dA-thNK . . . THNK . . . thnk_**

. . . started to wobble and shake. Its tongue rattled. Its joints moaned.

"You can let go, Oleo," Dusty said below.

Oleo released his grip on the chain and landed on what weren't actually blades but thick strips of metal, fallen still and covered in gore. The rats had been too much for the Machine to handle.

**_ra . . . DA—thnk THunK RA . . . da_**

While the Machine continued to break down around them, Dusty came snarling at Oleo like she meant to tear him to pieces.

"Why did you do that?" she asked, pressing her bleeding muzzle to his.

He glanced left and right, looking for escape.

"You shouldn't have jumped in here!" she said. "You put us both at risk."

"I . . . ," Oleo said. "I couldn't let you become dog food. You hate dog food."

The snarl slowly left Dusty's lips.

**_THOCK!_**

The door of the factory popped open, and heavy boots came tromping in. Dusty and Oleo crouched in the Machine's heart and held their breath.

"I've never heard it make that sound before," the musta-chioed man said.

### ra...da...THrrNK!

The Machine gave one last shuddering screech before it sighed a final greasy sigh and fell quiet.

"Let's get outta here," the mustachioed man said. "Before the boss rolls in."

His footsteps moved toward the Machine's tail end, and Oleo heard the sack sliding off the metal tree. He remembered the wet splat he'd heard after Dusty had entered the Machine's mouth.

"Dusty," Oleo whispered. "Doesn't that kibble have your throw-up in it?"

*"Phht!"* she huffed, silencing him.

They waited while the man bundled up the sack—kibble, vomit, rat parts, and all—and exited the factory with the other man, the door slamming shut behind them.

Dusty snorted. It almost sounded like a laugh. "Mutts probably won't notice a difference between my puke and their regular food anyway."

Oleo dared a small smile. He felt as if he were in on the joke. As if he weren't a mutt after all.

As the Machine cooled and clicked, the foxes leapt out of the pit and padded down the dead tongue toward the tail end. Dusty sniffed at the kibble that had spilled along the tube's crusted edges. "This has been here awhile. It shouldn't have any vomit or rat guts."

She gathered up a mouthful, so Oleo did too. It was warm and slippery on his tongue.

He followed Dusty's iron-orange tail out of the Machine and through the factory toward the leveled shelves and the brightening window. The fuzzy shadows shrank from him now too, as if his tail were made of flames.

# FOUR

*CRUNCH*. "*OW*." *CRUNCH*. "Ouch." *Crunch*. "Ow!"
The Milk Truck echoed with the sound of Julep eating kibble. He licked his lips and scowled at Oleo. "Thanks for getting hard food when my face is hurt, *mutt*."

Oleo sighed. He preferred the slurring and stumbly Julep.

Cozy leaned in to Oleo and whispered, "Pet food is his favorite."

Oleo smirked. So that was why Dusty went all the way to the dog food factory.

"You want some?" Cozy asked. "You earned it."

Oleo sniffed at the kibble. He licked up one of the little bits and chewed it. It was startlingly crunchy. Musky sweet and bitter compared to the chicken scraps and fish guts he'd eaten back on the Farm.

"Aren't ya gonna eat, Dusty?" Julep asked. "This pile doesn't taste like Oleo spit."

Dusty sneered from her crate cave. "I'd rather choke. But

someone can get this disgusting stuff off my fur before I have to taste it myself."

While Julep continued to crunch and wince, Cozy and Oleo went into the crate cave and cleaned Dusty. The fats and corn dust tasted salty and sweet. Beneath, the vixen's fur smelled of raspberries. And now that she'd thrown up the contents of her stomach, her breath no longer stank of cursed rabbit meat.

Dusty didn't tell stories like Oleo's mom once had. She wasn't kind and instructive like Mia's and Uly's moms, and she wasn't funny like B-838. But there was something reassuring about her. Dusty's gait was as pointed as her single fang. She showed by example that so long as he kept his eyes wide, his nose forward, and his ears alert, it was possible to survive the City.

Oleo wished R-211 could meet her.

Outside, the air grew brighter by a whisker as a weak sun finally broke over the skyscrapers. But the air didn't grow any warmer, and the world remained cold and colorless. It wouldn't be long before snow filled the sky.

But the thought didn't frighten Oleo as it had before he'd left the Milk Truck. Now that he'd been dragged through a machine's oiled innards, he knew how it worked. And he couldn't help but wonder . . .

Did the Skinner also have a tail?

**W**HEN THE STRANGER finished speaking, the alpha found herself nuzzling up a pillow of brown needles to support his head. It was only when her nose passed his fang that she remembered herself and flinched back.

"Thank you," the Stranger said with foggy relief. He rested his head, and the wince left his eyes.

Beyond the pine branches, the snow had stopped completely. It left behind an unnerving quiet. As if the storm were daring the foxes to come out into the open.

The alpha had an unsettling feeling that something big was coming. And not just in the story.

"Why won't you tell us who you are?" she asked the Stranger.

His eyes remained closed, but his breath was shallow and stilted. He seemed to be ignoring her.

"So now the foxes go back to the Farm, right?" the beta asked.

"Yeah," the runt said. "Does Oleo use the Skinner's wires to fill the Farmer full of Blue until all his skin melts o—"

"*Phht!*" the alpha said, tuning her ears past the branches.

She heard the sound of tiny claws scampering across the snow. Little huffing lungs. The needles parted, and a squirrel poked his wispy ears inside.

It saw the foxes and froze, paws clenched, tail twitching.

The alpha lunged.

**T**HE KITS SPLIT the squirrel three ways, the Stranger politely turning down a haunch. The fresh kill put a perk in the siblings' whiskers and some salty comfort in the alpha's belly.

"Is that machine what got you?" the beta asked the Stranger, licking blood from her beard. "'Cause we can kill it if you want."

"Yeah!" the runt said. "I wouldn't be scared. They call me the *Fang*."

"No one calls him that," the beta said.

"It was not . . . ," the Stranger said, ". . . the Machine."

The runt looked disappointed and sniffed for squirrel leftovers.

"So what happens next?" the beta asked.

"Like all good foxes," the Stranger said, "Oleo was learning how to survive in his new environment. But he was about to learn just how connected the City really is. As connected as any forest. From the towering buildings to the streets and sidewalks to the water running underneath. From the humans and their dogs to the wildlife that hides in the cracks. Oleo was about to learn that even the smallest of actions can bring a whole city crashing down."

# THE MAD
# HOUNDS

# ONE

**T**HE SUN ROSE DARK and red and ignited a drizzling rain. The strange light crept into the Milk Truck, bloodying the dust motes and making the milk bottles gleam darkly.

In a fit of frustration, Julep had torn off his bandages and was up on his paws for the first time in weeks, pacing from one end of the truck to the other. Or he was trying to, at least. He high-stepped a forepaw, then wavered and set it down. He lifted a hind paw, swayed, and set it down. Every couple of steps his body would go stiff and start to keel over, but Cozy was there to nudge him upright again.

"I'm *fine*," Julep snarled through his wincing.

"I know," Cozy said, muzzle at the ready.

Oleo was in his crate, watching the weather through the back door. The rain was turning to sleet, pelting the truck in icy pings and creating little explosions along the river. It wasn't snow yet. But it wasn't far off.

Oleo now knew that he was capable of saving himself. He could save other foxes (whether or not they appreciated it). And he knew how to beat a machine. But even if he could make it all the way back to the Farm, sneak past Grizzler, hide from the Farmer, and rip the Skinner's tail from the wall, how could he break through the wire mesh of the cages? How could he convince the Farm foxes to leave?

"If I have to spend one more minute in this truck," Julep snarled, "I'm gonna pluck out my own whiskers. I *need* to go outside."

Cozy's eyebrows furrowed.

"I'll be *fine*," Julep told her. "If any danger comes, I'll run. Watch."

He fixed his eyes on a moldy milk bottle in the corner, then swayed and stumbled toward it. He knocked over two crates, kicked three bottles, headbutted the wall, and whimpered every time his paws hit the ground. But he made it without falling over.

"See?" Julep said, panting and blinking back tears.

Cozy's brow remained furrowed.

He nodded outside. "Look, it's raining. Humans *hate* rain. We can go to the park and have it all to ourselves."

Cozy glanced out at the sleet and grimaced. During the weeks that Oleo had spent with the City foxes, he had seen Cozy avoid water at all costs. She flinched at every splash and took exaggerated leaps over gutters to keep her paws dry. She remained in the Milk Truck at the first grumble of thunder.

Julep hadn't seemed to notice.

"Come *on*," he told her. "We can raid the trash for hot dogs!"

"Hot . . . *dogs*?" Oleo asked, disgusted.

"You're kitting me!" Julep said. "You never had a hot dog before?"

Oleo shook his head.

"You are in for a *treat*," Julep said. "Especially if they have popcorn."

"What's 'popcorn'?"

Julep got a dreamy look in his eye. "Imagine if clouds were covered in butter."

"What's 'butter'?"

"*Ohoho!*" Julep said.

Cozy pawstepped anxiously. "Maybe we should ask Dusty."

"No, *wait—*"

"Dusty?" Cozy called toward the crate cave. "You wanna go to the park with us?"

The cave was silent a moment.

"You go," Dusty said roughly from the darkness. "It's time you all stopped relying on me so much anyway."

Julep grinned at Cozy, clearly pleased with this turn of events.

Cozy stared out into the drizzly morning. "You have to promise we'll come back at the first whiff of danger."

Julep nodded enthusiastically and then squinted away a headache.

Cozy looked to Oleo. "Will you walk on Julep's other side to keep him upright?"

Oleo stood from his crate. Anything was better than sitting in the truck stuffed up with his thoughts.

"For the last time," Julep snarled. "I don't *need* help." He smirked at Oleo. "Especially from a mutt. All the humans would probably come outside to pet him and murder us."

Oleo scowled. Julep still hadn't thanked him for rescuing him from Veteri. Or for bringing him kibble from the Machine. In the old stories, Mia and Uly were always grateful when one stepped in to save the other. But Julep was as stubborn as walnuts.

"Fine," Oleo said. "I won't come then." He lay back in his crate.

Cozy sighed miserably. And it might have been Oleo's imagination, but it seemed that Julep looked surprised. Maybe even hurt.

Julep recovered by rolling his eyes. "Tame."

He hobbled toward the back doors and hopped into the rain. Cozy glanced back at Oleo, then joined Julep.

Oleo rested his chin on the rough wood of the crate. He watched the sleet chew through the sky and tried to convince himself that the rotten weather had stolen his appetite.

There was a creak as Dusty crept out of her cave. She was still roughed-up from her tussle with the Machine. Patches of fur were missing, and her paws dragged when she stepped. Flecks of spittle gathered in the corners of her lips, while gummy tears collected around her red-veined eyes.

Dusty padded to the back doors, grabbed hold of the loop of fabric, and tugged them shut. She turned back to her cave and froze when she saw Oleo.

"I thought you left."

"Julep doesn't want me there," Oleo said. "Why'd you close the door?"

"I can't stand the sound of the rain."

"Me either," Oleo said.

His ears were dreading the moment when the cold pang of sleet turned to softly drifting snow.

Dusty moved toward her cave.

"Is this all we do in the City?" Oleo asked, then swallowed. "Just . . . survive?"

Dusty didn't turn around. "Do you have a better idea?"

Oleo's words stuck in his throat again. He'd always thought that having Mia's and Uly's tales romping through his head would prepare him for the world—make him brave and clever and capable of handling any horror that came his way. That it would feel like an adventure.

But as the foxes scavenged food where they could—alleys, trash cans, restaurants—trying not to get killed by humans or cars or poison in the process, Oleo was starting to realize that the old stories weren't as useful as he'd hoped. The City was not the forest. Its monsters were nothing like Mr. Scratch or the Golgathursh or the Snow Ghost. They were too fast, too heartless, too oily and hulking, with skin made of metal. Too ugly and leering, with burned and bandaged limbs.

Dusty took another step toward her cave.

"Why can't we talk about our pasts?" Oleo blurted out, then tensed.

He expected Dusty to snarl at him, intimidate him, to try to frighten the memories of the Farm deep into the caves of his mind where they would be lost forever.

But instead, the vixen lowered her muzzle. "My mother used to tell me stories. About two young foxes who survived the horrors of the wild."

Oleo stayed quiet, not wanting to scare the moment away.

"In one of them," Dusty continued, "a young vixen was caught in a trap. But she'd learned things on her adventures, and she and her friend, a boy kit, found a way to set her free. Her paw was injured, but she lived."

Oleo's heart lit up. He knew that story.

Dusty squeezed her eyes shut. Her voice grew tight. "When my daughter was caught in a trap—a trap baited with dog food—I tried to use what I'd learned from that story." Her jaw trembled, moving the pink gash on her cheek. "But traps change. Humans change them. The old stories don't tell you that."

Oleo felt a squeeze in his chest.

"I broke my fang trying to open that trap while my daughter cried 'Mom, Mom, Mom' over and over again until the humans came for her." Dusty looked at Oleo and slurped some saliva back into her mouth. "Life isn't a story, Oleo. If you expect it to be, it will crush you."

She vanished into the dark of her cave. Oleo didn't stop her this time.

So much about Dusty made sense now. Her hatred of

dog food. Her knowledge of traps. Her disdain for stories, and her overprotectiveness of Cozy, the one vixen kit.

Oleo stared at his paws. Over the weeks, R-211's face had slowly faded behind the mesh of his mind. Maybe it was better not to think about his cousin anymore. To try to forget the Farm completely. To focus instead on surviving the City.

He got up, padded to the back doors, nosed them open, and stepped into the rainy morning. The sleet drenched his fur as he ran to catch up with the other kits. Cozy looked miserable, ears and nose dripping, but she still smiled when she saw him.

"Well, well, well," Julep panted, "if it isn't the mutt."

"Well, well, well," Oleo said, "if it isn't the fox who can't catch the mutt."

He splashed ahead toward the park, and Julep snarled as he hopped after him.

Unless Oleo was mistaken, it sounded a lot like laughter.

# TWO

**THERE WERE NO** humans in the streets that day.
Not even those who slept beneath the awnings, pungent in their bundled rags.

Still, Oleo and Cozy kept their whiskers sharp as the frozen rain pattered the empty streets. Julep kept his eyes fixed on the pavement a whisker in front of his wavering paws.

"How ya doin'?" Cozy asked.

Julep spoke between pants. "Like . . . I could . . . do this . . . *all day*. I'm just . . . worried . . . about *you guys*."

By the time they reached the park, the rain had eased to a sprinkle. It was high morning, but the cloud cover made it feel later. The park was small and rectangular, fenceless and shadowed by the tall buildings that surrounded it. A fox could run its length in two minutes. The far half was hidden by trees, whose branches tangled in a black mass. Frigid winds swept the leaves and grass, as colorless as the sky.

Julep limped toward a small pond, but Cozy stopped a dozen tails away, keeping plenty of space between her and the water.

"I'm . . . not hungry," she said.

"Your loss," Julep said.

He and Oleo continued around the pond's cement bank to a little cart on wheels that sat beneath a red-and-white umbrella, shiny with rain. A flock of pigeons had taken refuge under the umbrella, beaks tucked beneath their wings. As the foxes approached, the pigeons burst into the air. They landed on the bank and performed their silly marches to the far end of the pond, where they fluffed and cooed, waiting to see what these foxes were about.

"Ready?" Julep said.

"I think so?" Oleo said.

Wincing, Julep hefted his forepaws against the cart's trash can and rocked it back and forth until it tipped over, spilling wrappers and cups and a strange paper diamond with a bowed tail. Buried beneath it all were several half-eaten buns and fat pink tubes of meat.

*Hot dogs,* Oleo thought dreamily, and his nose was born anew.

"Are they safe?" he asked Julep.

*"Yesh!"* Julep said, his mouth already stuffed.

Oleo gently nibbled the nearest hot dog. It was squishy and salty sweet with little explosive fatty bits and hints of char that made his tongue ache with saliva. He devoured the rest, then sniffed for another. He decided that from that moment on, he would eat a hot dog every day, no matter the dangers. And if he could have six, he'd have six.

He tried not to think about how much R-211 would like them.

Julep spotted a lone hot dog and pounced at it. He batted it toward the pond and then bounded and snatched it up before it fell in. He shook it back and forth, ripping the pink flesh to bits.

Oleo laughed. He spotted a hot dog himself, then leapt and snarled it to pieces. He'd never pretended to hunt before. It made his limbs feel springy and put a pleasant bristle in his fur. The only problem was that whenever he shook his head back and forth, his ear tag whipped him in the eye.

"We gotta chew that thing off you," Julep said, gulping down the last of his hot dog.

"No way," Oleo said. "You'll break your teeth."

He tried not to let on that his heart wasn't ready to let go of it yet.

"Not if I rip it off real quick," Julep said, stepping toward him. "I mean, if it can't even shoot any lightnings . . ."

Oleo laughed. "Wait, what?"

"When me and Sterling first saw you, we thought you were a Zag."

"What the squip is a Zag?"

Julep's eyes went wide. "Zags live in the clouds. They throw lightnings at foxes and strike them down, leaving a smoldering pile of fur behind. They're *awesome*."

Oleo smiled despite the pinch in his heart. These were the kinds of conversations he'd had with R-211.

"What . . . happened to your friend?" Oleo asked. "The one who put me in that trap?"

"Sterling?" Julep turned away his muzzle and sniffed. "The Hidden Man got him."

The name brought a cold fear to Oleo's stomach. "Who's the Hidden Man?"

"He's the most dangerous thing out there," Julep said. "Poison can be sniffed. Dogs can be outsmarted. Even cars can be dodged if you're quick." He winked at Oleo, who felt a flash of the heater's warmth. "But the Hidden Man is invisible. He can sound like anything and look like anything. He hunts foxes."

Oleo scanned the surrounding buildings, the alleys between. Was the Hidden Man watching them right then?

*"Boys?"* Cozy said from the other side of the pond.

Oleo and Julep looked across the water. Cozy's paw was lifted, her nose pointed toward the park's far end.

Oleo traced it toward the tangle of dripping trees. Two shapes formed between the trunks. A tall red shape and a low black shape.

"What *is* that?" Julep said, squinting.

Oleo gave his head a shake, trying to stop his eyebrows from dripping into his eyes.

The tall shape became a woman, running through the trees. A dog ran behind her, dragging its leash. It was hard to make out through the stormy haze, but it looked like the woman was swinging something at it. An umbrella maybe.

Julep laughed. "Well, here's one mutt that isn't tame."

"Yeah." Oleo snorted. "Don't the humans usually lead the dogs around?"

"You got it backward!" Julep called to the woman and her dog.

The boys laughed.

Just then, the woman tripped and hit the ground hard. The dog leapt on her. It sounded like it was growling. It sounded like she was screaming.

"Is that dog . . . attacking her?" Oleo asked.

"No way," Julep said. "Dogs can't do that. They would die of shame."

The woman continued to scream as the dog shook its muzzle.

Julep's eyes went wide. *"Whoa."*

Oleo remembered the pain in his throat. Grizzler's crushing fangs. He had stopped being afraid of the City's dogs when he realized they were always on leashes. But this one . . .

The woman managed to throw the dog off of her and get back on her feet. She hurled her umbrella over her shoulder as she sprinted toward the nearest tree. The dog pursued her, strangely, rickety across the soppy grass, chomping at her heels.

"I *gotta* see this," Julep said. "Let's get closer."

Oleo didn't budge. He couldn't tear his eyes from the scene.

The woman leapt at the low branches and caught one in her hands. The dog leapt too, hooking her skirt in its fangs. The woman screamed and scrambled up the tree as the dog growled and yanked. When her hem tore loose, the dog lunged again and caught her shoe. He dropped to the ground, growling and shaking his muzzle, shredding the shoe to pieces.

The woman made it to the high branches, clung tight, and wept. The hound dropped the shoe and leapt up the trunk, again and again, barking and hacking as if it intended to kill her. But then the dog's body seized. Its paws dropped from the trunk as its muscles twitched and writhed. Its neck jerked from side to side as if something invisible were pulling its collar. Froth dripped thick from its jowls.

Fear caught up with Oleo. His hackles prickled. His toenails retracted. His tail hid between his legs. Julep was silent.

The dog's fits suddenly ceased, and it scanned the park with its gooey black eyes. It spotted the foxes and came jerking, stumbling toward them.

"*Run!*" Cozy called across the pond. "*Go!* Back to the Milk Truck!"

Oleo's paws went numb. The park wasn't wide enough to run around the hound, and they would have to head toward it to reach the alley that had brought them there.

"*How?*" he called to Cozy.

But she was sprinting *toward* the snarling hound.

"Cozy, *no!*" Oleo shouted.

"*Hic!*" Julep hiccupped, spinning Oleo around. "I-I can't run. I'm broken. I— *Hic!* Please don't—*hic!*—leave me."

Oleo felt a strange sort of relief when he realized Julep was more scared than he was.

"I won't," he told him.

Oleo turned his nose toward the nearest alley, but it was blocked by another hound with the same twitchy, unpredictable movements. The next street over had an old man, collapsed on his back and swinging a broom handle at another dog, which had the old man's arm in his teeth.

"Um, um, um," Oleo said, breathless, swiveling his

muzzle from street to street. Nearly every direction echoed with snarls and screams.

The only way out was away from the Milk Truck.

"There," Oleo said, padding toward the skyscrapers.

Julep set a limping pace, whimpering with every step. Oleo wanted to move faster, but he couldn't leave Julep behind. They had just stepped off the grass and onto the sidewalk when—

*"Hey!"*

Oleo yiped in fear when Cozy ran up beside them.

"I thought you sacrificed yourself," Oleo said, shuddering with relief.

"Nope," she said, out of breath. "Just the pigeons."

Oleo glanced back to the park, where the black hound was ripping one of the birds to bits and feathers. Cozy must have run straight into the flock, scaring them into an explosion of wings and giving the hound a dozen new targets.

The foxes moved as quickly as they could, Cozy and Oleo leaning into Julep's shoulders to keep him upright, constantly checking behind and to the sides.

A shape flashed, huffing, past a side street.

"This way," Cozy whispered.

She led them to a brown dumpster that sat flush against a building, and they all dropped to their bellies and wriggled underneath. Julep flopped to his side and wheezed while Cozy and Oleo panted in fear, gazing into the rain-slick street.

A truck drove past, its tires going *ssshhhhhh* across the

wet asphalt. A crackled voice blared from the truck's speakers: *"Atternshern, serterzens. Plerz remern insired. Ahr repert. Stehr ehn yehr hrms."*

A pack of hounds loped past the dumpster, chasing after the truck. Their eyes were crumpled and leaking. Their breath was ragged, their jowls frothy. Cozy and Oleo shrank deeper into the shadows, pressing close to Julep. But the garbage masked the foxes' scent, and the hounds continued on.

A rat heard them coming and bounded out from behind a trash can. The hounds were on it in seconds, playing tug-of-war with its shrieking body before ripping it in half.

"What's happening?" Cozy asked.

Oleo shook his head. The question scared him. Usually, it was her who explained the City's mysteries to him. But as he studied the hounds' jerking movements, listened to their snarling madness, sniffed their thick breath permeating the rain-scrubbed air . . . something clicked.

"Miss Vix," he whispered.

Cozy looked away from him.

"She's from the old stories," he told her. "She was infected with the yellow stench. She attacked her students and gave them the yellow. That's how it works. A fox bites another fox, and it changes them. I thought only foxes could catch it, but"—he stared into the drizzling gray of the street—"it looks like dogs can too."

*And rabbits,* he realized.

The wind was colored with the same scent he'd smelled in Veteri. Mold and soiled straw. He hadn't known what to call it then. The old stories had described it as yellow, but he couldn't actually smell the words. That had to come from experience.

Oleo considered the events that had led to this moment. Julep releasing the rabbit from Veteri. Dusty catching and eating it, then vomiting its cursed meat inside the dog food Machine. Who knew how many hounds had eaten that infected kibble? Who knew how many more hounds they had bitten?

*Snfffff*

Cozy had closed her eyes and was sniffing deeply.

"What are you doing?" Oleo said.

Her eyes fluttered open. "I'm . . . smelling for ghosts," she said, sounding embarrassed. "They can tell you how to escape bad things."

Oleo blinked at her.

She looked at Julep, who had passed out cold. "We have to get him back to the Milk Truck."

Oleo's heart sank. "How? He can barely walk."

"I don't know," Cozy said.

Julep whimpered, paws twitching in his sleep. Hunting hot dogs was the best time Oleo had had since he'd left the Farm. He couldn't lose Julep now.

"The Brick Warrens," Cozy said.

"What are the Brick Warrens?" Oleo asked.

"Tunnels," she said. "They branch through the City's underbelly and carry the humans' old water and leavings." She pointed her nose far down the street toward a dark rectangle in a distant gutter. "The Warrens connect every drain and spit the water into the river. If we can get Julep down there, we can find our way home. Dusty will know what to do from there."

Oleo squinted, watching the rainwater vanish into the dark rectangle. "You sure you want to go down there, Coze? It's wet."

Cozy breathed deep and nudged Julep's ribs. "Julep. It's time to wake up."

He groaned, and his eyes slid open. He remembered where they were and stifled a whimper.

"Can you walk?" Cozy asked him.

Julep stared at the ground. "Just leave me."

*"No,"* Cozy and Oleo said together.

Julep only looked at Cozy. "I'll be okay. I'll hide here till my head stops aching. Then I'll limp back to the Milk Truck."

"I don't think those dogs are going anywhere, Julep," Oleo said.

Julep clenched his teeth. "I told you. I'll be fine."

Cozy snarled. "Pretty soon, those hounds will sniff us out. And they'll kill me too because I'm not leaving you."

Julep looked stubbornly away from her.

Oleo couldn't stop thinking about what Cozy had said about ghosts. He doubted that they could be sniffed in the air or that foxes from the Underwood could communicate with the living. But he did know some stories about dead foxes. Ones that might help.

How had Roa escaped Miss Vix in the Eavey Wood? The answer was, he hadn't. And he hadn't even had an injured fox to protect. But when Mia had looked back on that horrible day, she had wished that she had used her tail to tease her infected teacher away from her siblings, giving them a chance to escape.

"Julep will go by himself," Oleo said.

"*What?*" Julep said, head jerking upright. "I'm not sacrificing myself so you two can—"

"I wasn't finished," Oleo said. "Cozy and I will follow behind twenty tails or so. If one of those hounds comes after you, we'll run between and get it to chase us." He looked to Cozy. "With two of us keeping the hounds distracted, Julep should be able to make it to the drain." Oleo eyed the distance between them and safety—hundreds of tails away. "The three of us will meet in the Brick Warrens."

"You're a terrible runner, Oleo," Julep said. "Those hounds will catch you."

Oleo met his eyes. "You didn't think I could cross a street either."

Julep frowned. Then he huffed and slowly pushed up to his paws.

"Whatever you do," Cozy said, "don't get bitten."

"Thanks," Julep snarled.

He limped out from under the dumpster and into the open street.

# THREE

**C**OZY AND OLEO watched Julep as he limped toward the drain, which seemed to stretch farther and farther away. Oleo panted, glancing left, then right, down the street, watching for hounds.

Cozy nudged his muzzle. "I'll get the first one."

"Thanks, Coze." His panting calmed to a whisper.

Julep had barely hobbled ten tails when a high-pitched squeal ripped through the air. A tan ball of fluff came scuttling into the street. It was the pug from the restaurant. Only now its eyes were bulged and bloodshot. Its mouth hung open, and blood dripped from its sharp little teeth.

Julep froze as the little dog came twitching and huffing toward him. Cozy launched out from under the dumpster, sprinting between Julep and the dog. The pug rounded on her, but she ran rings around it—*too close,* Oleo thought— spinning it in frustrated circles before darting down a side alley. The little dog followed, yapping droplets of blood.

As Oleo watched its curlicue tail vanish around the corner, he couldn't help but wish that the short-legged dog had been his to distract. Who knew what would come next?

"Keep going!" Oleo hissed to Julep.

Julep panted, exhausted, but he started limping again.

Oleo waited until he was twenty tails away, then slipped out from under the dumpster. His lungs quavered. His knees trembled. His eyes darted left, then right, then behind. Every shadow seemed shiny with fangs, every sound foamy with breath.

Halfway to the drain, Julep slowed to a crawling pace. Oleo grew anxious. If Julep would hurry up a bit, they could make it to the grate without being spotted by another hound.

"Doing okay up there?" Oleo whispered, hoping to put some hustle in Julep's paws.

"I just . . . need . . . to rest for a sec," Julep said, then slumped to the street.

Oleo winced and stopped walking. He wished he hadn't said anything. He rocked from paw to paw as he scanned the abandoned streets. Something sloshed in a side alley, making Oleo jump. It was just a human dumping water out of a high window.

"I think that's enough rest, Julep," Oleo said.

Julep huffed. "Sorry. *Someone* made me cross a road, and I got hit by a *car*."

A heat built in Oleo's chest. He wanted to tell Julep that he hadn't forced him to cross that road. That Julep had been showing off. But Oleo didn't want those to be the last words he ever said to him.

Julep struggled to his paws, and Oleo breathed a little easier.

They continued on, approaching a section with an alley on either side. Oleo felt a tick in his whiskers moments before he heard the panting. Julep froze in the middle of the street as Oleo rotated his ears toward one alley, then the other, straining to determine where the sound was coming from.

As the panting grew closer, it doubled in his ears. Oleo went cold. It was coming from both directions.

Julep started to tremble. "Oh n— *Hic!* Oh no. *Hic!*"

A dog with gray fur, spiky with sleet, emerged from the alley on the left, its head whipping from side to side. From the alley on the right came a golden hound, its fur shiny. It was smaller than the other hound but more muscular. Foam spilled from its open jaw, and it made an awful hacking sound, as if trying to clear a bit of skin from its throat.

Oleo wanted to leap over Julep, sprint to the drain, slip inside, and not stop running down the dark tunnels until he reached the safety of the Milk Truck.

But as the gray hound came growling toward Julep, Oleo found himself lunging forward and striking it in the muzzle. He swiveled and leapt over Julep, headbutting the golden hound that thrashed in from the other side. Oleo's vision filled with dark lights, and he hit the asphalt hard, his fur scraping up rain and grit. He felt hot yellow breath against his throat and rolled away, the golden hound's fangs chomping at his face.

He had just gotten back onto his paws when the gray hound lunged back toward Julep, who flinched away just in time. Without thinking, Oleo leapt onto the golden hound's back and jumped off, kicking the hound onto its side and using the momentum to tackle the gray dog.

Julep snarled and retreated as the golden hound recovered and went after him again.

*"Nope!"* Oleo caught the golden hound by the tip of its tail and yanked.

The gray hound rounded and snapped at Oleo's face, ripping several whiskers out of his muzzle. Holding tight to the golden tail, Oleo shuffled backward, pulling the hound in a circle. He had no idea what to do now. His jaw felt raw, and his claws were slipping on the wet street. He couldn't hold on much longer.

He continued to circle until the golden hound's nose was pointed toward the gray hound . . . He let go. The golden dog lunged at the gray one, and for a moment, the two became tangled in a vicious fight, lashing blood from each other's faces.

*"Go!"* Oleo shouted at Julep.

Julep rose, trembling, and hobbled toward the drain.

The hounds noticed the movement and stopped fighting. Before they could go after Julep again, Oleo darted directly between them, drawing their muzzles toward his tail, before taking off aimless down the street.

The hounds chased after him, their hot breath snipping at his heels. Delirious, Oleo searched for an escape. Roa had briefly evaded Miss Vix in the old stories by hiding in brambles. But there were no brambles in the City.

Ahead, he saw a closed metal trash can sitting at the top of a sloping side street. He remembered what Dusty had said at the factory: *Dogs can't jump to save their lives.* Oleo picked up momentum and tried to leap on top of the trash can. But his muzzle smacked the lid, knocking the can over and sending him careening to the side.

For a brief moment, the hounds became confused and chased the spinning can. Oleo hopped up and stared back the way he'd come. The street stretched long and empty. His lungs and limbs were full of fire. He couldn't possibly outrun the hounds all the way back to the drain.

The trash can spun to a stop, and the hounds turned their gummy eyes back on Oleo. He saw his escape. He ran toward the hounds, dove beneath their clacking muzzles, and leapt inside the can. He ran his paws up the rounded metal, rolling it down the sloping street.

The gray dog sprinted alongside the can's opening, wheezing yellow-fouled spittle. It met Oleo's eyes and lunged sideways into the can, tripping him and sending them both tumbling around each other. Oleo panicked as his limbs flopped in circle after circle, the hound's fangs flashing at his chest, his tail, his eyes. The world spun outside, street flipping with sky, making it impossible to tell which way was up. He placed his hind paws against the can's bottom and kicked, then tumbled onto the asphalt.

The can continued to roll down the hill, the yelping hound unable to find its way out. Oleo lay on his side, chest heaving, and waited for the City to stop spinning.

*One down,* he thought.

The golden hound did not give him time to celebrate as it came charging down the hill. Oleo staggered to his paws and again ran without direction.

"Oleo!" Julep barked in the distance.

"We made it to the drain!" Cozy yelped.

Oleo slid to a stop, pivoted, and with everything he had left, sprinted up the hill, the golden hound skidding and fumbling to catch up. He reached the hill's top and turned in a great arc, rounding the corner toward the drain where his friends were waiting for him.

*"Yipe!"*

He felt a jerk and a sharp pain as the golden hound ripped hairs from his tail. It was right on top of him. He didn't have the energy to sprint anymore. He was winded. His head wouldn't stop spinning. And his paws stung so badly he worried they might break.

Just then, a figure stepped out from a side alley. It was dressed head to toe in blue and stared down the street with wide glass eyes. It held a needle in one hand and a metal pole in the other. The pole had a wire loop at the end.

It was Rubber Hands. The human from Veteri. Oleo remembered her gently massaging goo into the Ragged's burned skin. He remembered Julep's bleeding head, which she'd wrapped up to keep the life from leaking out of it.

The hound right on his tail, Oleo ran toward Rubber Hands, hoping she would save him. He leapt between the human's legs as she swung the pole in one smooth motion, catching the hound's throat with the wire loop before pulling it taut. The dog's momentum caused its body to fly forward, only to crash back down to the asphalt. Rubber Hands was on the hound in an instant, plunging the needle into its throat.

Oleo looked back long enough to see the snarl die on the golden hound's lips before its straining neck grew slack and its head thumped to the ground.

He made it to the drain and wriggled inside, falling through darkness and splashing into icy, paw-high water. Wan light shone through bars of shadow in the grate above. His breath made ghosts in the underground air.

Cozy looked miserable, shivering and lifting her paws, one by one, out of the sewer water. Julep lay on a dry hump, squinting away a headache. The kits looked at one another, shocked and panting, checking to make sure they were all unbitten.

Feeling spread through Oleo's body, waking the sting in his plucked whiskers and tail, the cuts in his paws from the asphalt.

"You'll never believe what happened out there," he panted. "The human. From Veteri. She caught one of the hounds with this wire thing. She saved my life!"

Julep laughed, a little out of breath. "She was probably just trying to get your collar back on."

Oleo's ears folded. "It wasn't like that. She might be good. Like . . . Miss Potter." *Or Fern,* he thought.

Cozy refused to look at him.

"You should've seen me up there, Coze!" Julep said. "I snarled so loud those hounds scampered away like frightened mice. I didn't need Oleo to distract them. I had it taken care of the *whole* time."

Oleo gritted his teeth. All the warm feelings he'd felt toward Julep in the park wilted in the dark of the sewer. He would have chomped Julep's ears if they weren't still healing.

For some reason, Cozy was scowling at Oleo. "Miss Potter was *never* good."

His ears perked. "You know the old stories?"

Without answering, she slunk down the dark tunnel, high-stepping through the water.

Julep joined her. "I'm just glad I didn't throw up those hot dogs."

An icy wind drew Oleo's attention up through the drain. Living in a story was difficult. But his confidence grew with every adventure. Veteri. The Machine. And now two hounds infected with the yellow stench.

If he could survive all that . . .

"I have to go back," he said.

Julep turned around. *"Up there?* Are you squipping crazy?"

"To the Farm," Oleo said. "I have to save my friends before the Farmer takes their skins."

Cozy kept splashing down the sewer tunnel, her tail fading in the gloom. Oleo felt a pinch in his heart. She didn't want to hear his story.

"Did you say their *skins*?" Julep asked.

Oleo nodded. "Once it starts snowing, he'll take them into the Barn. I have to get back there before that happens."

Julep gazed up through the drain. "You'll never make it out of the City. Those hounds will tear you to pieces."

The hounds weren't the only thing standing between Oleo and the Farm foxes. There was the Farmer and Grizzler, the cages, and the foxes' stubbornness.

"I have to try," he said. He swallowed the lump in his throat. "Even if I can only save my cousin."

Julep frowned. "You got lucky up there, Oleo. You might not be so lucky next time. Now come on. Stop trying to play hero."

He turned away, his tail fading with Cozy's.

Oleo took a deep breath of the underground air, trying to hold on to that feeling of confidence before Julep's words made it slip away. But he was tired. And he was already starting to shiver in the dripping dark of the Brick Warrens.

He decided he would return to the Milk Truck and rest up. Once the Black Hours fell, he would slip out and find his way back to the Farm. He wished Cozy and Julep would go with him—lend him their City bravery. But he would do it alone if he had to.

He padded to catch up with the others.

The deeper the foxes crept through the dark tunnels,

the more the drains came alive with sounds. Sprinting feet and shuffling paws. Screams and choked barking. And it may have been the stormy light or Oleo's imagination, but it looked as if some of the draining water dripped red.

# FOUR

**A**FTER A LONG, sloshing journey through the sewer, the foxes came to a glowing circle of evening gray. They stuck their muzzles through the opening and sniffed up and down the river. The air was cool and honeysuckle clean. The Milk Truck lay beneath the bridge, glowing softly.

Cozy nosed open the Milk Truck's doors, and they slipped inside. The air smelled danker than before.

"Dusty!" Julep called, panting. "You won't believe what just happened! I saved our lives."

Dusty didn't respond. She was hunched in her crate cave, illuminated by a crack of clouded moonlight. The vixen's back convulsed. Her ribs swelled and collapsed. Her tail writhed. Julep folded his ears and quietly slipped outside.

"Dusty?" Cozy said, padding toward the cave. "You okay?"

Dusty's head slowly lifted. Her eyes gleamed dully. Her

lips dripped with saliva. Oleo's heart started to pound when he remembered that Dusty hadn't wanted to go out when the rain was falling. Just like Miss Vix had refused to cross the creek . . .

Dusty may have thrown up that rabbit, but the yellow was still inside her.

*"Cozy!"* Oleo yelled.

Dusty lunged, knocking Cozy onto her back. Cozy barely managed to press her paws against Dusty's chest as the vixen hissed and clacked at her snout. Dusty was twice her size and thrashing madly. Cozy's legs started to buckle.

Oleo leapt, tackling Dusty off Cozy and rolling the vixen across the floor, knocking down the crate cave and shattering bottles. They struck the wall, Oleo on top, and he straightened his legs, pinning Dusty down.

Dusty lashed and choked, bending her neck in impossible angles to snap at his ankles. Oleo stepped back and back, moving his paws down Dusty's chest to escape her gnashing teeth until she was free enough to coil upward and chomp at his face.

He winced as the vixen's fang clacked shut just a whisker from his nose. Cozy had seized Dusty's tail and was pulling her back. Dusty tried to round on her, but Oleo clamped onto the vixen's scruff.

"Go!" he screamed at Cozy, his mouth full of fur. "Get out of here!"

As Oleo spoke, his teeth released just enough for Dusty to wriggle free. She righted herself, cranking open her jaws to clamp around his throat. But before her fang could sink into his fur, a tower of crates collapsed onto the vixen, burying her.

Cozy stood where the tower had been, staring wide-eyed.

"Run!" she screamed.

As Dusty thrashed beneath the crates, Cozy and Oleo leapt out of the Milk Truck. They turned and threw their forepaws against the doors, pushing them shut. Dusty slammed her muzzle into the opposite side, whining and gurgling with rage as she tried to force it back open.

The kits took off down the riverbank and arrived at the mouth of the Brick Warrens. Cozy slipped inside, but Oleo froze. A pain bloomed to life, white and sharp, in his chest. He looked down. Blood pattered on the frozen mud.

"Come on!" Cozy called from the tunnel. "Before she gets those doors open!"

Oleo wavered in shock. "She bit me."

Cozy saw the wound and fell quiet.

Oleo began to shake with disbelief. "She bit me, Coze. That means I have the yellow now. Soon, I'm gonna start acting like those hounds. Like . . ." He looked into Cozy's mismatched eyes. "You have to leave me."

Her face crumpled. "Squip no."

*THOOM! THOOM! THOOM!*

Upriver, the Milk Truck rocked and strained as Dusty threw her weight into the doors over and over again.

"If you don't move your tail this *second*," Cozy snarled, "I'm going to go let Dusty out so she'll chase you in here."

Oleo blinked and then slipped into the tunnel. They walked until they could no longer smell the honeysuckle, then crouched, small and silent in the darkness, noses pointed toward the circle of gray. They tensed when the Milk Truck's doors crashed open and watched as a silhouette passed the tunnel's entrance. It no longer walked with Dusty's arrowed confidence, but tumbled in fits and starts.

The sight broke Oleo's heart so much that he briefly forgot his pain. Dusty might not have been much of a mom, but she had kept him alive. She had shown him how to survive the City. He wondered what she would think of him now that he had saved Cozy's life. From Dusty herself no less.

Cozy stared toward the crooked silhouette. "Instinct prevails," she whispered.

There were no tears in her eyes.

They ventured deeper through the tunnels until they found Julep's flower scent.

"Where were you?" Cozy asked, voice tight.

Julep hesitated. "I . . . I thought you were right behind me. Is Dusty . . . ?"

"She's gone, Julep," Cozy said. "Fewer tails to watch over."

This time, it was Julep's turn not to respond.

He sniffed sadly, then looked up. "Wait. I smell blood."

Cozy remained silent.

"Dusty bit me," Oleo said.

"*What*?" Julep said. "But . . ." He swallowed deep. "Well, get him out of here, Cozy! He's infected!"

"He isn't changed yet," Cozy said. "Oleo's still Oleo."

"But-but he's gonna turn into one of those *things*."

"He's staying with us," Cozy snarled.

Julep grumbled to himself, then slumped against a wall. The sewer dripped.

"We'll have to sleep here tonight," Cozy said.

"It's cold," Julep said. "And wet."

"And not full of mad hounds," Cozy said.

*But it might have a mad fox,* Oleo thought with a shudder. *Soon.*

The foxes tried to make themselves comfortable in the dripping underground. Their haven was gone. Dusty wasn't there to guide them. And the City was crawling with mad hounds.

But that wasn't the worst part.

Wincing, Oleo lay on his unbitten side and licked a smear of blood from his shoulder. His wound pulsed and stung. What was going to happen to him?

A warm body snuggled up against his back. "I wish I could clean your bite," Cozy said. "But I might get infected."

Oleo sniffled. "Thanks, Coze."

She softly laid her tail over his side and pressed close. "Let me know if you suddenly feel like biting me, okay?"

Oleo nodded, eyes filling with tears. Would he even be able to talk by then?

Cozy's breath grew soft and rhythmic. But as the night wore on, Oleo couldn't sleep. Part of it was the pain in his chest. Part of it was the thought that he'd never get back to the Farm and save his friends. But mostly, he couldn't stop wondering what it would feel like when he turned. Would he stop caring about Cozy? R-211?

When all was quiet save Julep's snores, the faces appeared, dripping and contorting in the sewer's gloom. Their dry whispers echoed deep into Oleo's ears, all the way down to his throat.

*Thirsty,* the voices said.

*So thirsty.*

*But what to drink?*

Oleo's stomach contracted. His tongue ran dry.

*Not water,* the voices said.

*Never water.*

*You could* drown.

*So what then?*

*You know.*

*Red.*

*Pumping underneath.*

*Then you could drink your fill.*

*A pond's worth.*

*A* swamp's *worth.*

*Thirsty.*

*So thirsty . . .*

×   ×   ×

Above the sewer . . .
  Above the City . . .
  The clouds opened . . .
  And it began to snow.

"**W**HAT?" **THE RUNT'S** eyes were wide with disbelief. "*No.* No, no, *no.* Oleo can't die now. He's the *hero.*"

"Yeah," the beta said, sounding more worried than usual. "He was just getting good at things. Who the squip's gonna save the Farm foxes now? It's snowing!"

The alpha's whiskers twitched, and she watched the snowflakes multiply beyond the pine branches.

"I did not say Oleo died," the Stranger said. He had closed his eyes again. "Only that he was infected."

"But you can't come back from the yellow!" the runt said.

The Stranger didn't respond.

"Will they ever see Dusty again?" the beta asked.

"They . . . will not."

The runt whimpered. "I hate this story."

He was close to tears. The beta's brow was crumpled up. The alpha worried this story would ruffle her siblings' fur beyond their mother's smoothing.

"Don't grieve for Dusty," the Stranger said. "She's with her daughter in the Underwood. And before she died, the vixen taught the fox kits everything she knew. Things that would help them survive the horrors still to come."

"There's *more?*" the runt said.

"Of *course* there's more," the beta snapped. "What do you think, they lived happily ever after in the *sewer?*"

The alpha was only half listening. The snows had kicked up again, blowing in from north and south, lashing at the pine tree from both directions. If they left now and moved quickly, they could get back to the den before the drifts made the journey impossible. Before winter closed its jaws around the wood completely.

The alpha was about to tell her siblings it was time to leave when the beta leapt to her paws.

"So now what? Do we just listen while Oleo slowly loses his *mind*?"

The runt gulped. "There's gonna be a Golgathursh in the Brick Warrens."

"No," the Stranger said, lifting his head. "There are no monsters in the belly of the City. And there are ways to survive. Filthy water to drink. Rats to hunt. But the foxes were not safe. Not with a fox whose yellow scent thickened with each passing day . . ."

# HOUSE OF
# SILK AND
# INCENSE

# ONE

**I**N THE SUNLESS days and moonless nights of the Brick Warrens, Cozy didn't leave Oleo's side. His wound was healing, and she could no longer smell blood. But he was feverish and fitful. The heat coming through his fur was like metal on a summer day.

He talked in his sleep. "Go away!"

And even though Cozy knew he wasn't talking to her, she answered, "I'm staying right here."

Oleo had saved her life. And she wanted to do the same for him. Or at least lick his ears to keep him soothed while the yellow spread through his body.

When Cozy first met Oleo, his fur had smelled like nothing. It had taken her a while to remember why that was familiar. Oleo had reminded her when he brought up the Beatrix Potter story—one of her favorites when she was a kit. The cruel woman had kept Mia in captivity for weeks, feeding her only oatmeal and leeching the scent from her fur until even Mia's mother could not smell her.

It was not a story about the goodness of humans. Cozy

wondered who had lied to Oleo to make him see it that way. To make him trust humans more than any fox should.

Oleo no longer smelled like nothing. The more time he spent away from the Farm, the more his true scent came through. Something tart and sweet. Cozy wanted to hold on to it with her nose, to finally understand the real Oleo. But his true scent was quickly clouding over with yellow.

"Leave me alone!" Oleo snarled.

"*Shh shh shh*," Cozy said.

"I won't do it!" Oleo said, muscles straining. "I won't!"

She smoothed his hackles with her muzzle, afraid his voice would echo down the web of dripping tunnels and catch the ear of a mad hound that would wriggle through a drain and find them. Oleo's spasms calmed to shudders.

Life in the sewer was all sounds and smells—Oleo's snarls and yellow stench, Julep's snores and healing head wound. The only light was a faint winter bloom from a distant drain. Cozy had sniffed out an old shirt a ways down the tunnel and dragged it to their sleeping spot, trying to make it feel more like a den. But she couldn't stop the wetness from soaking through to Oleo's fur. Or to hers.

*Drip!*

A drop of water splashed a little too close, and Cozy scooted away. When she wasn't tending to Oleo, she sought the driest spot on the shirt and folded her paws over her ears, trying to muffle the gurgles and drips that haunted the brick tunnels. She had avoided water since she was two moons old. But there was no escaping it down here.

Oleo's body tensed again. "I'll *make* you quiet!"

"What's he saying now?" Julep asked from across the tunnel. He'd kept his distance from Oleo ever since they'd come to the sewer.

"*I'll tear you open!*" Oleo said.

"He's just . . . ," Cozy said, "talking about how he'd like to tear open a trash bag and find a nice juicy steak for us."

"Cozy," Julep said.

"He isn't snapping at us yet."

Julep scoffed. "Yet."

"I'm warning you," Oleo said. His grumbles were becoming more snarled.

"We have to leave him, Coze," Julep said. "If he tries to bite you—"

"He won't," Cozy said, trying to sound hopeful. She looked at Oleo. Her skin twitched along with his. "He talked to me a bit today. Normal talk."

"Great," Julep mumbled to himself.

She didn't tell him that Oleo had refused water. Or that he wasn't making sense. *Can't drink,* he'd whispered. *I gotta pull the Skinner's tail out. The voices say if I have water in my mouth, the Blue will sizzle me.*

Cozy adjusted Oleo's head until he looked more comfortable. Two weeks had passed from the moment Dusty had eaten that infected rabbit to the moment she attacked them. Oleo still had time. But time for what, Cozy didn't know.

"I don't know why you like that kit anyway," Julep said. "He's bad luck. Ever since Oleo showed up, Sterling died, I got hit by a car, and Dusty turned into one of those . . . *things.*"

The dark of the sewer seeped into Cozy's heart. She had lost so many foxes. If the yellow took Oleo and if Julep's head didn't heal, it would feel like losing her mom and three brothers all over again.

"You know what Dusty would say," Julep said.

*Dusty isn't here anymore,* Cozy wanted to answer.

Whenever she thought of the vixen, she felt a clench in her chest as if she was about to feel something. She never did.

She found the shine of Julep's eyes. "Oleo saved your life. He saved you from the hounds. And Veteri."

"I wasn't that hurt," Julep grumbled. "I had it taken care of."

"He saved mine too," Cozy said. "In the Milk Truck."

Julep huffed. "If I hadn't run away, Dusty would have *bitten* me, Cozy. What did you want me to do? *Bleed* on her?"

Cozy's whiskers ticked. "I thought you said you weren't that hurt."

Julep's teeth clicked shut. "You've changed since Dusty died," he said. He rolled over and faced the wall.

"Two Eleven!" Oleo cried.

His paws scampered sideways, as if he were running away from something. Or toward it.

When they'd first crawled into the sewer, Cozy had caught a piece of Oleo's tragic story. She had tried to escape before it could scrabble into her ears. But Oleo's words had echoed down the tunnel faster than Cozy could move. And now they were lodged in her heart.

She wanted to tell Oleo that he would return to that

Farm someday. That he would free his friends from those cages. That their skins would be safe. She wanted to tell him that if he never made it out of this sewer, if the yellow overtook him, that she would go and free those foxes herself.

But Cozy didn't know where the Farm was. And Oleo was too sick to tell her.

She waited until he ran himself to exhaustion and then snuggled up against his side. His fever kept her paws warm, even in the damp belly of the sewer.

"*S*nrrrr!"

Oleo growled so loudly that Cozy leapt away before she was completely awake. As his muzzle thrashed side to side, she stepped backward, angling her paws down the tunnel, ready to run.

"*I'll rip out your heart,*" Oleo snarled into the darkness.

"That's it," Julep said.

He got up with a grunt and limped down the tunnel.

"Wait!" Cozy cried after him. "He's still harmless! He can't even sit up!"

Julep scowled back at her. "I'm *hurt,* Cozy. You said so yourself. If he comes after us, I won't be able to run. You'll be halfway to the river before Oleo turns me into mouse-meat. Do you want me to become like him?"

Cozy didn't have a response, and Julep kept limping, his tail fading in the blackness. Her heartstrings felt tugged in opposite directions.

*Drip!*

The sewer's watery sounds flooded into Cozy's ears and brought a thought bubbling up from somewhere deep. She couldn't wince it away this time.

"My mom can help us!" she called after Julep.

The sound of Julep's pawsteps stopped. "Your mom's dead."

"That's the thing . . . ," Cozy said. "She's not." The words made her throat feel raw.

Julep padded back into view. "What?"

Cozy stared at the wet bricks beneath her paws. Back in the graveyard, whenever Julep and Sterling had whispered about their families' fates, she had let them believe everyone in her family had died too. It was easier that way. Then she didn't have to talk about it.

"Why would you lie about something like that?" Julep asked.

Cozy's head felt heavy. "Dusty didn't like us talking about that stuff."

"So you just let me and Sterling feel *sorry* for you?" A growl swelled in Julep's throat. "When you have a mom you could have gone back to this whole time?"

Cozy's jaw trembled. "My mom thinks I'm dead. How do you think that feels?"

"Not as bad as watching my dad die in front of me," Julep whispered.

Guilt rose hot and uncomfortable in Cozy's chest. She gazed down the dark tangle of the Brick Warrens, heart pounding. "My mom isn't dead. But she does spend all her time with them."

Julep's ears folded. "Huh?"

Sloshes echoed down the sewer, drying up Cozy's voice. She already felt that she'd said too much. "Ghosts . . ." She swallowed and tried again. "They talk to her . . . Kind of. It's hard to explain."

Julep frowned. "Ghosts aren't real, Cozy."

Cozy gave him a look. "You and Sterling talked about ghosts all the time. Zags too."

Julep dipped his head. "We were just kits back then."

Cozy sighed and stared toward the wintry light down the tunnel. "Ghosts are foxes or other creatures that have died. They stick around as sounds or smells after the rest rots away. If you know how to listen, ghosts can warn you about the things that killed them. If you don't, they can drive you mad. My mom knows how to listen."

Julep didn't respond, and Cozy was grateful.

"One of the ghosts is named Bizy," she continued. "She died from the yellow." She looked to Oleo, writhing and snarling on the ground. "My mom can ask her if she knows how to save him."

Cozy had always felt a thrill whenever her mom channeled Bizy's stuttering voice to tell the tale of Miss Vix. But after Cozy left the Linen Closet, she couldn't stand to think about a kit who lost all her siblings.

Julep gazed up at the sewer's arched ceiling. "If you go up there, the hounds will get you."

Cozy sniffed down the tunnel. "I can smell the buildings through the drains. The bakery's just down the street. If I continue past that, I can keep sniffing until I smell the Ladies' House. They're always burning incense."

"Who're the Ladies?" Julep asked.

Cozy didn't respond. Even saying their names made her muzzle numb.

"You can't just go to a human's house," Julep said. "They'll *kill* you."

Cozy tried to swallow, but her throat was too dry. The only thing that scared her more than returning to the Ladies' House was the thought of never going back at all.

"Fine," Julep grumbled. "Let's go. Which way is the bakery?"

"But . . .," Cozy said, "your head's still hurt."

"Yeah," he said, squinting an eye. "But you need me there to protect you."

Cozy's ears flattened. In his current condition, Julep would be about as useful as a splinter in the paw.

She sniffed at Oleo. "Who'll keep an eye on him? What if a rat bites his toes?"

"With all that snarling?" Julep said. "The rats are probably terrified of him. Besides"—he sneered at Oleo's twitching muzzle—"I'm not staying here with him."

Cozy bit her lip. She would never forgive herself if she came back to find Julep bitten, reeking of yellow.

She waited for Oleo's spasms to settle, then placed her muzzle to his ear. "Oleo?" she whispered. "Can you hear me?"

His breath was wheezy. His teeth clacked together—*klik-klik klik-klik*. She tried not to let it scare her.

"I'm going to my mom's," she told him. "I'm gonna find a way to get the yellow out of you."

Oleo suddenly seized and bared his fangs at the air. "Go away."

"Only if you know I'm coming right back," she said.

She gently touched his side, and a spark leapt from his fur to her nose. Oleo's snarling faded to a gurgle, and his muscles relaxed against the damp concrete.

Cozy headed down the tunnel at a trot, trying to outpace the yellow spreading through her friend's body. Julep hobbled behind.

"Come on, Julep!" she said.

"I'm *coming*," he said, limping to catch up. "I did get hit by a *car,* y'know."

"Right," she said, skidding to a stop. "Sorry. Take as long as you need. But hurry."

# TWO

**C**OZY FOLLOWED HER nose through the sewer, past drains that spilled scents of laundry, then yeast, then the raw marrow of the butcher, until they arrived at a grate that held a whisper of incense.

She scaled a set of metal stairs and stuck her nose into the frozen night. The air tingled her nostrils. No yellow. She wriggled up into the gutter and then stuck her muzzle back into the sewer to clamp onto Julep's scruff and help him the rest of the way out.

The streetlights beamed, illuminating a light snowfall. Chimneys and manhole covers puffed clouds. The concrete was frozen underpaw. This part of town usually bustled with shoppers, come to peer through clean windows at the brightly colored clothing. But now, the streets were as quiet as the sewers.

The foxes padded along the slushy gutters, past buildings made of brown stones.

"Okay back there?" Cozy whispered over her shoulder.

Julep blinked, focusing on the ground in front of him. He was panting too much to respond.

*SHHHOOOOoooommmmmm*

Somewhere in the distance, a shot rang out. Cozy had heard the explosive sounds from the safety of the sewer. The humans were hunting the mad hounds with their black sticks. If they spotted the foxes, the humans would shoot them too. She tried to hurry Julep along.

The foxes reached the Ladies' House—a two-story building, slick with melting ice. The front window glowed with a neon human eye purpling the snowfall. Cozy's heart grew as icy as the air.

Julep noticed her trembling. "You okay?"

Cozy only swallowed.

She slipped down the narrow space between the house and its neighbor. Drips fell from the eaves' icicles, splashing in the alley's puddles and into her fur. The scent of incense blossomed from a triangular hole in the house's bottom slats. This was the hole Cozy's mother had wriggled through the night she'd slipped out and met Cozy's father. The hole Cozy had fled through all those moons ago.

She wriggled through, Julep on her tail, and they entered the space between the walls. The wall's inner supports scraped Cozy's right shoulder while the pink insulation squished against her left. Dust and sharp particles drifted from the dry wood.

They came to a vent that sat loose on its screws. Cozy peered through the black metal whorls into the gloom of the house. The front room felt as dark and cavernous as it had when she'd still had milk teeth. The air still stank of lavender and sweets.

"Looks clear," Julep whispered.

He squeezed past Cozy and pressed his nose into the vent, squeaking it open.

She stopped him with a touch of her muzzle. "I think maybe you should stay here."

Julep's expression crumpled somewhere between hurt and anger. "Why did you have me come all this way, then?"

*I didn't,* Cozy thought.

She wanted Julep next to her, to face the house, the Ladies, the upstairs bathroom. But more than that, she wanted him and his injured head safe and sound between the walls.

Cozy gazed back toward the splintered light of the alley. "I need you to stand guard. Yelp if you smell danger."

Julep lowered his muzzle. "I'm not *that* hurt, Cozy."

"I know you're not," she said, and licked him once on the cheek.

She shook the snow from her fur, nosed open the vent, and entered the Ladies' House.

# THREE

**C**OZY CREPT AROUND the waiting room's edge, behind the shaded lamps, past the patterned wallpaper, and beneath the upholstered chairs. The grandfather clock ticked. *Nic Noc. Nic Noc.*

She avoided looking at the many framed photographs that covered the walls. But the black eyes still seemed to follow her around the room. In every picture, the Ladies, pale and grim, posed beside smiling customers in fancy suits and dresses. One of the Ladies was bony, with a slanted tooth poking through her lips. The other was large, with thick makeup covering her face.

Treacle and Cakeface.

Cozy and her brothers had named the Ladies the first time they'd snuck out of the Linen Closet. Cakeface was always smearing white goop across her cheeks while Treacle ate little candies and sucked the leftover sugar from her snaggletooth.

Cozy paused beneath the blood-red tassels of a corner

table and gazed into the house's depths—down the hall hazy with incense, through the darkened foyer, to the beaded curtain of the Spirit Room. She looked back to Julep, a broken silhouette behind the vent. She let out a slow breath and continued on.

The hall was low-lit by glass bulbs held by metal stems and leaves. Pipes gurgled behind the walls, and out of the corner of her eye, Cozy thought she could see baby kits' faces pressing through the wallpaper, stretching and contorting the patterns. She fixed her eyes on the carpet and padded faster.

She entered the foyer, passed the leather stink of the shoe bin, and arrived at the base of the staircase, just a few tails from the beaded curtain of the Spirit Room.

Cozy had just placed a paw on the first carpeted step—

*"Spirits!"*

—when a high voice pierced through the foyer like a branch shrieking against glass. Cozy scrambled behind the shoe bin and then peeked around it, whiskers alert.

The Ladies were in the Spirit Room. She could see them through the hanging beads. They sat at a table draped with a black cloth, empty chairs all around. Their eyes were closed and fluttering, and they held each other's bejeweled hands. Their opposite hands lay on the table on either side, as if clasping invisible ones.

"If you can hear me," Treacle shrilly whispered, "please say something!"

*THUMP*

Cozy jumped when Cakeface's meaty hand slapped the

table, jostling a glass of cherry liquid and making Treacle squeak.

"You're not *convincing* me, darling," Cakeface barked. "You must begin quietly, then slowly build into a crescendo that sounds as if you are dragging the spirits, clawing and screaming, through the veil. Listen." She cleared her throat, and her deep vibrato filled the air. "Spiiiiiriiiiiiiiiiiits! Wherever you're hiding . . . wherever you dwell . . . speak to me now!"

"That's what I said," Treacle said.

"That's what you *squeaked*," Cakeface said. She knocked back the last of her drink and huffed. "We were blessed with the Sense, darling. We just have to convince our customers that we have it. Do it again."

The moment the Ladies closed their eyes, Cozy hurried up the stairs.

Her steps grew heavy as the memories came back to her.

Sometimes, when their mom left the Linen Closet and the incense crawled up the staircase, Cozy and her brothers would sneak into the hall and huddle at the top of the steps. They'd aim their ears toward the beaded curtain and listen as the Ladies spoke in their otherworldly voices. The kits gasped along with the customers when actual scratches responded:

*Scrtch Scrtch Scrrrrrtch*

Strangely, there had been no scratches when the Ladies spoke this time. As if the spirits were preoccupied.

Cozy reached the second floor, which reeked of mold and neglect. The walls and floor were bare. Cobwebs clotted the corners. The upstairs looked much more like the sort of place a ghost would visit.

Cozy sniffed left, then right, then padded toward the Ladies' dressing room. She passed a long hallway that ended at a white door and froze. The Linen Closet. Where Cozy and her brothers had been born and lived their first moons, hidden among the hole-ridden sheets.

Dusty once told Cozy that fox mothers tried to keep their kits secret—waiting until they were big enough to bite and fight for themselves before introducing them to the world. But it wasn't easy keeping restless baby kits in such a small space. So Cozy's mom had channeled the voices of the dead, allowing the ghosts to possess her tongue, so they could deliver their dire warnings.

*Hush!* she would say. *I'm receiving a message!*

Her eyes would roll back in her head, showing only the veiny whites so it looked as if she were staring not at the back of the Linen Closet—but *through* it.

Cozy could almost hear her brothers' whispers coming through the closed door.

*Who is it this time?*

*It better not be that salamander again.*

*Yeah, no one cares how it died.*

*Listen!* their mother would say with eyes of white. Then she would speak in a whine or a stutter, or a voice so gruff it made Cozy fearful of her own mom.

*Don't leave the closet while Mom's at work today,* she once said in the pinched, panicky voice of the rabbit that had been skinned and boiled by Miss Potter. *The Ladies are stomping up and down the hallway and might squish out your guts!*

While her brothers gulped and kneaded their paws,

Cozy would roll back her own eyes, listening for the ghostly voices. They never spoke to her.

Cozy continued down the hall, remembering the day a new scent bloomed through the house—as dark and sharp as a fang. The day the footsteps came thumping and pattering down the hallway. The day the closet door swung open wide.

*How did you not catch this?* Cakeface said.

The Ladies stared down at the kits, who trembled and crouched, trying to hide themselves among the sheets. Their mom was nowhere in sight.

Treacle wrung her hands. *I thought Aura was just getting, you know,* rounder. *You said yourself I've been overfeeding her.*

*Pinhead!* Cakeface spat. *The naughty thing has gone prowling, and now* you *need to take care of it.*

Treacle frowned, unable to hide the tooth poking through her lips.

*Quick now,* Cakeface had said. *While they're still too small to struggle.*

Cozy and her brothers had watched, too afraid to leave the closet, as the Ladies swept around the house. Cakeface caught their whimpering mother by the collar and dragged her into the dressing room while Treacle fetched some soft candies and brought them to the closet. The smell of sugar had eased Cozy's brothers' trembling, and they had chewed the candy, tails wagging. Cozy didn't eat any. She couldn't huff that dark scent from her nose. It had spread through the whole house.

Cakeface departed downstairs while Treacle carried

Cozy and her brothers, one by one, down the hall, where she plopped them into the bathtub before leaving to get one last thing.

Cozy had been the only kit who couldn't stop shaking in the tub.

*It's okay!* her brothers had told her.

*She fed us sweet stuff!*

*She's nice!*

They couldn't smell the blooming darkness like she could.

Now, many moons later, a different scent stopped Cozy in her tracks. It oozed into the upstairs hallway—a wet breath of rusted pipes and black mold, with just a hint of lilac soap.

The bathroom. Its door was cracked open.

Cozy's breath grew shallow. The snow on her fur melted down to her skin, shivering every inch. She reminded herself that the bathtub led to the drain. The drain led to the Brick Warrens. The Brick Warrens led to Oleo. She had promised she would save him.

With that thought, Cozy took a step forward, pressing close to the wall opposite the bathroom door. Another step, and her eyes watered over with fear. She squeezed them shut and took a third step and a fourth . . .

As she passed the dank air of the bathroom, the memories came flooding in:

*Her brothers panting happily in the bathtub while she scrambles up and over its slippery edge, trying to hide from that sharp, dark scent.*

*Seeing the doorknob, high overhead, and swearing if she made it out of here, she would learn how to open one.*

*Crawling behind the cold porcelain of the toilet as the bathroom door creaks open.*

*Treacle shaking out the sack, counting the kits, and wondering if one is missing . . .*

*The* skreek *of the faucet and the watery* blub *of the filling bath as each of Cozy's brothers go whimpering into the sack.*

*Hooking her paws over her ears, unable to muffle their miserable howls as Treacle drops the sack with a splash.*

Mom!

Mommy!

Mom-glp!

*Their words becoming gurgled . . .*

*and then bubbled . . .*

*and then—*

### *rrrreeennnk*

Cozy slowly opened her eyes to discover she was directly across from the open bathroom. She gazed into the green darkness within, expecting to see her three brothers staring back, shivering, unbreathing, fur dripping on the tiles.

There was nothing there.

*Drip!*

A single drop from the faucet got her paws moving again.

# FOUR

**COZY STOOD IN** the dressing room doorway and waited for her heart to stop hopping. The room was low-lit. Mirrors reflected snowy streetlight from the window, making the bangles and sequins sparkle and the silk of the dresses glow.

The room looked empty. But then Cozy noticed a movement behind the window's long curtains. A fluffy tail, more white than red, curled in front of the wall vent.

"Momma?" Cozy's voice was barely a squeak.

The curtains shifted, and a fox's face pressed through, revealing a nose, a muzzle, eyes, and ears.

Cozy's eyes began to sting. Her mom's creamy fur had grayed. Silver hairs threaded her muzzle. Her collar, which had once shown waning and waxing moons, was faded and frayed.

"Little One?" Her mom's voice was rough, unused. "Is that you?"

Cozy smiled through her tears. "Hi, Momma."

*"Hallo, Little One!"* her mother responded in a nasally voice. *"L-L-L-Little One!"* she said in a voice as bright as a kit's. And gruffly, *"Well, well, well. If it isn't the young vixen."*

Cozy's heart squeezed when she saw that the milky blue in her mom's pupils had clouded over completely. Cozy had always wondered why her mom had remained in this house. Why the moment Treacle had drowned her babies, she hadn't slipped through the vent, escaped the Ladies and this house's dripping horrors, and fled into the City.

But Cozy understood now. Her mother had gone blind.

"It's so wonderful to finally hear you," her mother said in her own voice. She sniffed toward the wall. "I've heard your brothers. They speak to me from the pipes." She turned her clouded eyes back to Cozy. "But this is the first time I've heard you. I can almost *smell* you."

Cozy flinched. Her mom thought she was a ghost. She could smell Cozy's fur, damp with snowfall and believed her drowned daughter had finally crawled from the bathtub to speak with her.

"I'm real, Momma," Cozy said around the tightness in her throat. "I survived."

*"No,"* the gruff voice said. Then, in the skinned rabbit's voice, *"You were washed down the drain . . . with the others."* And in Bizy's stutter, *"Y-y-you're one of us n-now."*

Cozy's paws ached to step forward. To let her mom and the ghosts sniff her fur so they knew that one kit survived that awful day. But something told her the gruff voice wouldn't like that.

"I need to ask Bizy a question," Cozy said.

"*Wh-wh-what is it?*" her mom responded in the kit's bright voice.

"Yes," she said gruffly. "*What could a ghost possibly need from another ghost?*"

"*All our business is done,*" the skinned rabbit said.

But Cozy's wasn't. Her thoughts went plunging back to the moments before the tragedy. When she had told her brothers that she wanted to venture into the hall, down the steps, through the beaded curtain, and into the Spirit Room. To find out once and for all what made those scratching sounds.

*But Momma told us to stay in the Linen Closet,* one of her brothers had said.

*The rabbit says it's not safe.*

*The Ladies'll stomp our brains!*

Cozy had snarled at her brothers. *You're all a bunch of scaredy-paws!*

She had yelped those words as loud as she could, hoping to scare her brothers into joining her on the adventure downstairs. Moments later, the steps had come down the hallway, and the Linen Closet door had creaked open . . .

"It was my voice, Momma," Cozy said, lips numb. "That got us found."

Her mom was silent for a time. Then a growl built in her throat, slow and gravelly. "*You stupid little—*"

Cozy took a step back.

"*N-n-n-no!*" said Bizy. "*It w-w-wasn't her f-fault.*"

*"Those kits would have spilled out of the closet eventually,"* said the skinned rabbit. *"They were getting too big."*

*"N-n-n-nothing stays s-secret long. N-n-not in this house."*

The growl in her mother's throat faded. The gruff voice did not respond. As if the other voices had convinced it.

Cozy blinked back tears. She'd been carrying this guilt half her life. And now it was gone. Simple as that.

More than ever, she wanted to curl up between her mom's paws. For her to lick the fear from her whiskers and ears. Cozy could make a little nest in the basket of silks and remain as undetectable as a ghost in the Ladies' House. She wouldn't have to worry about the hounds or food or the sewer or . . .

Something shivered in the depths of her mind. Oleo was waiting for her.

"My friend," Cozy said. "He's sick. He caught the yellow. Does . . . Does Bizy know how to get rid of it?"

Her mom lowered her head, as if listening. Cozy strained her. Snow tapped on the window glass.

Finally, her mother whispered, *"You c-c-c-can't."*

"What?" Cozy said, stomach sinking.

*"You c-c-can't."* Her mom spoke with Bizy's voice.

"B-but I have to do *something*," Cozy pleaded. "I can't just go back to the sewer and watch him turn into—"

*"You c-c-can't,"* her mother said, raising her voice. *"You c-can't! You c-can't! You can't! You can't! YOU CAN'T! YOU CAN'T! YOU CAN'T!"*

Cozy retreated toward the door as her mom howled

the words over and over. Screaming as if everything was lost.

"I'm s-sorry," Cozy said over the howls. "I didn't mean to . . . I have to go."

Before she could flee down the hallway, footsteps came hustling up the staircase.

# FIVE

OZY'S MOM DID not stop screaming—"*YOU CAN'T!
YOU CAN'T! YOU CAN'T!*"—as Treacle's shadow
stretched down the hallway.

Cozy frantically searched the dressing room and spotted
the basket of loose silks. She leapt inside, vanishing in a
rainbow of material as Treacle swept through the door.

"Aura, Aura, *Aura! Shh, shh, shh.*"

Cozy watched through the cracks in the basket as Treacle
cradled Cozy's mom in her arms, pressing her muzzle to her
chest and smoothing her whiskers until her howls dwindled
to whimpers.

"There, there," Treacle said. "What big bad thing frightened you this time, hmm?"

"Did you give her toxo medicine?" Cakeface bellowed up
the steps.

"*You* were supposed to give it to her!" Treacle screeched
back.

Cozy sucked in her stomach and drew her paws in tight
to make herself small among the silks. She tried to calm

her panicky lungs so Treacle wouldn't notice the basket was breathing.

"Darling?" Treacle called into the hallway. "I didn't know we had a fox fur!"

Cozy held her breath. Treacle had spotted her tail.

"I don't know *half* the clothes we own!" Cakeface called back.

Cozy squeezed her eyes shut as Treacle's thin fingers lifted her tail from the silks. She tried to relax her muscles so her tail would feel like a dead thing.

"It's *beautiful*!" Treacle said, rubbing Cozy's tail between her fingernails and waking the nerves in Cozy's teeth. "You've been hiding it from me!"

"I probably stuffed it away so the sight of it wouldn't hurt Aura's feelings!" Cakeface shouted.

Treacle sniffed and set Cozy's tail back in the basket. Cozy released a breath into the silks.

"Oh, but that's *silly*," Treacle cried. "Aura can't tell this fur was a fox once!"

She seized Cozy's tail again, and Cozy's entire body was yanked from the basket. The dressing room whipped at an angle as Treacle tried to toss Cozy around her neck. Cozy screamed. Treacle screamed. She released Cozy's tail, sending her flying through the air, striking the wall, and thudding to the floor.

"What's happening?" Cakeface called from downstairs.

While Treacle shrieked and shook her hands, Cozy looked for her mom to save her. But her mom had vanished like incense.

Treacle pulled a dress from its hanger and hurled it at Cozy, who was already scampering out of the room and down the hall. Cozy flew down the stairs, two at a time. When she reached the bottom, the beads to the Spirit Room parted, and Cakeface poked her head through. Cozy sped up, claws slipping on the foyer floor as she rounded toward the waiting room and—

*CRACK!*

*"Oof!"* a voice said.

She ran headfirst into something and fell back hard. Her vision doubled, then came back together . . . as Julep.

"Are you okay?" he said, shaking the pain from his head. "I heard you scream!"

Before Cozy could tell him to turn around, *run*, a black piece of material fell over them. Strong hands gathered up the edges and jerked it beneath their paws, bundling them in an awkward pile before dragging them across the floor.

The tablecloth fell slack, and Cozy blindly nosed her way to its edge as something heavy scraped the floorboards. The black cloth slipped from Cozy's eyes, and she found that Cakeface had dragged the shoe bin from the front door and turned it sideways, blocking Cozy and Julep in the alcove beside the stairs.

Treacle pattered down the steps, saying, "Oh, oh, oh," as Julep wriggled out from under the cloth. Cozy pressed into the alcove's corner, and Julep leaned against her side. His shaking made hers worse.

The Ladies towered over them—one with eyes popping like an insect's, the other's sunken like a beast's.

"How did they get in?" Treacle whispered.

Cakeface frowned. "Probably the same way Aura snuck out."

Cozy eyed the space between the women, wondering whether she could bound over the bin and slip through without getting caught. But Julep couldn't run in his current state. And she couldn't leave him.

"Do you think they're"—Treacle wrinkled her nose—"*infected?*"

"They don't look infected to me," Cakeface said.

"I don't think you can tell just by—"

"*I can.*"

Cozy's breath came quick through her nose. The dark scent was blooming through the house again. It smelled as thick as thunderstorms, but also sharp, like rotting meat. Cozy had always been able to smell human scents trickling through the cracks in houses. But she had never stuck around long enough to consider their *quality*. How it changed with the human's feelings . . .

Cozy realized she was smelling the Ladies' fear. She knew the more scared humans were, the more dangerous they became. And right now, fear flooded the house. Of course, now that her nose had untangled the scent, it was too late. Too late for her. Too late for Julep. Too late for Oleo.

"What do we do with them?" Cakeface asked.

"They're young," Treacle said with a shadow of a smile. "Look at their shiny little noses."

"Young enough not to struggle?"

Treacle wrung her hands. "Oh, I don't want to do that again. I swear I heard those little gurgles for days."

Cakeface sniffed. "Wear earmuffs."

Julep pressed into Cozy. "What are they talking about, Coze? What does she mean 'young enough not to struggle'?"

Cozy knew, but she couldn't make herself say it. The Ladies were going to drown them.

Cozy gazed up the stairs, hoping to find her mom running down the steps to place herself between the Ladies and her only surviving kit. To snarl her disapproval.

Her mom wasn't coming.

"You know," Cakeface said, gazing into the Spirit Room. "Our darling Aura won't live forever."

Treacle's eyebrows lifted. "True. We'll have to replace her eventually."

Something changed then. In the Ladies' scent. It grew lighter. Sweeter. They were becoming less afraid.

"Well, we cannot afford them both." Cakeface's scent soured again as she grimaced at the foxes. "We'll pick one, and you can"—she scraped a wad of makeup from the corner of her lips and flicked it—"*handle* the other."

Treacle frowned, her snaggletooth poking through her lips. "Why don't we free the one we don't keep?"

"And have it torn to shreds by those infected dogs?" Cakeface scoffed. "It will be a mercy, darling. Besides, it might sneak back in here and scare the customers." She smiled at the kits, cracking the makeup on her cheeks and showing lipstick-stained teeth. Julep whimpered. "Which one is cuter?"

Treacle tilted her head. "It could be nice to have some masculine energy in the house."

Cakeface gasped and clapped her meaty hands. "I know how we'll solve it! Go fetch some candy and Aura's old collar. The one with the stars. Let's see which one of these little darlings comes to us."

Cakeface kept a careful eye on Cozy and Julep while Treacle whisked around the house, returning with the collar, some candy, and—Cozy's heart went cold—something Cakeface had not requested . . .

*The sack*. It might have been Cozy's imagination, but she thought she could see lumps in the worn burlap—silhouettes where her brothers' bodies had been.

Cakeface took the sack while Treacle crouched beside the shoe bin. Their scent became an unsettling mix of sweet and storm cloud, sunshine and rotting meat.

Treacle held out a bit of sticky brown candy, the collar hanging open in her other hand. She grinned, bunching wrinkles around her ears. "Which of you darlings would like a sweet?"

Cozy looked from the candy to the collar. She couldn't decide which was worse: Stepping forward and suffering her mom's fate—collared and trapped in this horrible house, haunted by gurgles for the rest of her days. Or remaining in the alcove and suffering her brothers' fate—stuffed in a sack and held underwater until her life streamed out in bubbles.

But it wasn't her fate Cozy was worried about right then. She nudged Julep's side. "Go."

Julep whimpered. "What's happening?"

"Everything will be okay, Julep," Cozy said, blinking so he wouldn't see the tears. "Just go and eat that candy. Let the Ladies put the collar on you."

Julep gave Cozy a broken look, then sniffed toward the sweet in Treacle's fingers. His stomach made a squelching sound. He padded toward the woman, low and slow.

"That's it . . . ," Treacle said, her scent growing sweeter.

"We'll name him Astra," Cakeface crooned. "Get it? Aura and Astra."

Julep reached the candy and sniffed it. He took it between his teeth and started to chew. Treacle, licking her snaggletooth, slowly, delicately looped the open collar around his neck.

Julep stopped chewing. Cozy thought she heard more grumbles in his stomach. But those grumbles grew into a growl.

"No!" Cozy yelped a moment before Julep snapped at Treacle's fingers.

*"Gah!"* Treacle screamed, yanking back her hand.

For a moment, Cozy thought the tip of the woman's pinkie was dangling. But it was only the fingernail. The alcove flooded with the scent of fear.

"See what *masculine* energy gets you?" Cakeface yelled. She brought the sack down around Julep and swooped him up, wrapping the top into a knot.

"No!" Cozy howled. "No! No! No!"

"Perhaps this one *is* infected after all," Cakeface said, taking the collar and handing Treacle the sack, Julep's shape struggling at the bottom.

Treacle sighed grimly. She stuck her broken fingernail in her mouth and carried the sack up the steps while Julep thrashed and snarled inside.

Cakeface waggled the collar at Cozy. "We'll try with you in a minute. Here's hoping you're smarter than your friend."

Cozy fell into a shaking panic. It was happening again. Treacle was going to drown Julep. Cozy would see his blue smudges in every puddle she passed, hear his bubbled voice whenever it rained.

She wanted to run from this house. To flee the City and never look back. She wanted to drop to her stomach and fold her paws around her ears to muffle the awful sounds that were about to come trickling from the upstairs bathroom.

But the moment Treacle reached the top of the steps, Cozy's fear changed. Her paws felt light. Her muscles strong. She wasn't a helpless baby kit anymore.

Cozy lunged forward and leapt off the shoe bin, snapping at Cakeface's chin. The woman blanched and stumbled back, and Cozy hit the floor running. She flew up the stairs, her paws barely touching the steps, and reached the bathroom door just in time to feel the wind of it slam shut against her nose.

She leapt, trying to hook her paws around the handle and open it, but the handle was round. Her claws wouldn't catch. She threw her weight into the wood, again and again, even kicking it with her hind paws, trying to get it open.

The door wouldn't budge.

Cozy heard the metallic shriek of a knob turning within. Splashing water. The glug of the filling bathtub. Her lungs heaved. Her breath refused to catch. The sounds made her feel as if she were drowning.

*THUMP THUMP THUMP THUMP*

Cakeface was stomping up the stairs.

Cozy kneaded her paws, uncertain what to do. She could hear Julep's muffled whimpers. She couldn't let those whimpers turn to bubbles. She had to save him. But how? She couldn't get into the bathroom. The only way would be to somehow stop the water before—

Something clicked in Cozy's mind. The house's clues fell together: The gurgles in the walls. The scratches in the

Spirit Room. Her mom vanishing from the dressing room like incense . . .

Whenever the Ladies asked the spirits a question, it was Cozy's *mom* who responded with scratches.

*THUMP THUMP THUMP*

Cozy ducked just as Cakeface swiped at her with the tablecloth. She dodged around the woman's ankles and flew back down the stairs. She rounded to the waiting room and slipped beneath the chairs, nuzzling through the loose vent.

Cozy entered the space between the walls.

# SIX

**C**OZY WRIGGLED BETWEEN the squishy insulation and sharp wooden supports, making her way past
the holes in the house's siding and through the cave-like
space beneath the stair. She arrived at the vent to the Spirit
Room, where her mom must have listened to the Ladies'
voices, waiting for her cue to scratch.

Cozy tracked gurgling sounds to a faint silver glinting of
pipes. She sniffed along them to a rusted joint, which bent
the pipes upward toward the second floor. Pressing her
back into the inner wall, she used her claws to scramble up
the insulation.

She reached a wooden beam and balanced along it
toward the mildewed stink of the bathroom. The beam
ended in a dark depression. She leapt into a crawl space, its
wood warped by years of moisture, and listened in the
damp darkness.

On the other side of the wall, she heard muffled splashing. Treacle grunting. Bubbled screams. "Oh, *please* don't
make this more difficult than it already is!" Treacle said.

Cozy spotted a pipe that ran into the bathroom wall, and she attacked it. She bit it, headbutted it, struck it with her forepaws. The pipe held strong.

On the other side of the wall, she could no longer hear Julep's thrashing. "There, there . . . ," Treacle said. "That's it. Let go."

Cozy leapt, bringing her full weight down on the pipe, which folded her body painfully in half. She slid off and leapt again. Then again and again, bruising her ribs against the metal.

The pipe loosened with a squeak, and a sheet of water sprayed into Cozy's eyes. She redoubled her efforts, slipping and sliding, hitting the pipe with everything she had. The pipe broke free from its joint and vomited water, filling the space between the walls faster than it could leak through the cracks. Cozy tried to jump out of the crawl space, but the water weighed down her limbs.

"Oh!" Treacle screamed on the other side of the walls. "What's happening?"

The liquid from the broken pipe flooded to her paws . . . her knees . . . her shoulders. She leapt again and again, trying to hook her claws on the beam she'd dropped down from. After the third jump, the water came up to her ears. It enveloped her muzzle and slipped up her nose.

Cozy gagged and spluttered. Water was everywhere. It bent the space, flooding it with darkness, making it impossible to tell the distance of things. The pink insulation blobbed and wavered around her. Her lungs heaved as her breath bubbled away. Her hind knee struck an edge, and she gazed down in horror. The beam was submerged beneath her now.

Cozy paddled weakly upward, desperate to hook onto something, anything, nose straining to break through the water's surface. But then . . . She was falling. No, not falling. *Hurtling* along a dark current. It swept her through the walls, tumbling her upside down and backward. Insulation whipped past her ears, a wooden beam scraped her hip before another cracked her between the shoulder blades.

Just when she couldn't hold her breath another second—when her lungs quit their hitching, and her swimming paws fell slack—the water swept her toward a splintered light. Cozy felt a scrape along her sides, a pop, and then a release.

The water shot her into the cold evening air.

# SEVEN

**C**OZY'S BODY SPUN to a stop on the frozen concrete. She hacked up water and drew in raw, painful breaths. She blinked at the clouded sky, snowflakes tumbling onto her eyelashes. She saw the hole that had spat her out of the Ladies' House. She saw the purple eye, glowing through the window.

Cozy struggled to her paws. Julep was still inside. In the bathroom. In the tub. In the sack. But before she could slip back into the alley, the front door burst open, and a wave of water came cascading down the front steps. Cozy hid behind the curb as Cakeface stepped into the doorway, eyes wide, makeup smeared.

"What did you *do*?" she screamed into the house.

"I didn't do anything!" Treacle screamed back. "I was taking care of our little problem!"

"Look at my Spirit Room!" Cakeface said, cradling her dripping cheeks. "Ruined!"

"*Our* Spirit Room!"

The Ladies stepped out of sight.

Cozy shivered in the gutter. She needed to muster the energy to run back into the house, through the walls, and up to the bathroom. To find a way to save Julep . . . if he was still alive.

But before she could take her first step, Julep slipped through the front door and down the steps, leaving a wet trail behind him. Cozy could only stare in shock as he sniffed her out behind the curb and collapsed against her side. They pressed their wet fur close, trying to soothe each other's shudders.

"What happened?" Cozy said. "I thought you were . . ."

Julep blinked his damp eyelashes. "I don't know," he whispered. "I was in the sack . . . I couldn't breathe . . . Then that lady screamed. Her hands let go. I tried to get out of the sack, but the top was tied. I thought I was done for. I saw a light coming through the sack's corner. The threads were weak there. Like something had chewed it. I scratched and bit at the corner until it broke open. Then I wriggled out and swam to the surface just as that lady was running out of the bathroom. The floor was covered in water."

A warmth spread from Cozy's chest right up to her ears. She'd done it. The broken pipe hadn't stopped the water. But it had distracted Treacle long enough for Julep to escape.

"*Brr,*" Julep said, shaking the water from his coat. "It's a good thing you didn't go in that sack. You probably wouldn't have been able to chew through it like I did. You would have drowned."

Cozy smiled and let the tears spill. "Probably."

Julep hadn't noticed her fur was also drenched. She

licked the frost from his whiskers, grateful to be able to do so.

"Did you talk to that ghost?" he asked, jaw shivering.

Cozy swallowed ice, which made her chest go cold again. "No," she lied. "I didn't."

She had returned to this house to find a way to heal Oleo. But she was leaving with nothing.

*"Ugh,"* Julep said. "What a waste of time."

He trotted toward the drain.

Cozy looked toward the Ladies' House. In the window, beneath the glowing purple sign, her mom stared out with milky-blue eyes.

After Treacle had drowned Cozy's brothers, the woman had gone searching for the missing kit and left the bathroom door open. Cozy had crept from behind the toilet and into the hallway, away from the tub and the sack and the lifeless lumps inside it.

At the end of the hall, she had heard her mom scratching at the dressing room door, whimpering for her babies. Cozy had wanted to go to her, to sniff her fur through the crack. But the Ladies were looming. So Cozy had flopped down the stairs and sniffed at the walls of the waiting room until she smelled summer pouring in from the vent. She had slipped through and escaped the Ladies' House without saying goodbye to her mom.

Two days later, Dusty had found Cozy pawing through some trash. Cozy was just two moons old, her tummy sticking to her ribs. The moment she had seen the vixen, she padded right up to her and pressed her face into her belly fur.

*Hello, cozy little kit,* Dusty had said.

The name stuck.

Cozy's eyes started to burn, melting the snowflakes in her lashes. She realized something that had never come to her before. In order for Dusty to bring Cozy, Julep, and Sterling into her life, she'd had to break her own rules about leaving foxes behind. The vixen's iron-orange fur shone a little more brightly in Cozy's memory.

"Bye, Momma," Cozy whispered toward the window. She lowered her head, and for the first time she shed tears for her other mom. *Bye, Dusty.*

"Come on, Coze!" Julep called from the drain. "It's *freezing.*"

Cozy looked at him, shivering a ways down the gutter, and her head quirked. Julep should have died in that sack. But he had said its corner was worn away, the threads thinned, as if something had already chewed it . . .

Like one of Cozy's brothers, trying to escape.

Cozy took one last look at her mom in the window. Maybe ghosts did exist. Maybe, in their invisible way, they could save foxes from suffering their horrible fates. Maybe.

A shudder ran down Cozy's spine. It wasn't unpleasant. She bounded to catch up with Julep.

**T**HE ALPHA FELT soothed by the end of this story. Warmly haunted in a way. She wondered whether some scary stories were just tragedies that hadn't been addressed yet.

Her siblings clearly didn't feel the same. The runt and the beta were silent. Their muzzles hung heavy. She could smell the fear coming through their fur.

The smaller kits weren't used to stories like these. They were used to simple tales about foxes tracking tricky prey. About grumpy chicken farmers and unreachable grapes. They had never heard stories about drowned babies. About moms who were unable to care for their own litter. About an infected kit who was doomed to die.

The alpha's mom had warned her about the horrors of the world so she would be extra careful as she guided her little brother and sister through the wood. The alpha was meant to protect her siblings from the darkness.

"Why are you telling us this story?" she asked the Stranger.

He met her eyes without flinching. "Why do you think?"

There was no snarl in his voice. No fiendishness.

The alpha considered the Stranger's fading eyes. His crusted wounds. Which of the foxes was he? Julen? Oleo? *Sterling?* Had the kit somehow sur-

The alpha looked at the frightened expressions on her siblings' faces. She wanted to get them back to the den. To tell them that the stories were not true. That the Stranger's wounds had made him delirious.

But what if the runt and the beta needed these stories? If wild foxes didn't learn about the dangers humans pose, they would be as good as dead once the last of the trees fell.

That was what scary stories were for . . . wasn't it?

"Do you want me to continue?" the Stranger asked.

The alpha looked to her siblings. The runt and the beta looked at each other, then to their big sister.

"Go on then," the alpha told the Stranger.

She could barely hear her own voice over the howl of the storm.

# RUBBER
# HANDS

# ONE

**OLEO WAS NOT** in the sleeping spot.

"Where did he go?" Cozy whispered, wide-eyed.

"Don't ask me," Julep said. His fur prickled with goose bumps.

They stared at the shirt where they had left the snarling kit. It was still warm. His yellow scent lingered in the underground air.

"Oleo?" Cozy called. Her voice echoed through the Brick Warrens.

"Are you nuts?" Julep whispered. "Don't let him know we're here!"

Cozy took a step toward the darkness, but Julep quickly snagged her tail. "*Whoa, whoa, whoa!*"

She tugged her tail from his mouth and scowled. "What?"

"What do you mean 'What'? You want to go searching pitch-black tunnels for an infected fox kit who might kill us the second we find him?"

"Yes," she said, and she took off.

"Cozy, wait!"

Julep romped to catch up, but the tunnel wavered in his vision. His head still pounded something fierce, and just an hour ago he'd almost drowned.

He limped after Cozy's tail as she flew down the long stretch of darkness, her cream-colored fur briefly illuminated by the snowy light of the drains. He watched the shadows, sniffing for yellow and listening for dripping breath. How was he supposed to keep Cozy safe when she refused to stay by him?

A new drain came into view, and the air grew bitter with car exhaust. Julep's paws slowed as he approached Cozy, who had stopped a dozen tails from the drain. She stared at something—a shadow in the slanted streetlight. Its back spasmed. Its head trembled violently.

"Oleo?" Cozy said softly. "You okay?"

Oleo's head turned in erratic spirals toward her. His teeth jittered. *Klik-klik-klik-klik.*

The sight made Julep numb with fear. "Cozy, *please*," he whispered. "Let's get out of here."

"We were so worried . . ." Cozy told Oleo. She placed one paw in front of the other, gently approaching him.

Julep knew he should bound forward and place himself between Cozy and the infected kit. That's what an alpha would do. But any sudden movement might make Oleo attack.

"How are you feeling?" Cozy asked, taking another step.

As if in response, Oleo angled his trembling muzzle toward the drain, a rectangle of night swirling with snowfall. Julep sniffed at it and smelled a scent sharper than the frozen wind—so clean it burned the back of his throat. The scent brought back flashes of needles and bandages, shambling laundry, and a snarling rabbit.

It smelled like Veteri.

"Cozy, *wait!*" Julep hissed as a wisp of silver slipped through the drain. It looped around Oleo's throat, tightened, and hauled his body upward, writhing and gurgling, toward the grate.

"No!" Cozy yelped.

She lunged to catch Oleo's tail, but Julep ran and tackled her, biting her scruff and pressing her to the wet bricks. She snarled and struggled beneath him, but Julep held on with every bit of strength he wished he'd used on Sterling the day they'd met the Hidden Man.

"Get *off* me!" Cozy said. "I have to save him!"

Julep looked up just as Oleo vanished through the drain. He was replaced with eyes. *Human* eyes. Covered in circles of glass. The eyes turned away, and Oleo's gurgles faded into the night.

"*Rrg!*" Cozy rolled, throwing Julep off and thumping his head painfully against the bricks.

She tried to leap toward the drain's steps, but Julep forced himself to his paws and blocked the way.

"Why did you stop me?" she snarled. "I could have saved him!"

"That was the human from *Veteri*," he said. "Oleo must have followed her scent here because he's stupid enough to think she helps animals." He softened his voice. "Don't you be stupid too."

Cozy's snarl sharpened . . . then faded. She sniffed toward the drain. "I don't know what she plans to do with him. I couldn't smell her sweat."

Julep didn't understand. But he didn't need to. "Oleo's gone, Coze. Just like Sterling and Dusty. It's just you and me now. More food for us."

Cozy's muzzle crumpled again. "Get out of my way, Julep."

The words felt like fangs through his heart, but he refused to let it show. "Oleo's sick, Cozy," he said, widening his stance. "If he bites you, you'll *die*."

"I know that," she growled.

She tried slipping past him to the steps, but Julep threw his weight into her, pinning her to the wall. The two strained against each other.

"If you know that," Julep grunted, "then why do you want to go after him?"

"I don't have to tell you!" Cozy said, writhing.

"I'm trying to save your life, Cozy!" Julep said, his strength failing. "Why are you stopping me?"

"Because I want Oleo to tell me where the Farm is!"

Julep's limbs gave out, and he collapsed to his side. The foxes panted clouds. The wind moaned through the drain, sprinkling their fur with snowfall.

"Why do you want to know that?" Julep asked.

Cozy squeezed her eyes shut. "I know I can't save Oleo," she said, tears in her voice. "But he knows where more foxes are. Ones locked in cages, about to lose their *skins*. I can't just sit here knowing that's going to happen." She opened her eyes. "The City is mean, Julep. You know that. It chews up foxes, poisons them, buries them, drowns them, *infects* them. Most of the time, there's nothing we can do about it." She gazed up at the drain, flakes tumbling onto her snout. "What if this is different?"

Julep swallowed. *What if it's not?* he wanted to say. *What if you die like Sterling and Dusty?* He kept his muzzle shut. The words made him feel like a coward.

Cozy pushed past him and placed her paw on the first step. "I'm going. Now. Before I lose the human's scent."

Julep sighed and struggled to his paws.

"No, Julep," Cozy said. "I can't wait for you this time. I'm sorry."

"I can keep up," he said, trying to blink the throbbing from his eyes.

Cozy didn't argue. She simply leapt up the steps.

"Cozy!" he called after her.

But she had already slipped through the drain into the night.

"I demand that you stay," he whispered to the falling snow, then slumped to his side.

This felt like the end of something. But what, he didn't know.

# TWO

JULEP AWOKE IN darkness. He lifted his heavy head from the shirt and sniffed at the underground air.

"Cozy?"

His voice echoed down the empty tunnel.

Julep swallowed. What if she hadn't made it? What if she was lying dead somewhere, mud collecting in her creamy fur? Or worse, what if she was wandering, rickety, through the streets, mouth dripping, eyes gooey, as she prowled with a pack of mad hounds?

What if Julep was the only fox left alive in the City?

He felt a shudder coming on and flexed his muscles against it. He clenched his teeth, snarled and scowled, until the shudder became something else. A heat in his ears. A prickling in his hackles.

What was Cozy thinking, traveling across a city crawling with maniacal hounds? Just to try to save some Farm foxes she'd never even met?

"She *wasn't* thinking," he said aloud.

It was bad enough that she'd kept an infected fox kit around. They should have abandoned Oleo the second he was bitten.

"*Psh,*" Julep said. "We should've left him in that trap!"

Ever since they'd met that kit—if that's what Oleo really was—he'd brought nothing but death and misfortune, replacing Julep's best friend with cars and curses. Sure, Oleo might have come to Veteri to fetch Julep, but he was the reason Julep was there in the first place. Julep never would have crossed that road if Oleo hadn't put him up to it.

Besides, Julep was just about to escape the tomb when Oleo showed up. And it's not like Oleo carried him. Julep dragged himself out of that basement. And it wasn't his fault that cursed rabbit had escaped. The evil human had given him stuff that made him act funny.

If it weren't for Oleo crossing that street, the hounds would still be their same stupid, leashed selves, and Dusty would still be alive.

"No question," Julep told the darkness.

He had tried to be Oleo's friend. He really had. Whenever he'd called the kit a mutt, Oleo winced as if Julep had bitten him in the face. Sterling never winced. Sterling would come up with an even better insult, and he and Julep would go back and forth until it was clear that they were both tame mutts and they could go back to being foxes again.

"*Real* foxes," Julep grumbled.

He sniffed a tear away. What would Sterling think if he could see Julep spending so much time with the Foxoid Being they'd caught together? What would he think of

Cozy following this muttish creature as if Oleo were the alpha of the group?

Julep's jaw tightened when he remembered one of the last things his dad ever told him. *Alphas forge the path for other foxes. They learn from the stories of the past in order to show others the way forward.*

His dad had said this moments before leading Julep down an alley fragrant with fish meat. He had found an open can of tuna and tasted just a little. Julep's dad had grown up in the wild, so his was a forest wisdom. He didn't know that poisons looked different in the City. Not like the bright reds and yellows of the forest. But invisible. Hiding in any kind of food.

Julep's dad had choked in front of him. Mouth foaming. Tongue swelling. Eyes bugging from his skull. Julep, just a baby at the time, had run in terror from his own father.

Several days later, Dusty and Cozy had sniffed Julep out beneath the metal steps of a bar. But he never forgot the smell of that tuna fish. He carried the memory of it in his nose, warning Dusty, Cozy, and Sterling away from foods that held those bitter undertones. And he never tried new things before the others. Even when he'd raced Sterling to the cat food, he always let him win.

"That's how you survive the City," Julep said quietly.

Oleo never should have survived as long as he did. He'd been lucky crossing roads, breaking into Veteri, getting wild hounds to chase him. But his muttness had finally caught up to him. And it had gotten Dusty killed.

The heat returned to Julep's ears, bringing a tingling comfort in the underground cold. Now that Dusty and

Sterling were in the Underwood with his dad, it was Julep's duty to step up as alpha.

He staggered to his paws, legs bowing like wet branches as he slowly limped down the tunnel. He would return to Veteri. He would find Cozy. And after he saved her life, Julep would leave Oleo there.

# THREE

JULEP STRUGGLED UP through the drain and into the street. He sniffed the flurries of snow for yellow and searched for hound-shaped silhouettes. The street was empty.

He was about to set off when a familiar scent caught his nose, tangy and warm. He padded to a fire hydrant and found a puddle melting through the slush. Cozy had marked this spot. He sniffed along the sidewalk and found another marking by a trash can. Then another by a newspaper box. Cozy's pee led *away* from Veteri.

Julep limped along her scent trail. The frosted air tightened the skin around his skull, making his headache feel bigger than his head. Without Cozy there to hurry him along, he flopped into a shadow every few dozen steps, waiting for his eyes to stop throbbing.

*SSSSSHHHHHOOOOOMMMMMmmmmmm*

"Populated areas first!" a man shouted in the distance.

Julep hefted himself to his paws and hurried away, afraid the humans would end him with their black sticks.

Cozy's markings led him along the same route the kits had taken days before. It led to the park. He limped to the cart where he and Oleo had hunted hot dogs and crouched behind it. He sniffed the air for Cozy's trail, but it had gone cold. As if something had chased her.

Julep blinked his tired eyes toward the park's tangle of trees. It was as white as bones between the trunks. A single lamppost lit an orb of fluttering snowflakes, casting branchy shadows, which stretched serpentine across the snow.

*Hehh*

                                                            *Hehh hehh*

                        *Hehh hehh hehh*

        *Hehh*

Julep could hear the hounds huffing in the trees. Even in their mindlessness, they had returned to a place they knew.

"What sort of crazy path did you take, Coze?" Julep whispered to himself, wondering how he was supposed to cross through the park without getting bitten.

A snowy gale whirled across the pond, and something screeched nearby.

*RRREEENNNK*

He crouched, heart thumping, only to realize it was the cart's tipped-over trash can scraping against the concrete. In the trees, the hounds stopped their huffing, and Julep held his breath, waiting for them to come sniffing after the sound and discover a tasty kit instead.

Nothing emerged from the shadows.

The wind continued to gust and lifted something out of

the snow. It was the paper kite that had fallen out of the trash the day Julep tipped it over. Its tail waved limply in the half-frozen pond water.

He had watched children fly these things. They sprinted across the park while holding a spool of string, making the kites swoop across the sky. Julep imagined clamping onto the kite's tail, breaking into a sprint, and riding the wind up and over the trees before landing safely on the opposite side. That was impossible, of course. But it gave him an idea.

He sniffed out the kite's string and followed it to its spool. He took the spool in his mouth and walked it once around the trash can's flat sides. The spool rattled between his teeth, unwinding as he limped across the crunchy grass. The string grew taut across the water.

Julep stepped beneath the snow-heavy trees onto a bed of dead, wet leaves. He crouched, fighting the urge to pant, and widened his eyes for rickety shadows. When the shadows kept their shapes, he set down the spool. He took the string between his teeth and yanked as hard as he could.

The string leapt out of the pond, flinging up a perfect line of droplets before pulling the trash can into the pond with a loud splash.

*RRREENNNNKKKK*

*SPLOOSH*

Gooey eyes turned in the darkness. Dry noses sniffed. Julep made himself small against a tree trunk as a dozen uneven pawsteps squished across the leaves to investigate the sound. He quietly moved around the trunk, barely avoiding the nose of a wheezing, skeletal dog. He darted to another tree before a large red hound could spot him, then quickly crept around it as three more hounds limped into the lamplight.

The hounds swayed around the pond but kept away from the water's edge, their dead eyes watching the trash can bob on the broken ice.

Julep panted with relief. These infected hounds were even more gullible than the regular ones. If any came sniffing after him, he'd simply give the string another tug, splash the pond, and distract them again. He wished Sterling were there to see his trick.

Julep retrieved the spool and continued to unwind it through the trees. His confidence withered when the string ran out a hundred tails before the park's end. He turned in a circle and spotted a small brick building that smelled of human leavings. He quickly limped to it and hid behind its drinking fountain.

His vision throbbed in and out of focus as he searched the lamp-bright spots for gummy eyes and dripping teeth.

*Hehh*

                                        *Hehh hehh*

                    *Hehh hehh*

            *Hehhhhh*

There was a flash of matted fur to his left. A pair of bloodshot eyes to his right. The air was thick with yellow breath, making it impossible to sniff where the hounds were walking.

A choking cough spun him around. Coming through the

trees was a pair of black gooey eyes, fixed on him. Julep backed away from the building but stopped when a white shape materialized to his side. Another hound had spotted him. And another. And another. Muzzles came fogging out of the darkness, hacking, growling, drooling strands of thick saliva.

The hounds circled Julep. He jerked his head left, then right, searching for an escape. He was surrounded. One of these hounds would attack first. But which one?

*SSSSSHHHHHOOOOOMMMMMMmmmmm*

A sound broke open the night, so skull-shattering that Julep thought something had hit him. But he was still on his paws. One of the hounds was not so lucky. It lay dead beside a splash of blood. The others turned to sniff at the trees.

A new scent spread through the chilled air, twining through the yellow . . . Burning leaves.

*SSSSSHHHHHOOOOOMMMMMMmmmmm*
*chk-chk*
*SSSSSHHHHHOOOOOMMMMMMmmmmm*
*chk-chk*
*SSSSSHHHHHOOOOOMMMMMMmmmmm*
*chk-chk*

Two more hounds fell, spraying black across the trunks. Julep searched the park for a human shape. The Hidden Man could disguise himself as anything. Leaves. Branches. Brick walls. *Everything* in the park was a danger now.

The hounds twitched their muzzles at odd angles,

sniffing the night for a target. Julep saw an opening between two of them and bounded through. One hound lunged at him with massive jaws, but the air exploded again—

*SSSSSHHHHHOOOOOMMMMMmmmmmm*

—and the dog flopped dead behind him.

Julep fled the trees and reached the edge of the park. He sniffed at the grass, the sidewalk, the street, hoping for a whiff of Cozy's trail. He caught the faintest hint of her scent and followed it to a wet spot on the sidewalk. His heart missed a beat.

It wasn't her pee. *It was her blood*.

Julep broke into a limping run.

# FOUR

**C**OZY'S SCENT STOPPED in front of a small brown house. A trail of red droplets led along the snow toward the backyard.

Julep slipped beneath some hedges and waited for his head to settle. The journey had caused a pressure to build behind his eyes, making the house swell and shrink, the bricks and windows pulse.

This was the Veteri woman's den. He could smell her too-clean scent seeping through the front door. His mind filled with images: shelves dripping with poison, walls hung with traps and gutting tools, floors sticky with fox blood.

Julep's paws wouldn't budge.

He frowned at them. "Come on."

He imagined Cozy inside the house, cowering in a corner while the human prepared its instruments.

Still, his paws refused to move.

Julep's fear bristled into anger. He shouldn't have to do this. Once a fox was taken by a human, they were as good as dead. Cozy should know that by now. Julep didn't believe what Oleo had said about some humans being good. Not for a second. When he became alpha, he would bring back Dusty's wise words: *Fewer tails to watch over. More food for us.*

But in order to do that, he had to prove himself. Alphas forged the path for other foxes.

Julep crept out of the hedges and sniffed along the trail of blood spatters, past two trash cans, to the backyard. The snow was pockmarked with animal leavings. He smelled a slice of inside air and followed it to the house's back door, which had a dog flap just like the one in Veteri.

Julep pressed his head through the bendy plastic. The house was dark. The walls were bare, save a cat-shaped clock with swinging eyes and tail, whose *tick tick tick* made his whiskers twitch. Leaning against the doorframe was the metal rod with the wire loop that had captured Oleo.

Julep pushed through the dog door, the flap pinching around his tail before snapping shut behind him. The blood spatters ended just a few tails from the door. Cozy's scent was lost in the stuffy air.

"Cozy?" he whispered, as loud as he dared.

Somewhere, the floor creaked. A door gently shut.

He crept across the squishy carpet, past a couch and chairs, and came to a hallway. At the far end was a room lit with cold light, wafting the zingy scent of the City's cafes. A human stepped into view, and Julep quickly ducked around the corner. She paced barefoot across the tile floor, mumbling to herself. "Just two more specimens," she said. "Two more brain stems."

Veteri was a foggy dream in Julep's memory, but he faintly remembered a figure dressed all in blue, with rubber hands and wide glass eyes. But now the woman wore a striped garment folded around her torso and tied with a strap. Her eyes were red, surrounded by puffy lids, as if she hadn't slept in days. Her gait was shuffling and uneven, and she kept scratching at scabs that glistened on her bare scalp.

She lifted a mug shakily to her lips and took a sip. She winced, swallowed, and continued to pace. "Three shots left. Enough for how many more? Six? Seven?" Another sip. Another wince. "*Hff.* If I'm lucky."

The moment she stepped out of sight, Julep slunk down the hallway and nosed open the first door he came to. The sight inside curled his toenails.

A collection of small children made of glass sat on a bed, their bodies wrapped in white bandages. Their silky hair stuck through in patches. A needle jutted out of one's eyeball. In the center of them sat a small, oddly lumpy form, different from the dolls, every inch bandaged tight. A tinge of burned meat hung in the air, sickly and familiar.

Julep continued down the hall, keeping an eye on the pacing woman as he sniffed beneath doors—bathroom, closet, human nest—until he found one that smelled deeper than the others. He nosed open the door and found three wooden steps, leading down into a cave-like space.

It was a garage, much like the ones Dusty and the kits used to search for food. The air was cold, haunted by car exhaust and just a hint of yellow. The only light was a tiny orange flame, flickering in the heart of a hulking furnace.

Julep crept onto the top step to get a better look. A dark

bulb hung from the ceiling over a silver table, exactly like the one he'd woken up on in Veteri. Something large and fuzzy lay on top. Julep tensed. It was a dog. Its gummy eyes were wide with shock. Its mottled tongue sagged out of its open mouth like a slug.

Julep's hackles relaxed. It was dead. This was the golden hound that had attacked him and Oleo in the City streets. What did the human want with a dead dog? Julep didn't think he wanted to know. Was she going to *eat* it? *No.* He definitely didn't want to know.

On a stand beside the table was a tray holding several silver instruments, including a mean-looking saw with dozens of teeth. Their metallic scent made the fur on Julep's paws prickle.

"C-Cozy?" he whispered.

In the far corner was a sink, draped with towels and blue material. On the wall above it hung a poster of a small hairy creature dressed in fancy human clothing. It stood before a giant striped tent, its long arms stretched wide. Its fanged smile seemed familiar, but Julep couldn't quite snag the memory. Behind the hairy creature was a hoop of flames.

Julep spotted a cage in the garage's far corner and drew a shaky breath. He limped down the three backless steps to the concrete floor. The dead dog loomed above as he carefully passed the tray, fearing its metal instruments might slide off and impale him.

"Oh," Julep said when he reached the cage. "It's you."

Oleo lay inside, paws twitching, eyelids closed and fluttering. His lips writhed, but his teeth could no longer clack together. His muzzle had been bound shut with shiny black tape. His breath came fast and hot through his nose: *A hehh a hehh a hehh a hehh.*

Julep's own breath started to mimic the sound, but he swelled his ribs, fighting against it. "I didn't come all this way just to save a *mutt.*"

Oleo could respond only with breath: *A hehh a hehh a hehh.*

The sound brought a sting to Julep's eyes. He widened them before they could get wet. "You always were worse than Sterling at comebacks."

*A hehh a hehh a hehh.*

Maybe if Oleo weren't in the state he was in, stinking of yellow, Julep would open the cage and chew the black tape from his muzzle and leave the kit to fend for himself. But what was the point of rescuing Oleo now? Just so Julep could watch another fox die in front of him, like his dad and Sterling?

A single tear escaped Julep's eye and rolled down his whiskers. He shook it away and sniffed. Beneath the yellow, he could smell Oleo's real scent coming through. Like dried apples.

"Maybe the human will take the pain away," he told Oleo, trying to keep his jaw from trembling. "Like she did for me."

*A hehh a hehh a hehh.*

Before Julep's guilt could get the best of him, he turned toward the stairs, determined to find Cozy and get out of there.

There was a creak in the hallway. As the human stepped into the garage, Julep thrust his head beneath the lower shelf of the metal table, its sharp edge scraping his back as he splayed his legs flat to wriggle underneath. He curled his tail into the shadow just as a *click* filled the garage with fluttering, greenish light.

Julep's nose followed the woman's feet as she swept around the garage. He readied his paws, waiting for her to turn her back so he could bolt out from under the table and up the stairs. When she swayed to his left, he stuck his nose into the open. But then she spun around, spilling an arc of coffee, which splashed his muzzle and made him retreat. When she shuffled to his right, he slid out a paw. But she knocked her hip against the table's corner, scaring his paw right back.

He was stuck.

Eyes pulsing, he watched the woman's shadow move across the concrete floor. She slurped more coffee, then set the mug on the tray, rattling the silver instruments. The sink came on, and the woman viciously scrubbed her fingers, as if she was trying to rub the skin off. Next, she shook out the folded pieces of material and wrapped them over her face, her bald head, and her body. She fixed her goggles to her face, then pulled rubber skins over her hands with a sharp *Snap! Snap!*

Rubber Hands stepped to the table, and Julep belly-crawled farther back beneath the shelf. He heard her rummage through the tray of instruments and a sharp *shhhhhink!* as she made her selection. The instrument's shadow—long and mean, with hundreds of teeth—rose into the air before descending toward the dog's carcass.

**KRNCH** *slrsh* **KRNCH** *slrsh* **KRNCH** *slrsh*

The sound of wet crunching was nauseatingly rhythmic. It vibrated the shelf against Julep's ears, making the rest of him tremble in terror. Black droplets dripped from the tabletop and pattered on the concrete. The blood reeked of yellow.

*"Hic!"*

The sawing stopped. Julep folded his paws over his muzzle, trying to stop the hiccups—*"Hc! Hcmph! Hc!"*—as the woman's shadow craned its head, looking around the garage. She began to crouch toward Julep . . .

*A hehh a hehh a hehh.*

. . . when Oleo's panting grew suddenly labored. The shadow turned its head toward the corner cage, sighed, and then returned to sawing.

**KRNCH** *slrsh* **KRNCH** *slrsh* **KRNCH** *slrsh*

Julep's hiccups eased.

Several gut-churning minutes later, the sawing finished with a wet *shhlck*.

Julep peered out from beneath the table as Rubber Hands carried the dog's head to the sink and plopped it inside. Julep had wanted Oleo to be wrong about this woman. But not *this* wrong. Rubber Hands didn't heal wounded animals at all. She cut their heads off.

Julep looked to Oleo, helpless in his cage. The kit had no business running with City foxes; his recklessness caused too much damage. But he didn't deserve to lose his head.

There was more clinking and shuffling as Rubber Hands busied herself by the sink. Soon, a green glow bloomed to life, as neon bright as an electric sign. She held up a small circular dish, which reflected green in her wide glass eyes. She grunted, satisfied, through her mask, then set the dish next to some needles full of brown liquid.

Julep's face crumpled with determination. When Oleo had crossed a road, Julep crossed it faster. When Oleo had hunted three hot dogs, Julep hunted four. And since Oleo had saved him from the clutches of this maniacal human, Julep would save him right back. And he wouldn't even get caught as Oleo had.

*SPLAT*

Julep jerked when a towel flopped beside the table. He held his breath as Rubber Hands crouched much too close and started soaking up blood from the floor.

How was he supposed to get Oleo out of the cage, up the steps, and through the dog door? The kit couldn't even walk.

Before he could think of an answer, a scent oozed into the garage. Crusted sores and charred flesh. The top step creaked, and Rubber Hands looked toward the door. Her shadow made strange shapes in the air. "Awake already?"

"*Hic!*"

Julep caught his hiccups again as long black feet came shambling down the steps, dragging strands of white.

# FIVE

**T**HE RAGGED'S PINK and twisted feet slapped across the garage floor, passing right by Julep's muzzle and filling his nose with its horrific stench.

In his hazy memory of Veteri, Julep recalled a pile of soft laundry. But this creature was hunched and skeletal. It wheezed like death itself and dragged its knuckles through the smears of blood. Its hands looked strong enough to rip a fox kit in two.

Julep watched from beneath the table as the Ragged hobbled to Oleo's cage. It unwound the wrapping from its arm and tried to squish it through the wires.

*"No."* Rubber Hands swept across the garage and took the Ragged's hand away. Her fingers made more symbols. "Only the dead ones. Remember?"

A numbness spread through Julep. He knew where Cozy was. The room of glass children. The bandaged lump among them. The Ragged must have caught her when she snuck into the house and wrapped her up. Julep hoped Cozy was still alive in there. He hoped she could *breathe*.

Rubber Hands opened the cage, removed Oleo's limp body, and carried him to the table. His ear tag panged against the metal above, making Julep wince.

*Shhhhhink*

Rubber Hands plucked her instrument from the tray, its teeth slicing through the air.

Julep stiffened as firm as stones. This was it. She was going to kill Oleo. Take his head and toss it in the sink. Julep had to do something. Right then. He had to save Oleo and rescue Cozy and get them both outside.

But if he snuck out now, the Ragged would seize him and wrap him up. Rubber Hands would saw him to pieces . . .

Julep watched, wide-eyed and helpless, as Rubber Hands's shadow lowered the saw toward Oleo. Julep's chest heaved. His ears pulsed. He didn't know what to do.

But a whisker before the saw touched Oleo's throat, the Ragged's shadow reached out and caught Rubber Hands by the wrist, stopping her hand.

Julep held his breath.

"I know you want to help," Rubber Hands said, prying the Ragged's fingers from her wrist. "But I'm using sharp things now." Her finger shadows moved. *"Not safe."*

The saw lowered again, and again the Ragged grabbed her wrist, this time with a smoky grunt. *"Oo oo."*

*"Mmph."* Rubber Hands made a slightly pained sound. "I know this is difficult to understand," she said, signing slowly, "but the sick in this specimen will make the sick in others go away." Her shadow pointed toward the sink and

the green glow of the circular dish. "In order to make more medicine, I need more neural matter. Understand?"

The Ragged held on to her wrist.

Rubber Hands sighed and set down the saw. Julep started to breathe again.

"Here," she said, walking to the garage's shelves. She shook out a plastic bag and gathered the bloody towels from the floor, stuffing them inside. "Carry this to the back door. *No trash yet.* I don't want the neighbors seeing."

Julep watched as the Ragged clasped its hand around the bag and dragged it up the steps and into the hallway. There came the rustle of another bag, followed by the sticky sound of the hound's headless body sliding off the table and flopping into the plastic.

Rubber Hands plopped the heavy bag by the steps and called down the hall, "Here's another when you get back!"

She removed her rubber hands—*Snap! Snap!*—took a sip of coffee, then went to the sink in the corner and scrubbed her fingers again.

Julep's paws began to tingle. Rubber Hands was distracted. The Ragged was down the hall. He wouldn't get another chance like this. But how was he supposed to get Oleo off the table without Rubber Hands spotting him? How was he supposed to get an unconscious kit up the steps and through the dog door?

Julep searched the garage. He saw the furnace and the sink, the steps and the bulging bag, the tray . . . and the shadow of a mug on top of it.

As Rubber Hands flicked the water from her fingers, he

darted out from the table and knocked his head against the leg of the tray. The coffee mug wobbled on the corner, then tumbled off and shattered across the floor.

Rubber Hands whirled with a gasp, but Julep was already scraping back under the table, squinting away a fresh headache. The woman huffed in disappointment. She collected the mug's shards and went up the steps.

The moment her shadow vanished down the hallway, Julep slipped into the open. He shook his hips and leapt onto the tray, clattering the instruments before bounding onto the metal table.

Oleo's breath came hot against his eyes. *A hehh a hehh a hehh.*

"You'd better live to appreciate this," Julep whispered.

He grabbed Oleo by the scruff and dragged him off the table with a *thunk*. Oleo didn't yelp, but his breath quickened.

There was a creak in the hallway. *Slap-slap, slap-slap.* Julep quickly pulled Oleo to the bulky plastic bag and, holding his breath, nuzzled it open.

"*This* is how you save someone," he whispered to Oleo, trying to dispel his own fear. "You made me climb stairs."

He jerked and nudged Oleo into the bag and, without looking at the headless thing within, folded the plastic over him.

Julep quickly hid under the table again as the Ragged's shadow darkened the stairs. It clasped the heavy bag and hauled it up the steps with a grunt.

Every inch of Julep wanted to stay beneath the table, but he had to move before Rubber Hands returned. He crept on soft paws, across the garage, up the steps, and into the hallway. He slipped behind the Ragged and tucked his tail, keeping close to the bulky bag in case the Ragged looked over its shoulder.

The bag slowly slid past the nest, the closet, the bathroom. Down the hall, Julep could hear Rubber Hands working in the kitchen, which bloomed with the scent of fresh coffee.

As soon as the bag passed the doll room, Julep slipped through the door. He leapt onto the bed, knocking aside the glass children to sniff at the misshapen lump. *Rainstorms.* He snagged one of the bandage's loose ends and quickly unwound it, revealing a cream-furred muzzle.

Cozy gasped. *"Julep!"* she whispered. "There's something here! Get out before it finds you!"

"It's down the hall," Julep whispered. "But we have to move quick." He pulled more wrapping away and noticed the blood leaking from her hind paw. "Were you bitten?"

"No," Cozy said. "I stepped on a splinter in the park."

The tears came before Julep could stop them.

"Julep," Cozy said. "I'm okay."

He nodded and sniffed. "I found Oleo. He should be by the dog door now. He was wrong about Rubber Hands. She's not good. We have to get out of here."

Together, they removed the rest of Cozy's bandages and then hid behind the door. They listened as the Ragged shuffled and wheezed its way back to the garage. The moment its shadow passed the doorway, the foxes slipped into the hall.

They reached the dog door, and Cozy nuzzled inside the plastic bag, dragging out Oleo. His paws were sticky with hound's blood.

"Quick," she said, slipping through the flap and reaching her muzzle back in. "Help me get him outside."

They each bit the loose skin of Oleo's back and lifted. Cozy pulled as Julep pushed, straining to get Oleo up and over the metal base, through the bendy plastic. But his body was heavy and limp and wouldn't cooperate.

"Why does he have to make everything so *hard*?" Julep grumbled.

He paused to work the ache out of his jaw, and a sound made his ear tick. He checked the hallway, and his blood went cold.

The Ragged was there. It stared at them with wet eyes, its jaw hung slack. Curled in its long fingers was a *needle*.

"C-C-Cozy," Julep whispered.

Cozy poked her head through the flap. "Get Oleo out of here."

She leapt over the unconscious kit and ran down the hall, stopping halfway to snarl warnings at the Ragged. Julep blinked in amazement. He realized that Cozy hadn't been treating Oleo like the alpha at all. She was just looking out for their most helpless members.

Cozy was the real alpha.

Cozy lunged at the Ragged's arm. But it dodged back, clasping her scruff with its other hand and sweeping her, snarling and snapping, into the doll room before slamming the door behind her.

Julep gulped. So much for the alpha.

The Ragged slowly turned its head. It came swaying down the hallway—*slap slap, slap slap*—raising the needle into the air. Julep seized Oleo's haunch. He clenched his jaw and strained his neck, jerking upward, desperately trying to get the limp kit through the dog door. But the moment he managed to lift Oleo's back half, his front half slid out of the flap and flopped to the inside floor.

A shadow rose over Julep. He turned, trembling uncontrollably. The Ragged filled his vision. It stared at him, fangs working, needle held high. Julep expected the needle to come swooping down, to stab him and Oleo over and over again until there was nothing left.

But the Ragged just held the needle there.

A droplet formed at its silver tip. Julep sniffed. It smelled like yellow.

"Oo," the Ragged said, and nodded toward Oleo. "Oo."

Julep's eyelids fluttered with confusion. He looked from the Ragged's eyes to the dripping needle. Why would it want to put more yellow in a kit that already had it? Then he remembered Rubber Hands's words: *The sick in this specimen can make the sick in others go away.*

In his foggy memory, Julep remembered the Ragged dragging Oleo into Veteri's depths. Oleo's muzzle had been speckled with blood. Just as Cozy's paw had been bleeding when she reached this house. The Ragged had caught them both and wrapped them up tight. Almost like he was trying to fix them.

Oleo had been dead wrong about Rubber Hands. But maybe the kit had sensed some goodness in Veteri. Just in the wrong place.

Julep stepped aside. The Ragged stuck the needle into Oleo's haunch, a plume of blood clouding the liquid within. It pushed the plunger with its twisted thumb, and the liquid vanished into Oleo's body. Leaving the needle in his haunch, the Ragged grinned at Julep, dug a fingernail into his nose, and ate what it found in there.

### Boom! Boom! Boom!

A pounding came at the back door, scaring Julep off his paws. The Ragged whirled as Rubber Hands came hustling out of the kitchen.

Without thinking, Julep seized Oleo's scruff and hauled him behind the couch. He watched as the woman took the Ragged by the hand and quickly led him down the hall. They passed the doll room, where Julep could hear Cozy sniffing beneath the door.

Panic overtook Julep again. How was he supposed to get her out of there? How was he supposed to get Oleo through the dog door?

Rubber Hands led the Ragged into the garage. *"Stay,"* she said, signing. She placed a finger to her lips. *"Quiet."*

She shut the door, then hustled back down the hall, pinching her robe shut. She opened the back door, letting in a waft of stale burning leaves.

"Special delivery!" said a gruff voice. "*Secret* delivery, more like. What would the neighbors think, seeing me drag this to your back door?"

A shudder ripped to the tip of Julep's tail. He knew that voice. He knew that *smell*. He peered from the crack behind the couch. The Hidden Man stood in the doorway, dressed in sticks and leaves.

*No*, Julep thought. *Please no.*

"You took too long," Rubber Hands told the Hidden Man. "I had to collect my own specimens."

The Hidden Man sniffed. "The streets are crawling with animal control. I had to go to the park for your precious *specimens*." He dragged something heavy onto the stoop. A burlap sack, oozing blood. "I still expect to be paid."

*Ahehh-ahehh-ahehh-ahehh*

Behind the couch, Oleo's breath grew labored, moving loud and hot through his nostrils.

*No, no, no,* Julep thought, placing a paw over Oleo's nose to muffle the sound. *Not now.*

"Odd hobby for a veterinarian," the Hidden Man said, nudging the bloody bag with his boot.

"I'm not paying you to ask questions," Rubber Hands said.

"You're not paying much, considering how dangerous the work is."

*Snrrrrr*

Oleo's neck suddenly reared up. His head thrashed back and forth as his jaws strained against the tape that bound them shut. Julep placed his other paw on Oleo's muzzle, gazing up to see whether the humans had heard.

"Know what I think?" the Hidden Man said. "I think you had something to do with this little outbreak we're having. Maybe you let an infected patient escape that hospital of yours. The authorities might be interested in that."

Rubber Hands was silent a moment. "The authorities might also like to know what you do with the fox kits you trap. Bringing them to a vet? Releasing them in a different neighborhood so you can get paid to shoot them again?"

*Ahehh-snrr-ahehh-ahehh-snrrr-ahehh*

Julep had to use his full weight to keep Oleo's jittering head from thumping the floor. But the words Rubber Hands had said stirred something in his chest.

The Hidden Man smiled. "Seems we're at a stalemate."

Oleo's thrashing was becoming too much for Julep to contain.

*Snrrr-ahehh-THUMP-snrrr-ahehh-ahehh-THUMP-snrrrrrrrr*

"Eh?" The Hidden Man leaned through the doorway and peeked behind the couch. "Whatcha hiding in here?"

Julep glanced up just as something thin caught him around the throat and dragged him out from behind the couch. The thing tightened, cutting off his airway. He whipped his body back and forth, threw his neck in circles, trying to escape. But Rubber Hands pressed down her metal pole, pinning him to the floor. The more Julep moved, the more the wire crushed his throat, the less he could breathe.

The Hidden Man laughed. "*That's* your specimen, huh? And you let it run loose around your house? No wonder an animal escaped your clinic."

Julep had to stop struggling before he passed out. The wire loosened a little, and his panting came in panicked bursts. The Hidden Man's burning leaves and Rubber Hands's stinging scent clashed in the doorway, making it difficult to breathe. Julep's heart throbbed in his ears.

"Hold this," Rubber Hands said, handing the Hidden Man the metal pole.

Julep tried to slink through the open door, but the Hidden Man jerked him close.

Rubber Hands reached behind the couch and picked up Oleo, whose fits had settled. She drew the needle from Oleo's haunch, sniffed it, then looked down the hallway and sighed.

"You want money?" she asked, pinching Oleo's ear tag. "I'll tell you where you can make a lot more than hunting foxes."

She handed Oleo to the Hidden Man.

"Why's his muzzle taped up?" the Hidden Man asked. "He infected?"

Rubber Hands tucked the empty needle into her robe pocket. "Maybe not for long," she said as she went to a small desk, where she took up a pen and paper. She scribbled something, tore the paper free, and brought it back. "I've done work for them before."

The Hidden Man reached for the paper, but Rubber Hands pulled it back.

She nodded at Julep, still struggling to breathe. "You have to let me keep this specimen for the vaccine." She lifted her chin to the bloody sack. "And the dogs stay our little secret."

The Hidden Man held out the metal pole, exchanging Julep for the paper. He read it, smiled, and tucked it into his pocket. "Pleasure doing business."

From another pocket, he took out a white stick and placed it between his lips. He lit a small flame and touched it to the stick.

Rubber Hands's lips tightened. "Put that out."

"And why should I do that?" the Hidden Man asked, and

blew smoke into the house, where it coiled down the hall. "Why should I do that?"

Julep's eyes darted between the humans. The Hidden Man was going to take Oleo out and shoot him. Rubber Hands was going to saw Julep's head off. And the Ragged, in its innocence, would bind Cozy tight with its bandages, eventually squeezing the life out of her.

But Julep couldn't do anything with the wire around his throat.

**_OOH-OOH-OOH-AH-AUGH-AUGH-AUGH-AUGH_**

Down the hall, the Ragged screamed at the top of its wretched lungs. The garage door burst open, and the creature came barreling on fists and feet into the room.

*"Whoa!"* the Hidden Man said, stepping back from the doorway.

The Ragged paused beneath the cat clock and frantically searched the room, huffing deeply.

"It's okay, Ramses," Rubber Hands said, breathless. She signed the best she could with the pole in her hands. "There's no fire. It's *safe.*"

The Hidden Man laughed in disbelief. "You kept that burned circus chimp? How many laws can one vet break anyway?"

The Ragged saw the glowing ember of the Hidden Man's white stick and screamed again, deafening Julep's ears.

**_AUGH-AUGH-AUGH-AUGH_**

The Ragged threw open the door to the doll room and vanished inside. Again, Julep tried to leap out the open door, but Rubber Hands tightened the wire, cutting off his air.

## AUGH-AUGH-AUGH

The Ragged barreled back into the room, holding a roll of bandages. The Hidden Man saw it coming and bolted around the side of the house, taking Oleo with him. The Ragged didn't chase after the Hidden Man. Instead, it knocked Rubber Hands to the floor, forcing her to drop the metal pole.

The wire around Julep's throat went slack. He whipped his head back and forth, trying to shake the wire over his ears, as Rubber Hands reached for the pole. The Ragged continued to scream, wrapping her legs in wild circles.

"I'm *safe*, Ramses!" Rubber Hands yelled as the bandages wound up and around her torso. "I'm okay! He's not going to burn me! I need that specimen!"

The wire finally slipped over Julep's ears, and he scrambled toward the open door right as the Hidden Man stepped back into the yard. He was holding the black stick.

Julep froze in the doorway. Rubber Hands was in the living room, clawing across the carpet toward him. The Hidden Man was outside, raising his stick. *Chk-chk!*

"*Julep!*" Cozy called.

He turned and saw her in the hallway, behind the screaming Ragged.

"Cozy!" Julep yelped. "What do I do?"

"The Hidden Man!" she called, sniffing the air. "Run to the Hidden Man!"

Julep hesitated.

"*Trust me!*" Cozy shouted.

He stared into her mismatched eyes. Then he ran outside, toward the Hidden Man.

***THHHHHHHHHHHEEEEEEEEEOOOOOOOOMMmmmm***

The moment Julep's paws reached the snow, he felt a pain in his back. Everything started to bend and fade—the fence, the lawn, the sky. His hind legs stopped working. He fought against the blackness, forcing his eyes wide as he wobbled, aimless, dragging his paws across the snow.

*Funny,* Julep thought as the world blurred and darkened. The black stick sounded different than he remembered.

"**G**REAT," **THE BETA** said. "Now every-body's *dead*."

"Haven't you been listening?" the runt said. "That ragged thing gave Oleo a cure, and the Hidden Man doesn't kill fox kits!"

"You can't get rid of yellow with more yellow!" the beta snarled. "And the Hidden Man would never leave foxes alive. He's the Hidden Man!"

The alpha let her siblings argue. Her hope was starting to blossom again, though she wasn't sure why. The Hidden Man had caught the foxes. Oleo was still sick. And the alpha had a terrible feeling that she knew where they were going.

But Oleo was still alive. And Cozy had trusted the Hidden Man's scent. The foxes had made it this far. They had survived the many horrors of the City. Maybe they would survive whatever came next.

"So?" the beta asked the Stranger.

"Yeah!" the runt said, kneading his paws. "So?"

The Stranger's breath was growing thin as breezes. "That . . . ," he struggled to say, "is the end."

"*What?*" the beta said.

"*No!*" the runt said.

"Stories don't end like that!"

"Yeah! It can't end until all the foxes are as safe as dens!"

"I agree," the Stranger said. His voice had quieted

to a whisper. "This is only the end of my telling."

The siblings fell quiet as mice. The alpha nuzzled them close.

"When you hear a scary story that has nothing to do with you," the Stranger said, "you might be tempted to ignore it. You'll be better off if you do."

"What do you mean?" the beta asked.

"Yeah," said the runt. "You make no sense."

The alpha didn't understand either. She gazed through the parted pine branches toward the blood trail the Stranger had dragged across the snow, now buried in white . . .

Her throat tightened when she realized where it led.

"We need to leave," she said.

"No, we don't!" the runt said.

"What we *need* to do is find out what happens," the beta said.

They didn't get it. They didn't understand what this entire telling was building to. Why the Stranger had come to the wood and what it meant for them. The alpha was supposed to keep her siblings safe.

The Stranger watched the alpha with his fading eyes. With all the blood slicked to his fur, she hadn't been able to see the slight differences between him and a fox of the wild. She saw the wound at the base of his ear—where a tag would've been.

"Tell them," the alpha said. "Tell my siblings who you are."

The Stranger's eyelids fluttered shut. He licked the blood from his lips. He told them his name.

The siblings' jaws fell open in shock.

The Stranger gave a half smile and sighed, his breath fogging the crisp winter air.

He did not draw another.

# FOXFIRE

# ONE

**T**HE WORLD STROBED like a slow-beating heart. Consciousness came in blooms. Cozy's vision shrank and stretched. Sounds warped in her ears.

A rumbling darkness. Stuttered panting. A whistling, metallic wind.

She remembered watching Julep slump to his side. She remembered fleeing the house and running to him, horrified that her nose had been wrong. That the Hidden Man planned to hurt Julep after all.

She remembered the spray of red feathers sticking out of Julep's chest. Then a crack of sound. A pain in her haunch. And . . . nothingness.

Cozy tried to lift her tired head, but it was held down by something. Ropes. Woven in a net. Beyond was a solid metal compartment. The air was woozy with gasoline.

She could smell the others nearby. Faint. Julep's flowery fur. And—*a hehh a hehh a hehh*—Oleo. His yellow scent was breaking up . . . *fading*.

Life grew slippery again.

Cozy shivered awake.

A black wind nipped at her ears and nose. It froze her tears to blurriness. She seemed to be floating beneath an impossible sky—no longer a haze of City lights but an infinite swirl of prickling blues. It stretched so wide and black and deep that she worried she might fall through it forever.

The stars rippled and slipped . . .

And she woke to blinding light.

She squinted, trying to see beyond, but the white flooded her eyes. She could smell electricity coiling, Blue, trapped in metal.

A skeletal silhouette formed from the light. Its sweat bloomed sharp and thick. Leather hands seized her body as if it didn't belong to her. Fingers pinched her fur, scaring a faint snarl from her throat. They lifted her tail and peeled back her eyelids, prodded her ribs and scraped her gums. Cold metal dug into her stomach and swiveled deep inside her ears.

Cozy's heart thrashed wild. Her breath came quick. Her eyes swung left and right in their sockets, searching for escape.

Somewhere, Julep was whining. Oleo breathed heavily.

She saw a flash of silver, then felt a needle-sharp pain in the base of her ear. Brighter than the light.

This time, she was grateful for the darkness.

# TWO

**W**HEN COZY OPENED her eyes again, she saw crosshatched wires, reflecting red light. She had hoped she was waking from a nightmare, but this nightmare refused to end. She was in a cage.

She rolled onto her stomach, wooziness melting from her muscles. A wire floor cut through her fur and dug into the pads of her paws. Her ear throbbed, and something hung cold and heavy against her cheek. No matter how much she turned her head or strained her eyes to the side, the thing dangled out of sight. Above, on the cage's ceiling, red lines blazed warmth onto her fur. But they couldn't thaw the cold in her bones.

Beyond the wire wall blew a cold so bitter, she was convinced that breathing it would form icicles in her lungs. She saw an expansive lawn buried in snow. On one side sat a house, lacy windows lit by candlelight. On the other was a massive white building, like an eyeless skull in the winter night.

To her left was a frozen wood. To her right stretched

double rows of cages, just like the one she was in. Some of the cages held foxes, growing blurrier with each mesh wall. They had floppy ears and strange wide eyes. They stared at her.

Cozy whimpered.

"Why so sad, wild thing?"

It was the vixen in the cage beside hers. Her belly was as round as a stone.

"Where are Oleo and Julep?" Cozy asked in a panic. The boys were nowhere in sight or scent. Her heart ached to smell them safe.

"Who?" the vixen asked.

"The foxes I came here with!"

"Oh. Weird names. *Ju-lep* is on the far end of the cages." The vixen pointed her nose toward the candlelit house. "O-Three Seventy was sick, so Fern took him inside to nurse him." She shook her head in disbelief. "After he ran away, we thought he was dead for sure. But I guess he finally got his wish and became a pet."

*O-370.* Cozy had almost forgotten that name.

A word tried to creep into her mind—the name of this place—but she winced it away. She had smelled the Hidden Man's sweat. She'd known he wasn't going to kill them. But if she had realized he would bring them *here* . . .

The pregnant vixen tilted her head, flopping her ears and dangling her silver tag. "Your name's C-Double O Two?"

So that was what weighed heavy against Cozy's cheek. She fell to her belly and tried to paw the tag off her ear.

"Good luck with that," the vixen said. "Your tag is a part of you now."

Each time Cozy pawed at the tag, a sharp pain pierced through her ear straight to her skull. She stopped pawing. Her eyes filled with tears. She leapt up, placing her paws against the wire wall that separated her from the outside. It bowed outward but held strong.

"I need to get out of here," she whispered.

"Why?" the vixen asked. "With pretty fur like that, you'll be a breeder for sure."

Cozy dropped from the mesh. Her shoulders hunched. "Breeder?"

"Is Three Seventy really alive?" a fox in the cage behind Cozy's said. His eyes glittered red.

Cozy gazed toward the house and swallowed. "I hope so. He was infected with yellow."

The kit made a pained expression but quickly shook it away. "That's what he gets," he said, sitting tall, "for ignoring our ancestors' warnings."

The fox was Cozy's age—just leaving kithood—but she could tell he was deepening his voice, trying on an alpha snarl.

"Oleo's one of the bravest kits I know," Cozy said. "He saved my life. Julep's too."

"But he didn't follow the most important rule of all," the fox kit said. "He let his wildness get the best of him."

"Why do you keep calling him *O-leo*?" the vixen asked Cozy, jaw moving awkwardly around the word. "That's not his name."

"It is now," Cozy said quietly.

"We use different names on the Farm," the fox kit said.

There it was. The word. It flooded Cozy's head with images.

Endless cages. Hanging skins. When Oleo had talked about the Farm, it had felt so far away. But now here it was, cutting through her paws and burning her ears and waiting for her, cold and looming, at the lawn's edge.

Another fox's nightmare. Now hers and Julep's.

Cozy gazed across the Farm. This wasn't how she'd imagined it. In order to save these foxes, she had to be *outside* the cages. But she couldn't chew through the wires. Her limbs were limp with exhaustion, as though the cage was sapping away her wildness.

"I'm Three Seventy's cousin," the fox kit said.

Cozy's ears perked. "*R-Two Eleven?* But . . . the Farmer was supposed to take you into the Barn once it snowed."

"R-Two Eleven was my *old* name," the fox kit said proudly. "I'm *A*-Two Eleven now."

Cozy felt a tingle of hope. This was Oleo's best friend. He would understand.

"Oleo talked about you all the time!" she said. "How he wanted to come back here and save you!"

"Never thought to mention *me*, huh?" the pregnant vixen said. "Thanks a lot, Three Seventy."

"I'm not going anywhere," A-211 said. He tilted up his muzzle, angling his ear tag so it flashed beneath the red heaters. "The Farmer made me *alpha*." He nodded to the pregnant vixen. "Once Eight Thirty-Eight has her pups, it'll be my job to tell them the old stories. She's been training me as a storyteller so I can tame the wild out of them. That way they'll be grateful to enter the White Barn."

Cozy's heart tumbled. Sterling and Julep had always said

"tame" like it was a dirty word. But on the Farm, it was something to be *proud* of.

That's why B-838 wasn't gnawing at the wires to free herself and her unborn babies. Why A-211 wasn't trying to help her. The foxes' fur was scentless with contentment. Their eyes were clouded with calm. This was what the Farm did, Cozy realized. With constant food and shelter, it made the foxes as soft as pets.

She stared at the bleary shape of the White Barn, obscured by a thousand snowflakes. Her muzzle crumpled with determination. Ever since she was a tiny kit, she had survived horror after horror. And even though her fear had gotten the best of her many times, she always found a way through.

She studied the mesh and remembered the moment when she and Oleo had shut Dusty into the Milk Truck by pressing with all their weight at the same time.

"I need you to pass a message to Julep," Cozy told B-838. "If he pushes the wire from that end and we push from this one, maybe we can break it open together."

B-838 snorted. "I'm not pushing *anything*. And neither are you." She pointed her nose toward the house, at a black stick leaning beside the doorway. "After Three Seventy escaped, the Farmer started keeping his gun on the porch."

Cozy sniffed toward the black stick and smelled a hint of rotten eggs. This wasn't the kind that shot feathers and made foxes go to sleep. It was the kind that spilled their blood.

"You've been listening to Three Seventy's lies," A-211 said. "Haven't you?"

"He was saying some pretty crazy stuff before he left,"

B-838 said, and chuckled. "He thought the Farmer was going to *steal* our skins."

"It's true," Cozy said in a whisper. "Humans in the City wear them around their necks. I've seen them."

"That's the City," A-211 said. "This is the Farm."

Cozy was having trouble catching her breath. "I can tell you what the Farmer plans to do with us. I can smell his intentions."

A-211 gave B-838 a look.

"Listen to me," Cozy said.

She told them about the City. Everything she could remember. She started in the Ladies' House, when she was just a kit, then worked her way to Hawthorne Street and Sterling's tragic end. She told the Farm foxes how they had found Oleo and hadn't believed he was a fox at first. How he had tried to tell them about the Farm and how Cozy, Dusty, and Julep wouldn't listen. Each for a different reason.

She spoke long into the night, telling the Farm foxes about the return to the City, about the road and Veteri and how one escaped rabbit had unleashed a yellow madness into the streets. Cozy grew teary-eyed when she told them what happened to Dusty. How the vixen they had trusted had attacked Oleo. She told them how she had gone to her mom to try and communicate with ghosts to find a cure but instead learned how to smell a human's fear. And she ended by telling how she had used this trick to get her and Julep away from Rubber Hands. How they'd barely escaped with the fur on their tails.

Cozy finished her story and looked at the Farm foxes.

She expected to see horror written across their faces. For them to have felt the highs and lows of her experience and to understand the danger humans posed. All humans.

"The City sounds *awful*," B-838 said. She curled up around her pregnant belly. "Glad I'll never go."

A-211 gave Cozy a kind smile. "You must be so happy you made it to the Farm."

Cozy blinked in shock. "You don't understand. Oleo was telling the truth. Humans are *evil*."

"Not the Farmer," A-211 said in his alpha snarl. Then he brightened a little. "Three Seventy always wanted to go on adventures. He used to see badgers in the shadows and the Snow Ghost in the moonlight. Things that weren't really there."

"That kit was *obsessed* with stories," B-838 said.

"He made that stuff up about the Barn because he wanted to scare us," A-211 said. "To make me go on an adventure with him." His gaze burned red with the heater's light. "But I respect my ancestors. That's why I'm an alpha now."

Cozy whimpered. Arguing with the Farm foxes was pointless. The dangers of the City were sharp and immediate. Poison and traps and rolling tires. Thoughtless humans and mindless hounds. But the dangers of the Farm were quiet. Hidden. These foxes could relax and be comfortable while death came for them as slow and certain as milk curdling. So slow the foxes wouldn't recognize it until it was too late.

"The Farm is paradise, Double O Two," A-211 said. "The Farmer gives us warmth and shelter, and Fern feeds us twice a day. *Twice.*" He smiled at the walls of his cage. "You might think the mesh is here to keep you in. But really, it keeps the bad things out."

Cozy felt a slight stirring in her chest. She wondered which was worse. The Farmer, who drew out the foxes' deaths over many moons, feeding and caring for them before he stole their skins. Or the City humans, who did their killing quick.

A-211 nodded to Cozy's tag. "Now that you have a Farm name, you're one of us. You never have to worry about the City again. All you have to do . . . is stay."

Cozy's thoughts felt tangled up. The Farm foxes seemed so happy. They had a calmness about them that she had never known. Her muscles still felt melty from whatever the Hidden Man had shot her with. Sore from the Farmer's prodding. Her ear felt as if it would never heal. But she had to admit that the heaters above were slowly thawing the cold from her bones.

She watched the snowflakes tumble across the Farm. The white-dressed trees. The softly flickering farmhouse. Everything felt dreamy and strange. If Cozy was going to be a breeder, her death was still moons away. She doubted she would have survived that long in the City.

"What if I tell *you* a story now?" A-211 asked. "One our ancestors passed down. It might make you feel better."

Cozy didn't respond, but A-211 began anyway.

The story was about Beatrix Potter and how she had brought Mia, a helpless little kit, in from the dark of the wilds, warming her fur beside a crackling fire and feeding her rabbit meat.

Cozy listened, still droopy with exhaustion. The story

was nothing like the one she remembered. Like no other story she'd heard before. It had no cages or knives or boiling skins. No poison or shovels or sacks. It was about a little old woman who cared deeply about animals and who filled a young vixen with sweetness and hope.

It was the kind of story, Cozy realized, that she had always wanted to hear.

By the time Miss Potter was releasing Mia back into the wild to be with her mother again, Cozy found herself desperately wanting to believe it was true. To know in her heart that some humans could be good. That some places were just safe and nothing else.

Cozy wished her mom had told her stories like this one, instead of channeling the voices of ghosts to describe gruesome deaths. She wished the Ladies had been more like Beatrix Potter.

Oleo had been wrong about Rubber Hands. He'd invented stories about the woman, making her seem kinder, and nearly getting Julep and Cozy killed.

What if Oleo was wrong about the Farm too?

# THREE

**T**HE DAYS PASSED in endless flurries. Cozy's life became a dream.

When she wasn't sleeping, letting the sharp City memories fade to dullness, she was gobbling up bloody morsels or listening to A-211 tell stories of his ancestors. They weren't all as kind as the one with Miss Potter. But even the most terrifying of them felt distant, toothless. Lessons learned. Within the wired comfort of her den, Cozy found she could finally enjoy Mia's and Uly's adventures.

The Farmer, it turned out, smelled quite sweet. His gloved hands were gentle the next time he brought her to the Barn for his careful examinations. And when her eyes grew accustomed to the blinding light, Cozy noticed there were no skins hanging from the rafters. Just a green metal box in the corner. Nothing scary whatsoever.

A-211 told Cozy that the reason the Farmer's sweat had soured when he put in her ear tag was because he was fighting against her wildness, trying to make her part of the

Farm so she would be safe. She wished she had known that. She wouldn't have snarled so much.

Fern, the Farmer's daughter, smelled sweeter still. Like lemon soap. Her long fingernails scratched Cozy's ears through the wire, relieving itches better than her own claws ever could.

The fear Cozy had carried since kithood began to smooth away. Her muscles relaxed. Her tail grew pleasantly limp. She was safe now. Protected from the City and the winter wilds by the wires that surrounded her. She had heat and food and foxes to talk to—not about how they were going to survive, but about interesting outside scents or B-838's unborn kits or which bloody bits were the tastiest.

Beneath the Farm's wide, strange sky, Cozy felt far away from her cruel, old life. She only wished she knew how Julep was faring at the far end of the wire dens. And how Oleo was doing in the farmhouse.

Outside, snowflakes multiplied in the air, blurring the White Barn and the farmhouse until they became part of winter itself.

At the end of another pleasant, snowy day, Cozy curled up beneath the heaters and sighed, content. She listened to A-211's and B-838's soft snores and the hiss of the snowflakes as they melted on the tin roof of her wire den. Her breath turned to fog as it escaped through the wires, like ghosts in the night.

Fog.

Darkness.

Fog.

Darkness.

Fog.

A shape.

Cozy blinked. For a moment, it looked as if the steam of her breath had crystallized into something solid. But when her breath vanished, the shape remained.

She rose to her paws as it slowly loped across the lawn, cutting a line through the snow. It dragged something behind it. Something floppy and wide, growing whiter with flakes the closer it came.

Cozy sniffed the winter air and smelled something tart and sweet. The warmth in her heart spread to a wiggle in her hips.

"*Oleo!*"

"Hi," he said, dropping the floppy thing. He blinked his eyes, no longer gooey, and stared around the Farm. "How did we get back here?"

Tears of relief spilled down Cozy's whiskers. "I think the humans saw your ear tag and realized you'd escaped the Farm."

Oleo tilted his head to look at his tag. "Dusty once told me this proved I belonged to the humans. I wanted to rip it off when she said that." He gazed around the Farm. "But I don't think I ever would've found my way back here through all this snow."

Oleo looked unsteady on his paws, but he was standing all by himself. His limbs and muzzle were back under his control. The blood had been cleaned from his fur, and he no longer reeked of yellow. He smelled like apples.

"I'm sorry I dragged you into this, Cozy," he said. He looked toward the far end of the wire dens. "Julep too. I'm gonna get us out of here." His nose scanned to A-211. "All of us."

"But we don't have to leave!" Cozy said, tail wagging. "We can stay here, where there's food and shelter." She looked from A-211 to B-838, both fast asleep. "The Farm is good, Oleo. I've been in the Barn, and there are no skins in there." She smiled, hoping to get him to smile back. "I know you thought the Farmer was bad, but if you just talk to Two Eleven, you'll hear the t-truth."

Oleo sighed. He reached back and grabbed the floppy thing he'd dragged across the lawn. He shook his muzzle, clearing the flakes away. Cozy recognized ears. The fluff of a tail. But the rest of it was *wrong*. Flat and unnervingly smooth.

The winter cold twined through the wires. It found its way past the heaters and into Cozy's bones. "Is that . . ."

Oleo nodded. "Fern's dad gave it to her. I found it in her closet."

Cozy began to tremble. The wire cut into her pads again. The heaters burned her ears. Her peace froze like ice within her.

"Don't quit on me now, Cozy," Oleo said. "We have to find a way to get everyone out of these cages."

Cozy drew a deep breath and tried to shiver the numbness from her skin. "I . . . think I know a way."

*"Three Seventy?"* A-211 said, yawning awake. "Is that really you?"

"Hi, Two Eleven," Oleo said.

A-211 sat up tall. "It's *A*-Two Eleven now." He spoke with his alpha snarl, but it didn't sound so convincing to Cozy now.

The cousins considered each other through the mesh. It had been just over a moon since they'd last seen each other, and foxes grew a lot in their first year.

"So," A-211 said. "How was your little adventure?"

Oleo looked down at his paws. "It was the scariest thing that's ever happened to me." He looked to Cozy. "And the best."

A-211 smirked. "It's a good thing I didn't come with you. While you were gone, the Farmer made me alpha. But *you* . . ." He studied Oleo's disheveled fur, his thin frame. "You look like you got chewed up by a Golga—" His voice caught when he saw the flat, fuzzy thing lying in the snow. "Did you bring that from the City?"

"You know I didn't," Oleo said. "Smell it."

A-211 sniffed through the mesh. His eyes widened at the skin's acorn fur, the tip of its tail as white as the moon. His ears folded. Then, just as quickly, he straightened his back. "Listen to me, Three Seventy—"

"It's Oleo now," Oleo said.

A-211's muzzle snapped shut.

Oleo looked to Cozy. "We need to wake everyone up." He glanced toward the farmhouse. "Quietly."

Cozy stared down the long line of sleeping foxes, her breath fluttering with fear. She felt a splinter in her heart when she saw B-838. The vixen's pregnant belly rose and fell in sweet sleep.

"Don't do this, Double O Two," A-211 snarled.

Cozy scowled at him through the mesh. He had talked her into ignoring the Farm's dangers, unaware he was passing on the same lies that had been passed to him. But now that he'd seen the skin, he had no excuse.

A-211's snarl faded. "Please. We're happy here."

Cozy turned away. "Eight Thirty-Eight?" she whispered. "You have to wake up. I'm sorry."

B-838 grunted. She rolled onto her round belly and blinked through the wire. "Three Seventy?"

"Hi, Eight Thirty-Eight," he said.

"I could *kill* you, you know that?" she snapped. "We thought you were dog meat the second you stepped into those trees. Now get up here before I tell you what a stupid, *selfish—*" She saw the skin and her mouth froze. "Is that Nine Forty-Seven?"

Oleo bowed his head.

B-838 looked to Cozy, eyes twitching with panic. "You mean it's true? We're all going to be . . ."

Cozy swallowed and nodded.

B-838's belly began to heave. "You have to get me out of here! My babies!"

"Wake the others," Oleo whispered to her.

B-838 caught her breath and composed herself. "Hey!" she hissed at the fox a few cages down from hers. "Wake up!"

The fox stirred and saw the flat shape in the snow. He began to tremble and woke the next fox. The cages filled with yawns and murmurings. But when the foxes saw what lay crumpled before them, the Farm fell as silent as the snowfall.

They all looked to Oleo.

"Um," he said with a trembling voice. "You're probably feeling pretty scared and confused right now. You're realizing I wasn't lying about the White Barn." He tried to steady himself. "But if we want to get out of here, every one of us, we need to act now. Tonight. Before the Farmer wakes up."

The foxes looked at one another in their cages. They'd clearly never been asked to do anything before.

A-211 cleared his throat. "How long will we survive out there, Three Seventy?" he asked, loud enough for the others to hear. "A couple of moons? Maybe three?"

Cozy remembered the foxes she had lost. Sterling. Dusty. Her brothers. Almost one for every moon she'd been alive.

"We all know the stories," A-211 continued, turning his muzzle down the line of cages. "There's nothing out there but traps and teeth. And winter is the fiercest predator. Every fox knows that. If we stay on the Farm, we'll all live longer. And we'll be comfortable."

B-838 touched her nose to her pregnant belly. The vixen was probably wondering how she would feed her kits out there. Cozy wished she had an answer.

"I won't lie," Oleo called. His expression had crumpled. Not in a snarl. But in pain. "Life is harder out there. A lot harder. No one feeds you or brushes your coat. There are no tin roofs to keep your ears dry, or heaters to warm your fur. No mesh to keep you safe." His voice lifted. "But there are also a thousand beautiful sights to see and different foods to eat. Just wait till you try your first hot dog."

*"Woo, hot dogs!"* came Julep's voice, far down the cages.

"Foxes still manage to live good lives out there," Oleo said. He smiled at Cozy. "Good foxes, who watch each other's tails and protect each other from the cars and humans and hounds."

Cozy's fear melted just a little.

"Out there," Oleo continued, "you know how the humans feel about you. Foxes are vermin in the City." He looked straight at his cousin and placed a paw on the skin. "But on the Farm, we're vermin with nice fur."

The foxes held perfectly still in their cages.

"The stories our ancestors passed down scared us," Oleo said. "But they also showed us how to survive beyond the Farm. That's what they're for. To wake the wild that we all have inside us so we can survive anything that comes our way. Even if it's something a fox has never seen before." Oleo sat tall. "So. Who's coming with us?"

The cages rattled as the foxes whimpered and kneaded their paws with uncertainty. But then B-838 bowed her muzzle. And, one by one, the others did the same. Only A-211 ground his teeth.

Oleo exhaled in relief. "Cozy?"

Cozy's voice tried to slink down her throat, but she caught it. She told the foxes her plan.

# FOUR

"**P**USH!" **OLEO WHISPERED**.

The foxes pressed their heads into the mesh. They strained, digging their paws into the wire floor, pushing against the cages' outer walls with every bit of wildness they still possessed. Pushing with the fear of becoming like the skin in the snow.

Only A-211 remained in the back of his cage.

*"Push!"* Oleo said, a little louder.

The foxes pushed again, and the mesh bowed outward. The nails squeaked in the wood.

B-838 gave up with a gasp, collapsing in her den, so Cozy doubled her efforts, forcing her ears into the cutting wires, pushing past the crick in her neck, until finally . . .

*Rrrrr-queenk!*

Something popped loose.

Cozy's heart lifted. She looked right, then left, searching for the spot where the wire mesh had given out. She spotted it. By pressing into her cage's corner, Cozy had made the mesh bow around the divider, popping out a nail on A-211's side. A-211 frowned at the new hole in his cage.

*"Again!"* Oleo whispered.

The foxes panted in exhaustion. A life spent in cages had made them weak.

"Just a little more," Oleo called up to them. "You're almost out!"

A light blared through the snowfall. The farmhouse windows lit up.

Cozy froze as B-838 worked her paws. "Oh no, oh no, oh no."

Oleo, panicked, searched for solutions and saw the hole in his cousin's mesh. "Jump, Two Eleven!"

A-211 stared at the hole and swallowed.

"We can save these foxes!" Oleo said. "We'll work together to open their cages from the outside! We'll be just like Mia and Uly!"

A-211 looked to Cozy. He was trembling.

"Oleo will keep you safe," she told him. "He's good at that."

A-211 drew a shaky breath. Then he dipped his head and nuzzled into the cramped space between the wire and the wood support.

"That's it," Oleo said below. "You've got it . . ."

Cozy jerked her head toward the farmhouse. The front door was opening.

*"Yipe!"* A-211 yelped in pain behind her.

His ear tag had caught on the mesh. He wriggled, trying to free himself, but he was stuck.

Cozy leapt forward and hooked her fangs through the wires, taking the tag, cold and metallic, between her teeth. She yanked back hard and felt a pop. She tasted blood. A-211, ear freed, slipped through the wire and hit the snow.

*"Run!"* Oleo shouted as he sprinted toward the trees. "We'll come back for the others!"

Cozy watched anxiously as A-211 struggled to his paws. He was clumsy on the snow, a hind paw sinking, then a forepaw. The Farmer's shadow darkened the porch. Cozy could smell his sweat start to sicken.

Oleo paused at the forest's edge. "Come on, Two Eleven!" he called to his cousin. "You can make it!"

A-211 struggled, unable to lift his paws from the drifts.

"Walk lightly!" Cozy called down to him.

She swung her nose toward the house just as the Farmer grabbed the gun from the porch and pointed it toward the foxes. *Chk-chk!*

"Oleo!" Cozy yelped.

### *SSSSSHHHHHOOOOOMMMMMmmmmm*

An invisible line ripped through the flurries, splitting the winter air. A-211 collapsed, spraying red across the snow.

*"No!"* Oleo screamed as the shot echoed across the Farm.

The Farmer aimed his gun at Oleo, then lowered it when he saw Oleo sprinting back to his cousin's side. As Oleo sniffed and whimpered over the hole in A-211's chest, the Farmer set off across the lawn. He seized Oleo by the scruff and heft him to eye level.

"You're lucky my daughter likes you," he said.

Oleo hung slack in the Farmer's grip, face frozen in shock.

He didn't so much as snarl as the Farmer stuffed him into A-211's cage, found the loose nail in the snow, and forced it back into the mesh with the butt of the gun, pinning it to the wood.

The Farmer stooped again and snagged A-211 by the tail, lifting him so that his body swayed. Cozy didn't look away this time. She didn't fight the pain that drilled into her chest, right where A-211 had been shot.

The Farmer carried A-211 back to the porch and tossed him to the boards. He grabbed a hammer and a rattly tin and headed back to the cages, where he violently struck nail after nail into the bottom of the mesh, securing it down the line.

When he was finished, he hooked his fingers through the wire and gave it a sharp jerk. The nails stayed put.

On his way back to the farmhouse, the Farmer noticed A-947's skin lying in the middle of the snow. He picked it up, shook his head, and went inside.

Cozy looked at Oleo, who lay unmoving in his cousin's cage.

"I'm sorry, Oleo," she said.

He didn't even blink, and Cozy's heart broke for him. He'd finally made it all the way back to the Farm to save his best friend. And he had failed.

She pressed up against the wire wall between them, trying to lend Oleo as much comfort as she could. Cozy blinked toward the White Barn and tried to prepare herself for the slow death that awaited them.

# FIVE

**M**ORNING CAME, FROZEN and crystalline.
Cozy did not rise to meet it.

She watched the dawn break bright through the clouds,
sparkling the snowy lawn. Before the sun could warm the
air, the clouds bundled thick again, and the snow returned
with a vengeance, consuming the Barn and the farmhouse.
The wind cut at an angle, making flakes land in Cozy's fur
before melting beneath the electric heaters.

She wished the snow would cover her completely.

In the next cage over, B-838 had her tail wrapped tight
around her belly, as if trying to stop her kits from being
born. Her paws twitched and she whimpered with bad
dreams. The sight was too much for Cozy to take, so she
rolled to her other side.

Oleo hadn't moved since the Farmer stuck him in his
cousin's cage.

"Oleo?" she whispered.

No response. His breath was slow and slight. Icy breezes
ruffled his fur.

Since the moment Cozy had met him, Oleo had carried the Farm in his heart. Even when Dusty told him to shut his muzzle about the past, he had somehow kept the hope that he would return here someday and save his loved ones.

But not all stories ended well. No one knew that better than Cozy.

To survive the City, she had stuffed the memory of her brothers deep down inside her. But now that she'd seen Oleo fight for something that seemed hopeless, she realized that painful memories could be good things. They helped other foxes avoid danger and kept the brightest parts of the past alive. They helped her remember there was something to fight for.

By not talking about her brothers, Cozy had not only smothered their memory, she had drowned them a second time. Drowned them in silence. And now she would never be able to tell her brothers' story to her own kits.

"Hey."

A whisper twitched Cozy's ear. She lifted her head and looked at B-838, who was still fast asleep.

*"Hey!"* the voice said again.

Cozy blinked through the mesh. There, on the snowy lawn, stood three wild fox kits. They stared up at her, their fur flaming red against the snow. The alpha and the beta were vixens. The runt was a boy.

"Um," Cozy said, "yes?"

"We're here to rescue you!" the runt yipped.

*"Hush!"* the alpha said. "We haven't decided that yet."

"Yeah," the beta told the runt. "Shut your yap trap."

"I'll shut yours!"

*"Phht!"* the alpha huffed, silencing them.

Keeping her eyes on the wild foxes, Cozy turned her muzzle. "Oleo. *Look.*"

He didn't budge.

The alpha sniffed toward the White Barn. "What is this farm for?"

"It's a—" Cozy's voice caught. "It's a skin farm."

*"Toldja,"* the beta said, headbutting the runt's side.

The runt gazed toward the White Barn, a look of terror on his face.

"You must be Cozy," the alpha said. "Is that Oleo?"

"How did you know?" Cozy said.

The alpha breathed fog. "R-Two Eleven told us your story."

Oleo suddenly jerked upright. "You saw Two Eleven?"

The alpha nodded. "He found us. In the wood."

Cozy gazed back toward the porch at the spot where the Farmer had tossed A-211 the night before. The boards were streaked with blood, but the body was gone.

Oleo was up on his paws now, pressing his nose through the wire mesh. "Where is he? Can I see him?"

The beta lowered her head. The runt's ears folded.

"He . . . didn't make it," the alpha said.

Oleo's muzzle fell. Tears dripped through the wire floor.

"I'm sorry," the alpha said. "He seemed like a good fox. He told us everything that happened to you. To Cozy and Julep. He regretted not believing you about the Barn. I think that's why he told us. To make up for it."

"He told the story real good," the runt said.

"The best," the beta agreed.

Oleo turned away and stared into the trees.

The alpha looked at her siblings. The runt panted happily. The beta nodded.

"How can we help?" the alpha asked.

Cozy looked to Oleo, who was still gazing through the forest.

"I don't know," she said. "The Farmer fixed the mesh, so we can't break it open. Even with your help."

The wild foxes quirked their heads in thought. Cozy tried to think of something herself, but her mind was as blank as the snow. They had help now. They could draw from the wisdom of the Farm, the City, and the wild. But what good did that do if they couldn't open the cages?

Cozy turned to B-838, who had lifted her sleepy face from behind her tail. Her eyes were wet with tears. She had heard the news about A-211.

"Any ideas, Eight Thirty-Eight?" Cozy asked.

B-838 sniffed. "All my ideas are silly. Two Eleven always said so." She turned her muzzle toward her neighbor. "Hey! Wake up! There are foxes outside, and they're trying to save my babies."

The Farm foxes woke, and whispers swept up and down the cages as they tried and failed to think of an escape.

Everything went quiet. And then new whispers began at the opposite end of the cages. They passed from fox to fox like a rushing river, building with excitement.

B-838 listened to it, then turned to Cozy. "There's

a message from, um, *Ju-lep.* I'll never get over your weird names."

B-838 told her the message. A grin crept across Cozy's face. The foxes were going to give the humans a scary story of their own.

# SIX

**THE SNARLING BEGAN** at dusk. It was as quiet as mice at first. But it slowly grew to the size of engines.

The farmhouse door burst open, and the Farmer stumbled onto the porch, pulling on his boots. Cozy shook her muzzle and attacked the flimsy mesh, snapping at B-838, who flinched and whimpered in the opposite corner. Behind Cozy, Oleo jittered and thrashed in his own cage. Far down the line, Julep growled up a storm.

The Farmer reached the lawn's edge, and his face fell slack. "No," he said. "No, no, *no*."

Still snarling, Cozy tuned her ears toward the farmhouse.

"Dad?" Fern said from the doorway. "What's happening?"

The Farmer squeezed his hair in panic. "That exterminator sold us *infected* foxes."

In the cages, Julep, Cozy, and Oleo built into a howling madness. They squinted their eyes and whipped their muzzles and huffed saliva between their teeth. They growled and gurgled and paced their cages in jerky circles.

The Farmer frowned at the cages. He noticed that the Farm foxes were cowering from the ones brought in from the City. "Looks like our stock's still uninfected."

He looked back at his gun leaning against the doorframe, and his fear grew thicker than any Cozy had smelled before.

*No,* she thought. *Please.*

"But I can't shoot the infected ones," the Farmer said. "Their blood's contagious. It could splash into our stocks' eyes."

He ran past the gun, into the house and right back out again, pulling on gloves and carrying a sack in his teeth. The Farmer stomped across the snow to Cozy's cage, fishing keys from his pocket, then fumbling to unlock the door with his gloved hands.

Cozy felt a surge of panic at being the first one chosen, but she turned her snapping muzzle toward the Farmer. The door shrieked open, and his hand darted inside, snatching her by the scruff with his gloved fingers and wrenching her neck so far back she worried he would snap it.

Oleo attacked the mesh between the cages with everything he had, but the Farmer ignored him. Cozy tried to thrash as the Farmer dragged her toward the sack, but his pinching fingers seized up her muscles.

*Snrrrrrr*

The Farmer froze when something snarled in the wood. The alpha, fangs bared, darted from the trees, startling the Farmer, who dropped Cozy back in her cage. The alpha sank her teeth into his pantleg, shaking it to shreds.

*"Daddy!"* Fern screamed from the porch.

"Get Grizzler!" the Farmer yelled back, struggling to tear his pantleg from the alpha's teeth.

Fern moved to step onto the lawn but found two more foxes, the runt and the beta, snarling at her. She screamed and retreated into the house, slamming the door.

"She's gone!" Cozy yelped.

The alpha released the Farmer's leg and fled back into the wood, followed by her siblings.

The Farmer stumbled back across the lawn. Trembling, he lifted his pantleg and blinked at the pale flesh of his ankle. Blood pooled in his sock. The alpha's fangs had reached his skin.

"Oh god," he whispered.

He limped back to the farmhouse.

Cozy acted quickly. She needed to get onto the tin roof before the Farmer returned. She nosed open the cage door and reached around to the outside of the mesh, hooking her claws in the wire holes. Paw by paw, she climbed. Just as Dusty had scaled the mesh of the chicken coop.

Cozy reached the roof's overhang and craned back her neck. The tin jutted half a tail from the mesh.

"Careful, Cozy," Oleo said.

Cozy's limbs shook. The wires sliced into her pads. She only had one shot at getting over the lip of the roof. If she missed, she would tumble to the snow. The cage was too high for her to jump back up again.

She studied the tin sticking out against the winter sky. Snowflakes melted in her eyes, blurring her vision. She coiled back, then pushed off the wire with her hind paws, lunging back and up, hooking her forepaw around the roof's sharp edge. Her paw slipped on the melted slush, and she fell before jerking to a painful stop, her other forepaw still hooked in the mesh.

Whimpering, Cozy slipped her claws back into the wires. She hung heavy from the mesh, a new pain searing the muscles of her shoulder.

"It's okay," Oleo said, breathless. "Try again."

The farmhouse door banged open, and Cozy tensed. The Farmer came limping out, jangling keys. "I'm going to the hospital, Fern!" he called toward the window. "Stay inside!"

He gazed across the lawn and saw Cozy hanging from the cage. He frowned and went around the back of the house. His truck stuttered to life, then went slipping and sliding down the icy road.

### BAOWRAOWRAOWRAOWR

Cozy froze in fear as heavy paws came barreling across the snow. The Farmer had released Grizzler.

The hound reached the cages and leapt, briefly catching Cozy's tail in his jaws and nearly yanking her from the mesh. She curled her tail and curved her spine, scaling the holes with her hind paws to bunch up her body, trying to escape the dog's clacking muzzle.

### RAOF! RAOF!

Grizzler leapt higher, scraping his teeth along her haunch, then again, hooking the tendons of her ankle.

"Nuh-uh!" a small voice cried from the wood.

The runt bounded out of the trees and chomped his tiny teeth into the hound's tail. Grizzler rounded, taking the runt's body into his massive jaws and violently shaking him back and forth.

"No!" the alpha screamed.

She and the beta leapt out of the wood and clamped onto each of Grizzler's ears, trying to weigh him down. But Grizzler kept ripping his head back and forth. The runt howled in pain.

"*Climb*, Cozy!" Oleo shouted.

Cozy couldn't move. She could feel invisible teeth in her throat where the runt was being bitten. It was too much to bear. She unfurled her tail and flicked it back and forth, trying to catch Grizzler's attention.

The hound shook the foxes from his ears and spat the runt into the snow. He lunged again, his jaws clamping shut around Cozy's tail, sharp as a thunderclap. His weight dragged her downward. She flexed her claws, hooking them deeper around the wires, but they were quickly sliding out.

"Hold on, Cozy!" Oleo said.

He spun circles in his cage. Then he looked straight up at the ceiling and clenched his jaw. He leapt high and snapped, catching the heater's wires in his fangs. He hung a moment, muzzle clamped around the wires, then jerked and thrashed his body.

Cozy was slipping. Her nails slid from the mesh to their very tips. One more shake from Grizzler and she would plummet to the snow and be devoured.

## *POP*

## *KZZT*

There was a pop and a great flash of Blue. Oleo yelped and dropped limp to the floor of his cage, and all the heaters went dark. The sound and the flash were enough to startle Grizzler, who released Cozy's tail. He sprinted back across the lawn and vanished around the farmhouse.

Cozy looked to Oleo, who lay still in his cage.

"Oleo!" she cried.

He twitched twice, then rolled onto his stomach and gave his whiskers a shake. His fur was alive with static. "Keep climbing," he told her.

Cozy looked down, where the alpha and beta worried over their brother in the snow.

"Omega!" the beta said. "Are you okay?"

The runt peeled open his eyes, heavy with saliva. "It's the squipping *Fang* now."

The beta laughed, and the alpha shook her head, tears of relief dripping down her whiskers.

Cozy looked back to the roof's edge. Her limbs trembled worse than when she started.

"You got this, Coze," Oleo said.

Cozy closed her eyes and took a foggy breath. She didn't have this. Not even Dusty had been able to make it onto the roof of the chicken coop.

"Hey, kit," B-838 said.

Cozy opened her eyes.

B-838 smiled. "Don't mess this up."

Cozy gritted her teeth, bent her legs, and lunged off her hind paws, this time releasing *both* forepaws from the wire. They caught the roof and started to slip, but she bowed out her forelegs, digging her claws into the slick metal as she wriggled, tail spiraling, scraping her chest up and over the sharp edge.

Cozy collapsed on top of the tin roof, panting, eyes watering. Below, B-838 yipped in celebration.

Cozy slunk to Oleo's cage and peered over the side. Oleo scaled the inside of the mesh while she reached around the roof to press her paws against the top of the wire, bending it so that Oleo could squish his body through the tight space. He spun upside down, hooked his paws around the roof, and, with the support of the mesh against his back and Cozy dragging his scruff, pulled himself up and over.

The foxes panted at each other.

"You just did what I couldn't do," Oleo said.

"What's that?"

"You saved every fox on this Farm."

He licked her once on the snout, then padded to B-838's roof and peeked over. "I'll bend the wire as much as I can so your belly can fit through."

"You know what else would help?" B-838 said, grunting as she awkwardly scaled the mesh. "Keeping those comments to yourself, that's what."

Cozy padded to the very end of the cages.

"Your idea worked!" she said as she helped Julep struggle over the lip of the roof.

"I'm just glad the Farmer freed *you*," Julep said, squinting away a headache. "I couldn't have made that jump to the roof." His ears folded. "Don't tell Oleo I said that."

Cozy smiled at him, and they set about opening more cages. The Farm foxes scaled their mesh and leapt down to the snow. They hesitated, lifting their paws from the crunchy ice and sniffing for dangers. Then, one by one, they crept across the lawn and vanished into the wood in poofs of frost.

A few of the betas remained in their darkened cages, shivering and pawstepping.

"Come on!" Cozy told a pregnant vixen, pressing the top of her mesh. "You're free!"

The vixen didn't respond—only stared through the wire into the wintry unknown.

Oleo nudged Cozy's side. "Come on. We did what we could."

Cozy stared at the vixen a moment, then turned away.

She and Oleo leapt from the tin roof and belly-flopped in the snow. Cozy was ready to bound into the trees and escape this awful place, but Oleo sat, taking one last look at the Farm.

"It looks so small now," he said.

Cozy considered the cages, the farmhouse, the White Barn. This had been Oleo's entire world once.

She touched his side, and a small spark touched her nose. "We saved them, Oleo."

Oleo stared at A-211's empty cage. "Not all of them. *Oof!*"

The air burst from Oleo's lungs as something tackled him to the snow. For one awful moment, Cozy thought Grizzler had returned. But then she saw the blue splotches.

"*That's* how you save foxes," Julep said, pinning Oleo down.

Cozy was about to tell Julep that this was no time for playing, that Oleo was grieving for his cousin. But a snarl was already building in Oleo's throat. He lunged, driving his paws into Julep's chest and clamping his fangs around his ear, making Cozy wince for Julep's injured head. But Julep giggled and fought back, and the two wrestled each other across the lawn, rolling clumps of snow into their fur, and clacking together their cold fangs.

"Oh, great. Why not just kill each other the moment we escape?"

Julep and Oleo froze, each other's paws in their mouths, as B-838 dragged her belly up and plopped in front of them.

"Don't worry about helping the pregnant vixen across the snowy lawn, by the way," she huffed. "I'm *fine*."

Oleo romped over and licked her muzzle.

"Um," B-838 said, "those foxes are staring at us."

The alpha, the beta, and the runt sat a little way into the wood, eyes gleaming.

Oleo padded up to them. "Thank you."

The alpha bowed her head. "Thank R-Two Eleven."

"Well, *and* us," the beta said.

"Yeah!" the runt said. "And us."

The alpha curled a lip at them.

"Could you . . . ," Oleo said. "Could you take me to him?"

The alpha nodded.

She led the way.

T**HE FOXES JOURNEYED** away from the Farm, deep into the winter wood. Flakes piled in their fur until they looked more white than red. The clouds parted for the moon and made the snow shine.

They moved slowly, struggling through the powdery drifts—the Farm foxes used to roofs catching the weather, the City foxes used to grates draining the slush away. Only the wild foxes moved with ease.

B-838's eyes darted back and forth at the trees, the depths between them.

"One paw at a time," Oleo whispered to her. "Just like Mia and Uly."

They arrived at the pine tree—a dark, needled opening nestled in the white. The others remained outside while Oleo crept beneath the branches and blinked the ice from his lashes.

There was R-211, lying still on the bed of needles, his life a frozen pool around him. His eyes were closed, his mouth no longer tense.

A heat tingled in Oleo's ears, burning the cold away. He was angry at his friend. Angry at him for refusing to listen.

"We always talked about going on a great adventure together," Oleo said. "But when the time came, you refused to go. I needed you out there. Why didn't you come with me?"

A breeze brought snowflakes coiling under the

tree, ruffling his cousin's fur. The tingle in Oleo's ears started to fade. If R-211 had come with him, he couldn't have told the wild foxes their story. Oleo and all the others would still be trapped in their cages.

"You saved our lives," Oleo said. "When it mattered most. I just wish you could've—" His voice caught. Tears broke down his whiskers. "I wish you could've tried hot dogs."

Oleo lay beside his cousin and rested his muzzle on his cold neck. He didn't know how much time passed after that. It was just him and his best friend—or the memory of him—beneath the snowy pine.

Outside, B-838 whimpered and Oleo made himself get up. He pawed needles from the bare earth onto R-211's tail. The branches rustled, and then Cozy was there, digging up muddy swaths over R-211's paws. Julep came next, shaking the snow from his fur and finding loose branches to pile over the body. Oleo placed the final branch over his cousin's head.

Once R-211 was covered, the foxes sat in silence. The smell of blood was slowly replaced by the green scent of pine.

Julep sniffed, tears pattering on the needles.

"Two Eleven would have really liked you," Oleo told him.

Julep gave a half smile. "Sterling still would have thought you were a mutt."

Oleo laughed, spilling the last of his tears. For

the first time, he noticed that Julep's bluish smudges looked a lot like blackberry kisses.

Julep looked to Cozy. "Rubber Hands said the Hidden Man didn't kill fox kits. Do you think . . ." He blinked into the winter night. "Do you think Sterling is still alive out there?"

Cozy shivered. "I hope so."

The branches rustled behind them. "Um, I hate to be a burden, but . . ."

The foxes turned and found B-838 had crawled beneath the pine. She was sprawled on her side and breathing heavily. The bed of needles was wet and steaming.

"Oh!" Cozy said.

"What do we do?" Julep asked, paws kneading.

No one had an answer.

The alpha, the beta, and the runt slipped beneath the overhang and watched, perfectly still, while B-838 grunted and struggled. Baby foxes started to appear. They kept coming and coming, squirming on the pine needles, their tiny bodies slick with newness.

"Stop staring," the alpha told the wide-eyed runt.

In the end, there were eight pups. Three boys. Five girls. With sticky ears and squeezed-shut eyes and the tiniest sprigs of tails.

B-838 curled herself around them and licked the bloody goo from their little heads.

"What are you going to name them?" Julep asked.

"Not numbers," B-838 said. "But not weird names like yours either."

They all smiled at the new life wriggling and squeaking beneath the pine tree.

"You're gonna be a good mom, Eight Thirty-Eight," Oleo said. "Just like you were to me and Two Eleven."

B-838 smiled sadly. "So long as I don't mess up the stories."

The alpha sniffed toward the distance. "We should get back to the den. Mom probably thinks we froze to icicles."

"But-but *babies*!" the runt said.

The beta watched B-838 caring for her kits. "Alpha's right. Come on."

The wild foxes slipped out from under the branches and into the snow.

"Good night!" the beta called back toward the pine tree.

"Glad you didn't get turned into skins!" said the runt.

The alpha bowed her muzzle, and then the three foxes faded into the winter night.

Cozy watched the squirming babies with their shiny eyes and noses. "Can I help keep them warm?" she asked B-838.

"*Please,*" B-838 said. "I don't have enough belly fur."

Cozy sniffed out the three baby boys shivering on the needles and situated herself around them, gathering them up with her paws to the warmth of her belly.

Soon, the babies' needle-sized snores were squeaking through the pine. B-838 was fast asleep.

"What now?" Cozy whispered. "We can't go back to the City."

"No kitting," said Julep. "But . . . where do we live?"

Oleo thought about this for a few foggy breaths. He'd lived on the Farm. He'd lived in the City. But he'd never lived in the wood, where his favorite stories took place.

"I guess," he said, "we stay out here."

"That sounds hard," Julep said, gazing between the trees.

"No harder than what we just survived," Cozy said.

She, Julep, and Oleo smiled at the litter of eight sleeping pups. They waited for the wild to return to their whiskers.

SLEEP TIGHT,
LITTLE FOXES.

# ACKNOWLEDGMENTS

This is the end of a long, long journey. But before we rest, Mia, Uly, Cozy, Julep, Oleo, and I would like to extend our deepest gratitude to the following humans:

First, to John Cusick for steering me away from that first draft, which he eloquently called "a hat trick of publishing no-no's." Without that advice, the foxes would be wearing suspenders and living in tree houses and navigating much less interesting adventures. To the team at Holt Macmillan, past and present, thank you for making my books look and feel like haunted relics, and for cleaning up my mistakes. And extra fuzzy thanks to Junyi Wu for bringing the foxes' world to life with images more harrowing than any I could conjure with words alone. No one combines terror and adorableness like you do.

To my beta kit readers, Peter Lundmark, Beatrice Teigen, and Alice Garcia: You all caught things the professionals didn't and made these stories wilder still. To my adult beta readers, Mark Sorenson, Brittany Strickland, Alan Mouritsen, Breana Reichert, Susan DeYoung, and Kay Patino for braving early drafts and showing me clearer paths through the wilderness. To Mom and Dad for being fans no matter the quality of the content. And to Rebecca McGregor for sending me a small clipping about Beatrix Potter's taxidermy habit. May the world someday forgive us.

Thank you to the 2020 Newbery committee, run by the

delightful Krishna "serious as a Golgathursh" Grady. I'll never forget that fateful call during the black hours of the night. Your applause and laughter will echo through my heart forever. I promise to only ever use this spotlight for good.

To Hannah Garrett for reading these books out loud to me multiple times, even when her eyes hurt. And for laughing during the funny parts and crying during the sad ones. I wish you were here to celebrate the end.

To Christian Trimmer for your wisdom, patience, and incredible instincts for good storytelling. You pushed these stories beyond what I thought was possible and concocted some truly horrifying scenes that still wake the nerves in my teeth. The rabbit's and golden hound's blood is on your hands. And I couldn't love you more for it.

Finally, thank you to Chris Chambers, a bottomless den of intrigue, kindness, and the best darned poetry I've ever read. Chris, I will never be able to repay you for those dozens (hundreds?) of hours you spent helping me polish the language in these stories. You tracked the heartbeat of the wilderness. You made these characters breathe. And you reminded me daily of the joy of putting together simple words in new and exciting ways. This book is for you, my friend. Let's do this until we reach the gray lands . . . and beyond.

Thank you again, everyone. You make me grateful to be a children's author, and I could not imagine this adventure without you.

If anyone needs us, the foxes and I will be curled up in a den, fast, fast asleep.

Christian McKay Heidicker